HER
Hot Ride

BOOKS BY HEATHER VAN FLEET

Her Wild Ride
Her Rough Ride

HEATHER VAN FLEET

HER
Hot Ride

bookouture

Published by Bookouture in 2019

An imprint of Storyfire Ltd.
Carmelite House
50 Victoria Embankment
London EC4Y 0DZ

www.bookouture.com

ISBN: 978-1-83888-100-9
eBook ISBN: 978-1-83888-099-6

To Emma. I'll love you for eternity.

CHAPTER ONE

Archer

Whiskey, women, and wild nights. There was a reason the letter W was one of my favorites in the alphabet. Plus, the woman behind me in my bed currently tracing a nail up my spine was named Willa.

At least I thought she was.

"You can't give me ten more minutes?" she purred.

"Sorry, sweets." I glanced at her over my shoulder, stood, then winked. "Got places to be."

"How about *five* minutes?"

"No can do."

I bent over and grabbed my jeans, knowing that even one more minute was impossible. Once the sun hit my face in the morning, I couldn't sit still. I had a constant need to rise early. I lived to capture the day ahead. And already my mind was wandering away from the bed to the shit I had to do today. Tasks to be dealt with, brothers to keep in check, things to get in order for the club… Good old ADHD did a number on not only my mental state but my ability to keep a woman in my bed for longer than a month—sometimes less than that.

There was nothing wrong with Willa or any of the women I bedded. But most were groupies. And groupies were predictable, always looking for a forever with a biker who wasn't looking for more than a good time. Not that I blamed them. It was just that anything predictable didn't hold my attention for long enough; didn't challenge me, force me to focus, surprise me.

I love a good surprise.

I slid my jeans on, taking in Willa's wild blonde hair. Like every other woman I've been with in the past, she'd been trying her best to kiss me, and looked a damn mess because of it. No matter. Pretty little thing like her knew the rules like all the rest of them did: I, Archer Benedict, *never* kissed a woman. On the mouth, anyways.

"One of the boys will give you a ride home," I told her, nodding as I picked up my gun and tucked it into the waistband of my jeans.

Her lower lip pushed out into a pout. "Will I at least see you tonight for Flick's welcome home party?"

"I'll be around." I winked then snatched up my wallet before heading out.

With Niyol 'Hawk' Lattimore's house my main goal this morning, I let the door click shut behind me. It was Wednesday, which was also my favorite day of the week because anything with a nickname that started with "hump" was definitely worthy of being my preference. I walked down the hall, turned left, then stiffened at the sight of Talker, one of my club brothers, who was passed out on the floor in front of the couch that sat in the main lobby.

"Would you look at that." I chuckled under my breath and headed over to him, hovering. Had I ever been this stupid at nineteen? Yeah. I was that stupid now.

The guy was dressed in a pair of skimpy white briefs and nothing more—unless you counted the bright-red nail marks down his back. Least he got lucky.

I nudged him in the ribs with the side of my boot. "Wake up."

He groaned, rolled over onto his side. "Ten more minutes, Mom."

I smirked and decided to leave him there. Dumb kid.

The rest of the bar area was empty this morning, other than a cleaning lady.

"Morning." I nodded at the dark-haired older woman, armed with a vacuum cleaner.

She smiled tightly at me but didn't speak or make eye contact either. I was pretty sure she was scared of us all, which was why she only came in during the early hours.

The gravel lot was half filled today. A few guys lingered to the left of our body shop—prospects mostly, probably out taking a smoke break. They watched me, but I didn't acknowledge a single one of them as I stepped toward my bike.

As the VP of the Red Dragons, I should've taken the time to get to know the new guys more. But I also knew making nice would make them feel welcome... and feeling welcome would make them weak.

We were at war. There had been no deaths since February, for four months now, but we knew our enemies were out there, ready to pounce at any given second, and we needed to remain at DEFCON 4. Soldiers at the ready.

My brothers weren't stupid. Nor were they lazy. But they'd grown weak lately, weren't on guard as much as they should be either, mostly because of the women in their lives. That shit worried me too. Being blinded by the forever kind of pussy? Seemed pointless, honestly. Why have the same meal every night of the week when we had a never-ending buffet readily available right here? A *delicious* buffet of blondes and brunettes that managed to keep *my* ass happily sated, thank you very much.

For now, though, we'd agreed that the safest course of action was to do nothing about the war, and it was driving me fucking insane. More than anyone, I wanted to find our enemy, Pops, our former pres, and end this all before shit got even worse—before anyone else had to die.

I stepped up to my bike and studied her angles, bottom lip tugged between my teeth. All curvy, slippery, silver pipes, and a repurposed leather seat that fit me perfectly. I loved my bike almost as much as I loved sinking inside a woman for the first time. She was pretty—not to mention all mine—and I treated her like the queen she was, fixing her up on my own. I'd used old parts and combined them with new. I would've killed to run a shop of my own one day. But time was money in my world, and I barely had either of those things at the moment, which was why it was nothing but a dream.

As I straddled her seat, I couldn't help but stroke her handlebars. Smooth yet rough, my paint job good, but not the best. I revved the engine just once to give her time to warm up before I started toward Hawk's place at the back of the compound.

"You're late," Hawk barked at me from his door five minutes later. The tiny thing in his arms wiggled at the sight of me.

"Had shit to do." I shrugged, stepping up into his house.

"Yeah, well, we got places to be, remember?"

I yanked Biker-the-mutt from his hands and tucked him under my arm. His body fit against me like a football, and I kinda hated the fact that I loved the little shit. He was all black fur and beady little eyes, too tiny for my taste. But he'd been a gift from Hawk to his lady, Summer, last month. Something about her being so sick from her pregnancy. My brother was trying—willing—to do just about anything to make her happy. Stupid, was what I'd called my oldest friend the day he'd gone and picked up the furry dude. Who the hell gave a sick, pregnant woman more responsibility than she wanted to deal with? But it worked, becoming the perfect distraction for Summer—go figure. Apparently, he did know her better than anyone else.

I followed Hawk into the house and asked, "Summer gone already?"

Hawk grabbed a mug out of the cupboard in the kitchen. "Yeah. She left about an hour ago." He waved the mug at me, and I shook my head.

"She still puking all the time?" I watched him pour a cup, leaving it black, then taking a drink.

"Yeah." He frowned. "Only in the morning though."

"You better learn to glove that shit next time you wanna love it." I scratched the back of Biker's head, snorting under my breath at the same time.

Kids? Getting a woman pregnant? In *this* world? Hell no. I shuddered at the thought.

"Who you got on her lately?" I asked, wondering why he hadn't snapped at me.

"Chop today."

I nodded. Ever since Pops had declared war, we'd had all the old ladies followed.

Despite Chop being called the nice guy among the women around the club, I personally didn't like the guy. Or trust him much either. There was something about his pretty-boy face that rubbed me the wrong way, but I hadn't been able to put my finger on what that was yet. I would though. It's what I did. Read people, figured them out most of all. I may have sucked at staying on task, but I sure as hell knew how to get a good read on someone. For some reason, people showed their true colors around me.

"He's supposed to be tailing Emily too," Hawk added, "but she's been acting all weird. Not listening, leaving without warning…"

I cleared my throat, trying not to let my annoyance show. Hawk's little sister Emily was a certified pain in everyone's ass—especially my own. She'd made a life for herself outside the club once, but since that shit went down with Pops, we'd been protecting her and let's just say she didn't like it much.

I got it. The woman wanted her independence. She wanted to take care of herself and maintain the freedom she'd enjoyed prior to becoming part of the club. She wanted normalcy in a world that wasn't ever meant to be normal. But the thing was, she was Pops's daughter, a part of this world whether she liked it or not. Hawk had accepted that, being Pops's son. The sooner she figured that out, the better off we'd all be.

"What else has she been doing?" I asked.

"Ignoring Summer. And me. Staying home and doing nothing." He shrugged. "It's messing with Sum, and I don't like it."

I scowled, remembering what I'd seen on my way into the club last week: Emily in the parking lot, leaned up against her car, crying. I hadn't taken the time to stop and ask if she was okay. The less I had to be around the little junk puncher the better. I'd never understood her, and after a long day at work, my dick had other plans that didn't involve comforting a crying chick who I wasn't interested in fucking.

"Maybe it's her ex or something. Maybe they're in contact."

"Doubtful. He moved about a month or so ago. Somewhere outta state." Hawk took another drink of his coffee then sighed. "We just need to make sure she stays put."

"God knows she ain't gonna be honest with you." I laughed at the idea. Emily was the ultimate version of closed off, and no one could break her vault, not even Summer from the sounds of it, and they were best friends.

Hawk grunted. "Guess a brother's love ain't the same as being her friend."

"Wouldn't know." My family was long gone. To the point where I barely even remembered what it was like to have one. It was probably why I didn't understand my best friend's need to keep this woman safe. It was obvious she wasn't looking for help. But Hawk was standing in as club pres until Flick got home and I'd never question his motives.

"As long as she does what she's told and doesn't cause problems, I'm not gonna worry anymore." He shrugged.

"You don't think she'd take off, do ya?"

"Wouldn't put it past her." He scowled. "Emily thinks with her heart, not her head."

"If you don't trust Chop to keep his eye on her, then you should assign someone else."

"I would. But everybody hates her. She's stuck up and snooty. Never even bothered to give this place a chance." Hawk shook his head, wincing.

I opened my mouth then snapped it shut, not sure what he wanted me to say. If the woman would just relax a little—pull that giant stick out of her ass—then maybe she'd be more tolerable.

"Unless…" Hawk's eyes narrowed, but his lips ticked up on one side at the same time.

I knew that fucking look. "Fuck no. Not happening. She hates me."

"She doesn't *hate* you," Hawk said, laughing. "You test her. Which is why you're the perfect candidate."

I gritted my teeth, hissing through them a big, fat, "Fuck no."

Challenging her? Pushing her buttons with my smart mouth? Yeah, I was guilty of all that, sue me. Hell, I bet I could tame the little lion with the snap of my whip if I had to. But the thing was, I didn't *want* to. Emily annoyed the hell out of me for some reason. Five minutes in her presence and I was ready to pull out my eardrums, maybe yank the hair from my scalp while I was at it. All spiteful and shit, what with her dirty, snooty looks and thinking she was better than everyone else… Drove me damn nuts. No way would I ever be her little lion tamer. Not when I wasn't in the mood to run the circus.

"Come on. You ain't got nothing going on right now." Hawk smirked. "God knows your dick's gonna fall off soon if you don't stop screwing random women at the drop of a hat."

"I've got monthlies." I scowled. "Always cover my shit, unlike you."

"How about this? You watch her for a bit. Keep her here. See if you can't pick up on anything new. You see through people. Have that ability to know what they're thinking."

"I don't have ESP. And I'm sure as *hell* not gonna be your little sister's babysitter."

He smirked at me, knowing he had the power to tell me what to do.

"I'm not fucking her." I smiled, thinking of the only thing that could put him off.

Hawk's upper lip curled. "You know that's not what I mean."

"What if that's all she needs? A good dicking can do wonders for a woman." When it came to the ladies, I was the best at the job. Always made my intentions known to the women I took in: I wasn't relationship material. Hell, I didn't even kiss on the lips. But I fucked well and ate a woman out even better. If anything, I was the perfect candidate for a little fun.

But I wouldn't touch Emily. She was cute and all, what with her dark eyes and dark hair, but she wasn't my type. Wasn't blonde. Wasn't bright and cheery-looking either. If anything, Emily was more like me than any other woman I'd known, and fucking my little twinkie wasn't something I was interested in doing.

"Six weeks," he continued. "That's all I'm asking. You watch her, read her, keep her occupied. Then hopefully we'll have Pops taken care of and Emily will be free to leave." He shrugged one shoulder. "With Flick coming home tonight, that means we're one day closer to taking real action."

"Two weeks," I countered, ignoring the bit about Flick. Our pres had been living the high life in Texas with another club. Said he was looking to make alliances in the war against Pops. Nobody argued with him.

Hawk folded his arms. "Four weeks. That's the lowest I'll go."

Good Christ. Hawk had lost his ever-loving mind. "Fine. But your ass owes me." Not that I really knew what he wanted me to do with her. It wasn't like I was about to come over and play Monopoly with the chick every night. Only way I knew how to lighten up women was by spreading their legs and putting my mouth under their skirts.

Hawk reached out, took my hand, and shook it. When he opened his mouth to speak, a car pulled into the driveway outside, cutting him off. Biker yipped in my arms, and Hawk and I took off toward the front door, stopping short at what was there.

"Speak of the devil," he muttered, pushing out of the house.

When Emily got out, I couldn't stop myself from cringing at what I saw. Ho-lee-shit, she looked bad. Red face, tears, pink nose… It was as if she'd been crying all day—possibly all night.

With intentions of spying, I snuck out the side door of the house, set Biker in the grass to piss, and started listening from the backyard.

"Why are you home already? Aren't you supposed to be with Sum, helping out with that cheer camp shit she does in the summer?" Hawk asked, following her up the walkway to the little dollhouse-looking place that served as Emily's home.

"I've got a headache. Wanted to come home early. Talker was supposed to come follow me back, but he never bothered to show up."

I groaned, rubbed both hands over my face. *Talker* was supposed to come and follow her home? That dumb motherfucker was currently half naked and passed out in the lobby at the clubhouse.

"What the hell, Emily? You know you're not supposed to go anywhere without someone tailing you. Chop know you took off?"

"Nope."

"I swear to God…" Hawk growled. "You got a death wish or something?"

Even from where I stood watching Biker hiding in the tall grass, digging his nose into whatever dirt hole he'd found, I could still hear the annoyance in Emily's quiet words.

"Just leave me alone, please. I've got a headache."

"But—"

"I'm here, I'm alive, I'm fine," she murmured. "So please stop with the annoying big-brother routine."

"You know the rules," Hawk warned. "Yet you left without a tail. Again. Shit's gotta change, Em. Starting today."

Emily growled. "I'm not a prisoner *or* a Red Dragon, so you'd do good remembering that, *Hawk*."

I froze, imagining her hands on her hips, her brown eyes rolling too, waiting for Hawk to strike. Not that he would. The guy walked on eggshells around this woman more than anyone else. Let things fly that he probably shouldn't.

For years I'd tried to figure out Emily. Her quirks and tells were minimal, which drove me batshit crazy. Body language was supposed to be my skill set. It's what made me a damn good VP—and according to most of my partners, a fantastic lover too—but little lion Emily was impossible to read.

"Give me some credit, alright? I didn't go anywhere. I came back to your precious compound like a good girl."

"This is about your safety, damn it," Hawk barked.

"I have that… that *gun* in my glove compartment you make me carry too. What else do you want from me?" Emily groaned.

"A little cooperation until we figure this shit out would be nice."

I got it. The RD world wasn't her thing. But if she'd just wait it out a little longer, let us take down her father, then she could be free to do whatever the hell she wanted, wherever the hell she wanted to do it. Her not listening to the rules we put up for everyone at the club—not just for her—was only distracting us from doing what we needed to be doing. How could she not see that?

I picked up Biker, who sat on the toe of my boot, his eyes shut, fuzzy ears bent to the side. "Let's go, you little turd," I whispered.

"Well, excuse me if I don't feel like I should follow your stupid rules, brother. Now if you'd get out of my face and leave me alone, I'd *greatly* appreciate it."

Hawk growled out something I couldn't understand about the time I started toward the front of the garage. I wasn't surprised when I heard his boots shuffle against the gravel drive, and the door to his house slam shut a minute later. The guy had the patience of a toddler most days.

Thinking Emily would head inside too, I stood by the garage a few seconds more, waiting for another door to slam… a slam that never came. Instead, the noise of her creaky porch swing filled the air, followed a minute later by the sound of her mumbled curses.

Apparently, Operation Babysit was starting now.

I strode up the steps of the house and took a seat beside her on the swing without asking. If this was going to happen, then we needed to have a little chat first. Set some boundaries, so to speak.

"You sick or something? Lack of sex eating at ya? I may not like you, but I'm good for a roll in the sheets," I said, even though Hawk had made it clear she wasn't to be touched.

Emily pinched the bridge of her nose and rested her head back against the swing, all while Biker snuggled up next to her tits. "No. I am tired, I am stressed, and I have a headache. What I want is alone time. Which is apparently too much to ask for around here."

I studied her cheeks, how red they were. There were marks on her neck too. Scratches it looked like. I frowned. Had someone hurt her?

"No offense, but you look like shit."

She opened one of her eyes, upper lip curling. *This* was the Emily I could deal with. The backbone-wearing hard-ass.

"For the love of God, *leave,* Archer. Now."

I didn't leave. Instead, I smiled wider, having way too much fun pissing her off. "You're strung too tight, JP. Come to Flick's welcome home party with me tonight. I'll show you a good time."

"Yeah, no. Don't think so."

"I can get you drunk on my whiskey, then we can explore the cuffs I got attached to my headboard in my room. It'll be fun."

With an eyeroll, she lifted her middle finger and flipped me off.

"I'm not in any real danger," she said a minute later, surprising me. "If Pops wanted me gone, don't you think he would have come for me a long time ago?"

It was weird talking to a woman about club business. Still, this involved her more than it even did me in some respects, which was why I didn't mind much.

"Wish I had a manual for the inside of that fucker's head, just so I could give you a real answer. Either way, is it worth it? Risking your life like this?"

She stood and brushed her hands over the back of her khaki pants. "I'd probably be good bait, don't you think?"

"Maybe." The thought had crossed my mind before. If Emily left, Pops might come for her, and we'd have the opportunity to take him down, to end this war before anyone else got hurt.

Hawk had shut down that idea right away when I'd brought it up. But the thing was, I was tired of lying low and ready to end this once and for all. Probably more than anyone else in this club. Why? Because all this uncertainty left me unsettled. And as a man who couldn't ever sit still, I needed some goddamn peace for just once in my life.

Nobody listened to me though, despite my status as club VP. Which was why I was days, maybe even hours, from taking matters into my own hands, even if it meant sacrificing my life to make it happen. I would end this one way or another. I was just trying to figure out the hows and whens.

I knew *my* reasoning, but what about her? Why in the hell was Emily okay with being the RDs' bait when she didn't even like any of us?

"What're you hiding?" I asked, watching as she walked toward her front door.

From over her shoulder, her eyes narrowed back at me. "Nothing." A clenched jaw, twitching lips.

I stood and moved in closer. "Liar."

She turned around completely and folded her arms. "No. I'm not lying. I *don't* lie."

"You sure about that?" I backed her up against the door, capturing her there with my chest. I set my hands on either side of her face and saw her flinch. The sight of it had me frowning and dropping my hands right away, but I didn't move my feet.

"Tell me what it is. Or I go to Hawk."

"I'm not hiding anything." She blinked, face emptying of emotions.

"Bullshit."

Another twitch of her eyes.

Slowly, I stepped away and allowed her to turn around. Whether she realized it or not, she'd shown me too much. Now there was no way in hell I'd be letting her out of my sight. Hawk had been right to be worried.

"Someone will be by tonight to get you at eight," I called to her back.

Her shoulders stiffened and the hand on the doorknob froze. "No. I *said* I'm not going."

"Aww, JP. See, that's where you're wrong. I asked you to come and you'll come."

She lowered her forehead to the door. "Stop. Calling me. JP."

"You don't like that name?" I gasped, a hand to my chest.

"No." She swiveled to face me again. "Because I have a feeling it's insulting."

"What if I told you it's kinda badass?"

"Yeah right." She rolled her eyes. "Because you're always real nice to me. I'm supposed to believe the guy who once called me the 'hot version of a table'."

"Because you were." Then I looked her up and down, smirking. "Definitely not anymore though."

She flipped me off. "Go to hell."

Emily was sixteen or so when I'd first met her. A scrawny little thing with short legs and not a single curve. Brown bobbed hair, braces, full cheeks, and one hell of a sassy mouth that had eaten away at my nerves even when I was twenty. She and Hawk had never got along and were fighting long before they found out they shared both a ma and a dad. The second she'd opened her mouth, I could see why that was.

"I was kidding, JP. Seriously. You should learn to lighten up a little." I shrugged a shoulder.

She shook her head, dark eyes filled with exasperation. "Call me Emily." She poked me in the chest with her finger. "Or call me nothing."

"*Nothing?* That's boring. How can I jerk off to that name, huh? *Oh, God, Nothing, I'm gonna c—*"

She shoved me then, her face so red I thought she'd turned into a tomato. I almost called her that, but decided that maybe I needed to cut the dick routine. The problem was, though, I liked labeling people with nicknames and struggled most days not to do it. It was impulsive and blunt and, well, it was me. Who I was. If anything, I was like my old man in that sense. He'd been the same way when it came to nicknames, but for a different reason. I was creative, while he'd usually just been too drunk to remember real names.

Emily's latest nickname, JP, was my favorite, equating to the words Junk Puncher—like I said, total fucking badass. Last summer was the first time I'd seen her in four years, since I'd called her a hot table, and she'd remembered who I was just as much as I'd remembered myself. The guy who'd once teased her about looking twelve, not sixteen, and, well, "flat like a table" was apparently not forgiven. I'd been told to watch her, which she hadn't liked, and it hadn't taken much of my usual provocation before she'd kicked me in the nuts.

Hence the name.

"Sorry." I took a step back, pretending to give her space. "It's special to me."

"Special," she deadpanned, eyes narrowing.

"Oh, yeah. *Very* special." I winked, sliding out from around her. She followed me with her eyes from over her shoulder again, but kept her body pointed toward the door, her hand grabbing the knob once more. "In fact, it's so special it'll likely break my cold, dead heart if I can't keep using it. You understand, don't you?"

She turned her head away, her lips flattening. I couldn't help but zero in on the things from the side, mostly because they were abnormally red, kinda like her cheeks. The bottom one was bigger than the top and suddenly an image of them wrapped around my cock had me swaying even closer, breathing in the scent of her perfume. Oranges mixed with vanilla was a damn nice combo. One I'd never smelled on a woman before.

"Whatever, oh incorrigible one." She turned the doorknob and stepped into her house. Then she turned to face me, smirking as she said, "But I'm still not going to that stupid party."

CHAPTER TWO

Emily

I was anxious. Not to mention restless. I felt as if I was a ticking time bomb sitting around doing nothing.

I *would* leave this place… even though I didn't have a clue how. But I had a goal at least. A goal that had everything to do with the secret stash of letters hidden in my kitchen cabinets.

God, what I wouldn't give to go back to my old life. To the life I'd begun to build with Sam, my ex-fiancé. It wasn't that I missed *him* as a person. More that I missed the stable world we'd built together. Our giant, two-story townhouse, which was about an hour from Rockford in St. Charles, had been the place where we were supposed to start a family together after we got married. Suburbanized, quiet at nights, especially during the weekends— other than the sound of kids running through the streets. The big backyard was the reason he'd wanted to buy it in the first place, but only because it was filled with tall oaks that grew past our rooftop. Big enough for shade and a treehouse for our future kids, he'd told me. Kids I would not, in fact, be having any time soon.

Sam had put up a hammock a few weeks after we'd got back from our cruise last summer. I'd only laid in it a total of three times before my life had gone to hell and I'd had to basically start over.

I was pretty sure he and his new girlfriend took it when they moved to Des Moines for his job last month. I may have been the one to break up with Sam, but that didn't mean I was happy about it. He was too good for the trouble that seemed to come at me in the form of my family, which was why I'd ended it before it had truly begun. With things falling apart in my life, Sam didn't deserve to go down with me. Not when he had real life goals that went beyond motorcycle clubs, deadbeat criminal dads, and moms who ran because they were too scared to stay put and fight for what really mattered.

Either way, that part of my life was over now, and instead of planning *future* birthday parties for my and Sam's *future* kids, I was planning an ingenious way to escape this godforsaken motorcycle club once and for all.

Last month's letter was the eleventh one I'd received from my mom since she'd taken off with Pops. It had appeared in my teacher's mailbox at school in a plain, white envelope, alongside information about our summer work party, which was weird. The others had shown up in my PO box at the post office downtown. Why, now, would she send it to my work? Not only did it confuse me, it also wasn't good for job security. I couldn't imagine what the Rockford School District would think, not to mention *do*, if they figured out that I, a middle-school science teacher, had been associating with, not to mention *living* with, one of the worst-labeled MCs in all of the Midwest.

God, my life was so messed up.

I'd brought all the letters home with me and kept them under my kitchen sink. Nothing like hiding things in plain sight. If my brother, or any of the Red Dragons, found them—found out I'd been communicating with the *enemy*—then I was pretty sure they'd off me. Even with that knowledge, I couldn't throw them away. As dumb as it sounded, they were like a kid's stuffed teddy bear to me. Emotional support letters, really, proving that my mom wasn't actually gone, but more like on an extended vacation that was meant to keep me and my brother alive, safe, and out of Pops's clutches—not that the Red Dragons would ever see it like that.

I blew my bangs from my forehead, using the foot hanging off the porch swing to rock myself back and forth. The calm before the storm, that's what this all felt like now. Any day this week, another letter would show, this time with directions. When it did, I had my bag packed and ready, no second guesses.

No matter what happened, I needed to go find my mom and get her away from Pops once and for all. Then after that, I'd get us both away from the MC life altogether. For good. Yes, the Red Dragons claimed to want the same thing I did, but not with the same intentions. If they found my mom before I did, they'd treat her as a traitor. Kill her without warning for going with Pops instead of staying here with them. I wouldn't allow that to happen. Which was exactly why *I* had to find her first.

I was tired of waiting around, bottom line. Especially after what had happened last week.

At the thought, I couldn't help but shudder. A bike roared from the road then, pulling up into the drive a second after. I turned my head just in time to see a familiar red helmet as Talker skidded to a stop in the driveway. He was one of those bikers that rubbed me in all the wrong ways, even more so than Archer Benedict. The memory of Archer's hot body so close to mine lingered even hours later. I shook it off, not entirely sure I hated it as much as I pretended to.

"Yo," Talker said, kicking off his engine. He clicked his tongue, waving a finger gun at the same time. "We gotta go, woman."

I rolled my eyes and pulled my turtleneck up a little higher. The last thing I wanted was for rumors to start about me.

"*Yo,*" I said back, mocking him without the finger guns. "I'm not going anywhere with you tonight. I've got a headache."

"You ain't gotta choice. Got my orders from up top."

"And who would that be exactly?"

"VP himself."

I rolled my eyes. Freaking Archer. He was worse than my brother. I wasn't sure what kind of game he was playing.

"What does he want?" I asked, rocking myself back and forth again.

"Dunno. I'm just the messenger. Now get up, throw on something short, and let's go."

"Tell you what." I paused. "If your *VP* gives you any crap about me not going with you, then feel free to send him my way."

Talker shook his head, long brown hair falling over one of his eyes. His face was a mask of thinly veiled disgust, reminding me of a rat. If I were being honest, most days he smelled like one too.

"You don't get nothing at all, do you?" Talker's boots slid to a stop next to the porch. "None of you old ladies do."

I didn't bother to correct him. I wasn't anyone's *anything*, especially an old lady.

"That's why I don't believe in the sanctity of taking on an old woman." Talker continued doing what he did best: talking. "My boy Archer's got it just right." He clicked his tongue against the roof of his mouth, something he did a lot, even without the finger guns. "One pussy a month. One at a time."

"Barf," I mumbled.

Obviously not hearing me, he continued, "Hell, you'd be a good one to take on, temporarily. Especially with those tits of yours. Just a handful is right by me." He whistled, eying my breasts.

"Are you done insulting me yet?" I let my hand fall away and grabbed the back of the porch swing to sit up.

He shrugged. "If you don't show up with me, it's your ass that'll be handled."

"I'll take my chances, thanks." In other words, I'd rather die than show my face at the club right now.

*

Forty minutes later there was a knock on my front door. "Open up, JP. I know you're in there."

I kicked my feet up on my couch and turned the volume up louder on my TV, ignoring him. I wasn't sure why Archer suddenly cared so much about my whereabouts. The two of us barely spoke.

Another knock sounded, this one more forceful and with no words to accompany it. What did a girl have to do to get a little peace around this place? Silence came after his fourth knock, lasting an entire two minutes. But then I heard the lock engaging, followed by the crack of the door as it slammed against the wall. I squeaked, losing the bowl of popcorn on my lap, and struggled to pull the blanket up and over the pair of Sam's old boxers I was wearing.

"What in the hell are you doing?" I cried out, standing.

Archer stood just ten feet from my couch, smelling like an ashtray, a bottle of perfume, and some sort of liquor. Long pieces of his blond hair hung over his right eye, giving him a certain kind of sex appeal that I wished I hadn't noticed.

As much as I wanted to deny it, there really was nothing unattractive about Archer Benedict, physically. Full, pink lips that looked out of place on his pale skin, and a pointed nose that was model-worthy. He was a pretty boy who drank too much whiskey—liver failure would kill him before he even learned what the word "sober" meant.

Ignoring me, he took the remaining few steps inside, letting the door click shut behind him. I watched him through narrowed eyes when he lifted up picture frames and looked behind them, only to set them back down and move along. By the time he stood in my living room completely, he'd scoped out, turned over, and examined each and every item present.

"Are you looking for something?" I asked, pulling the blanket up higher on my chest then wrapping it around me like a towel.

The leather of his vest—better known as his cut—rubbed together when he finally stopped in front of me. His sharp gaze held mine. He was beyond intense, his eyes burning and prickling with a curiosity I did not like.

"Depends. You got something to hide?"

"No." I set a shaking hand on my hip and scowled, praying he didn't notice.

He studied me, those light brows of his furrowed slightly. Seconds later, he sat on my couch, uninvited, and patted the seat next to him. "Sit," he ordered.

My heart continued to race but, somehow, I managed to keep my breathing steady. "I'm afraid you're barking up the wrong tree if you came here to try and sleep with me."

"JP, JP, JP…" He sighed. Always with that stupid name. "If I wanted you in my bed, then there'd be no question: I'd get you there, very willingly, I'm sure." He grabbed my hand and yanked me onto the couch.

"Hey!" I pulled my arm back, just about the time his gaze locked onto my cleavage.

He smirked. "Trust me though." He winked. "I'm good with what I got at the moment."

Was my boob size being insulted again? "You mean your flavor of the month, right?"

"You jealous?" He quirked a brow, leaning closer.

I couldn't help but shiver. Other than the time I'd kneed him in the nuts, we'd never been this close. I hated that it intrigued me: the smell of whiskey mixed with whatever cologne he wore.

"Hardly," I huffed. "Disgusting is not my type."

He chuckled.

"What are you doing here?" I folded my arms.

"You're not at the club." He lifted both brows. "Care to tell me why?"

"Because…" I rolled my eyes. "I'm having an emotional self-care night watching movies and eating popcorn, that's why." That's all I'd been doing since Friday night.

He leaned back, kicking a foot onto his knee. "You're needed there tonight, yet here you are." He rubbed at his stubbled chin. "I don't like it when people ignore my orders."

I grabbed a handful of popcorn and shoved it in my mouth. "Well, excuse me if I don't listen to you. You're not my parent."

"No shit," he said with a laugh, pushing back to his feet before heading toward my room.

"What in the hell are you doing?" Setting down my popcorn bowl, I took off after him, only to find him in front of my closet, pushing aside hangers.

"This is like a grandma's closet. Don't you own anything that's not a turtleneck or a cardigan? It's summer, for fuck's sake."

My mouth fell open, then shut, then open once more. "Get the hell out of there." I grabbed his leather cut and yanked him back, but all that did was make him laugh more.

Hangers were thrown aside until he finally stopped on something. "Now *this* is hot." He tossed it at me with a wink.

"*This* is the lingerie I was supposed to wear on my honeymoon." It still had the tags on it in fact. The receipt was in my purse too, just like the receipts for all the other honeymoon clothes I'd bought. I hadn't been able to stomach returning anything yet. They were the last pieces of my old life, all I had left, and I wanted to hold onto them as tightly as I could.

"What the fuck would you wear that for? Aren't you supposed to be naked on one of those honeymoon things?" He folded his arms, and his eyes pinched at the corners.

I groaned and moved around him to shove the nighty into the back of my closet where it belonged. Where it would *stay*.

"Can you just leave, please? I'm not going anywhere but my bed tonight."

He looked around me toward my mattress. "That's not a bed. That's a SUV."

I rolled my eyes, tired of his insults. "It belonged to me and Sam. He liked his mattress super firm and I liked mine soft, so we bought an adjustable bed and—"

"Good Christ, woman. You're better off without him. Any asshole that can't fuck you into a coma every night without worrying about how firm his *mattress* might be isn't worth it."

"You have no filter, do you?" I sighed, taking a step back, hating the fact that his brash words could make my face heat so easily. Maybe I was a prude. Maybe *he* was right. Which was all the more reason why I wasn't cut out for the RD lifestyle.

"I do, when it's necessary. But you've got a right stick up your ass that *needs* pulling out." He reached into the closet, grabbing a pair of jeans this time, followed by a lace cami that I saved for when I wanted to dress up a little under my cardigans at work. I'd never worn it alone before, mostly because it showed my nipples.

"I do not, thank you very much," I huffed.

"You do. And you can thank me later for the fact that I'm gonna be the one doing it for ya." He winked, shoving the cami into my hands, his Irish accent growing thicker the bossier he got. "Now get dressed. Got a surprise for ya."

I flinched at the mention of a surprise. The last person who'd told me he had a *surprise* for me had done this thing to my neck with his teeth and his mouth. "No."

"Yes."

"No." I put a hand on my hip.

"Suit yourself." He pulled out his phone, typing something.

"What are you doing?"

"Leaving you with no choice."

Nosy, I yanked the phone down, eyes widening at the text on the screen. It was for Hawk.

Emily's hiding something.

"You wouldn't dare." I pulled the phone out of his hand before he could hit send.

"Then get dressed." He yanked it back, holding it over his head.

"Fine." I gritted my teeth together. "I'll go to your stupid *club* party."

He lifted an eyebrow at me—which was seriously so much harder than he made it look. "Just like that, huh?"

"What choice do I have?"

Archer studied me a second longer, brows furrowed. It was obvious he didn't trust me, which meant I needed to *make* him trust me. What if our discussion earlier today was all for show? What if he was keeping watch over me all of a sudden because he'd somehow figured it out that I was wanting to leave? This man could seriously ruin my plans, which meant it was best that I not only get under his skin as much as possible but try and convince him that we were on the same side. That he could trust me. He wasn't the only one who had ulterior motives.

"Go!" I shooed him toward the door, grinning, trying to relax. I didn't want to go to the club. Especially since *he* would likely be there. But if I stuck close to Archer, then maybe I wouldn't have to worry.

"I'm good right here." He folded his arms and leaned against my dresser.

I growled. "I don't give out free shows."

He rubbed his jaw, one half of his mouth sliding up. "If I was really interested in what you had under your clothes, JP, then I'd pay you for a look."

"If you're not interested, then why are you still standing there?"

He waved me on. "All part of the process. You know, getting that right stick out your cute little ass."

"I hate you so much." I shoved him toward the door then locked it the second he stumbled over the threshold.

From the other side I heard him laugh. But surprisingly, he kept any other comments he might've had locked up tight where they belonged.

Despite the fact that I wasn't a fan of Archer, I found myself leaning close to him as we walked into the club a half hour later.

"Why is it so crowded in here?" I asked over the noise. It smelled like an ashtray—a typical bar, really. But the men here were bigger and angrier than the ones Summer and I used to meet in college. These biker guys were all dressed the same too: black jeans and leather cuts with patches, all wearing some sort of facial hair as well.

There were also only three other women. I'd seen them all in passing before, but never up close. Two hovered over a couple of the older club members at the bar, while one of them chose to sit on a lap. The majority of the bikers sat at various tables throughout the room, but none of them looked familiar—not that I'd made much of an effort to get to know any of them.

Well, except for *my greatest mistake,* who was, thankfully, nowhere in sight.

Archer lowered his mouth to my ear, probably so I could hear him over the loud music. "Since Flick's coming back tonight, everyone's gonna be here."

I nodded then bowed my head, careful not to make eye contact with anyone. Already my nerves were shot. To think what these men might say or do to me if they ever found out I'd been receiving letters from my mom…

Archer guided me further into the club, stopping every so often to talk to people. He was so social, and it grated on my nerves a bit because I didn't have a clue as to why he wanted me here when there were three other women he could torment.

It was obvious I wasn't a welcome guest, and I was pretty sure it was because of my mom. In a way, I'd become a pariah to this club. Yes, it was my doing as much as everyone else's as I always hid away in my house. Other than coming here last summer, and then again last Friday with *him,* I tended to keep my distance from the main club. Unlike Summer, or Slade's girlfriend, Maya, I didn't belong here.

Regardless, the entire time Archer kept his hand on my back, which earned me a whole lot of looks, and not just from the men either. Weird looks. Angry looks. Looks of disgust in general from one woman across the room who was sitting on someone's lap. A beautiful blonde who looked just a few years younger than me. Long legs, lots of curls, and piercing blue eyes that said, *You're dead to me.*

I shuddered, breaking the eye contact. The last thing I wanted was to make a new enemy, even if I'd be leaving this place sooner rather than later.

More and more bikers came into the room, but there were no other women. Hands trembling, I pulled at the front of my red cardigan, immediately regretting my outfit choice. Not only did I look more out of place than usual, it was also hot in here. I'd worn the cami Archer had picked out, along with a pair of my nicest jeans, and kept my long hair down, so that it covered the marks on my neck. If I took off my cardigan, it would leave me too exposed. And though I wasn't really a prude by any means, I wasn't exactly comfortable showing the goods here either.

"Drink?" Archer asked, his mouth to my ear again as he urged me toward the bar.

"No, thank you, I don't drink anymore."

"Pity."

I frowned, ready to bite back, only for a tall figure to appear from the hallway by the dorms to my right.

Crap. *He* was here.

My body grew rigid, and I immediately bowed my head once more, using my hair to hide my face. *Please don't let him come over here, please don't let him come over here.*

Archer tugged me by my sweater sleeve onto a bar stool. "Sit. Don't move. I'll be right back."

My eyes widened. "What? No. You can't leave me here alone."

He patted the bar, whistling at someone behind me. "I gotta piss. Nobody will bug you."

"Please." I tugged on his arm this time and stood, pleading softly.

What if he comes over? What if he—

"Hey, Arch. What can I get you?" I looked to my left, spying a woman with gorgeous red hair and a friendly, if not weary, smile. A smile that fell a little when she looked at me. "Hey, I know you." She pointed a finger at me, waving it. "You came here with Chop Friday, didn't ya?"

I held my breath, chewed on my bottom lip. Next to me I could feel Archer's quizzical gaze. I gave the woman a stiff smile, nodding just once, praying she'd let it go.

"Yeah, he was pretty fucked up, wasn't he? I saw you running out, crying. Did he hurt you, honey?"

My face grew hot. I opened my mouth, unsure of what to say, only for Archer to grab my elbow and pull me away from the bar.

"Raincheck on the drinks, Tam," he told the bartender, then he started dragging me toward the hall, his fingers wrapped around my wrist, not hard, but enough that I could feel the pressure.

Just when I thought he was going to yank me right out of my flats by how quickly he was walking, we stopped in front of a room. He pushed the door open, and I stepped in behind him, thankful for the reprieve, the space away from Chop, until Archer shut the door, leaving us in the nearly pitch-black room together, alone.

"Stay," he ordered, already walking toward the window.

Despite the sudden flux of nerves in my stomach, I called to his back, "I'm not a dog. You can at least say *please*."

He ignored me and pulled the curtains back just enough to look left and right outside before shutting them and facing me again. "Sit on the bed."

My eyes widened. "W-what?"

"Sit. On. The bed. You look like you're seconds from passing out."

I shook my head. "I'm fine standing."

"Your face is ghost-white, and your hands are shaking. Now, sit on the bed and tell me what the hell's going on."

I flinched, not immediately saying no this time. I knew what he meant right then, but explaining things could get tricky. There was only one real explanation here though, and it couldn't be avoided. Chop had become pushy, stupid-angry-drunk, clamped his teeth down on my neck, and broken my skin as he bit me like a drunken vampire, all before I'd managed to get him off. Then when I'd got up to leave, crying, telling him to never talk to me again, he'd told me that he knew my secrets. That he would tell my brother if I told anyone about what had just happened.

I didn't ask how he knew. Didn't ask *what* exactly he knew either. I just ran, fear encompassing me like a storm in the night. Ran out of the dorm, out the club doors, and stood next to my car, struggling to breathe while I soaked up the blood on my neck with an old T-shirt I'd had in my trunk.

Archer walked to the bed and clicked on a bedside lamp. Seconds later, he sat in a chair in the corner of the room and pointed again to the bed. "Open that mouth, Emily. Use it. Tell me what the hell's going on with Chop."

My stomach tightened, but I lifted my chin and played dumb. "I don't know what you're talking about."

"I saw the fucking mark, JP. This morning on your porch. And again, just now, when I was talking to Tammy. Doesn't take a genius to figure shit out, and I'm responsible for watching over you now." He spat the words out like an angry viper, a vein bulging in his temple that made my stomach tighten even more.

"I'm fine. Chop and I are friends. We hung out together and watched movies a lot." Until Friday night. Until he'd tried crossing a line I'd never wanted to cross in the first place.

Archer got up from the chair, moved around the foot of his small bed, and stood beside me. He leaned a shoulder against the wall, his legs crossed at the ankles. Even after I'd kicked him in the balls last year, he'd never made a move to get back at me. Yes, he taunted me. Yes, he teased me. And, like now, he got all angry-bear on me too. But he was at least speaking to me, unlike most people at the club.

"So, he didn't hurt you," Archer deadpanned.

Panic rushed through me so quickly that the words came out before I thought them through. "No." With Archer, though, it was hard to lie.

"And those aren't *teeth marks* on your neck?"

I flinched, breathing deep. "They are, yes."

"From Chop," he clarified.

I nodded once, needing to be careful with how I worded this. "But I told him it was okay."

"How the fuck's that okay?" He snarled and pointed at my neck.

"Because I-I… I like it rough, alright?" It was a struggle to keep a straight face. But it was necessary as well. Nobody could know what had happened. Not when there was a small chance that Chop might actually know what my plans were. My secrets.

I looked at my feet, frowning. Tears stung my eyes but I refused to let them fall. Crying was exhausting, and I'd done so much of it lately that I was surprised the old ducts weren't dried out. When Chop would follow me and Summer into work, we'd share a few jokes, but that had quickly turned into him coming to my place every night after dark to hang out.

Last Friday afternoon, he'd asked me to come to the dorm. Said he wanted to see me, but he'd been drinking all afternoon and couldn't drive or walk. Because I was lonely and in desperate need of a friend, I'd driven to the club, no hesitation—despite the fact that the main house made me uncomfortable. Chop had been nothing but kind to me before that. Always checking up on me, always sweet, never pushing me around, never *ordering* me to obey his every rule. I enjoyed being around him. His companionship, in a way, reminded me of how it had been with Sam once—minus the attraction on my end.

I'd ordered pizza for us and forced him to drink a bunch of water, too. I thought he'd sobered up because at the end of the movie, he was still awake and alert. But it was only a matter of time before I realized I'd been very wrong about Chop… and his intentions toward me.

Archer looked down at me, his shoulder still propped against the wall, his muscular arms folded over his chest. His eyes were narrowed in distrust, but he didn't call me out on my lies this time.

"I don't like that guy. Never have. So, if you're scared of telling me the damn truth about what really happened between you two, then know that I won't fucking hesitate to put a woman-beater on the streets."

Despite his harsh words, my chest warmed at his confession. It was oddly comforting again knowing that he had my back. And that, alone, was enough to make me feel safer than I had been just minutes ago.

"I appreciate your offer, but I swear nothing happened," I insisted.

Emotions warred in Archer's gaze: distrust, anger, curiosity too…

A knock sounded at his door. "Flick's back," Niyol hollered from the other side.

"Shit." Archer unfolded his arms and stood up straight. "Stay here."

"What? Why?"

He shook his head. "It was a mistake bringing you to my room. Hawk will kick my ever-loving ass if he sees you in here."

"Why? It's not like we were 'doing' anything." I scoffed and made finger quotes with my hands.

He shook his head. "Doesn't matter. You being in my room means something to the brothers here. They'll either think I've taken you on as a monthly, or that I'm making you my old lady."

"Yeah, well, maybe you shouldn't have blackmailed me to get me here."

"Maybe *you* should try to be less of a whiny brat and have some fun every once in a while, then maybe I wouldn't have had to make you come."

I scowled at him.

He winked.

Then, when I couldn't handle his smart mouth any longer, I walked toward the window, ready to create my own exit.

"I'll just leave *this* way then." I yanked the curtains open and went for the window.

"Not happening." Archer tugged me back by the sleeve of my cardigan before I could get one foot out. "We've got guards everywhere. People will be even more suspicious of you if they see you scaling the wall."

"Then what do I do?" I threw up my hands. The last thing I wanted was to be stuck in here for an indefinite amount of time because *Archer* didn't want to mess up his *reputation*.

Another knock sounded. "Let's go, brother. All men out on the floor for arrival. You know the drill." This time it was Slade, my cousin, and one of Archer and Niyol's best friends.

"You wait in here," he whispered. "One hour. Please."

I rolled my eyes, knowing there was no way on God's green earth that I would *ever* wait in here. Still, what Archer didn't know wouldn't hurt him.

"Fine. Go."

He stood there, staring at me.

"What?" I hissed.

"Nothing." Then he turned and walked out the door, something clicking into place from the other side.

"What the hell?" I walked over, turned the handle. He'd locked the door. "Asshole." I hit the wood with the back of my fist, then kicked it with my toe.

That's when I realized what I had to do.

And exactly forty minutes later, when I had nearly paced a hole in Archer's floor, and finally told fear to take a flying leap, I opened the window and left.

The best part? There was not, in fact, a single guard watching me.

CHAPTER THREE

Archer

"You boys still know how to throw a good party." Flick grinned, downed another shot, then lit up a smoke—his fifth in an hour. Wrinkles covered his saggy, brown eyes, making me wonder what all he'd seen with them over the last few months.

"We learn from the best, Boss." I took a sip of my whiskey, trying to keep the conversation light.

Tonight was all about his return, preparation for the next steps in our war against Pops… but my mind was somewhere else: on the brunette in my room. My guess was JP was ripping my shit to shreds for revenge, pissed to hell that I'd locked her in. But it was for her own good. At least that's what I kept telling myself.

Knowing she was in there, possibly lying on my bed, did something funny to my gut. I'm guessing it's because I was attracted to the idea of the forbidden. And Emily was exactly that. Every so often, I looked to where Chop was sitting at the table next to ours, imagining my hands around his neck, squeezing until he had bruises on his throat that were ten times worse than the one he'd left on JP's neck.

Scratches and a bruise, fingerprint marks too. Motherfucking sick bastard was what he was. And for Emily to openly lie about it? That shit wasn't cool. There had to be a reason though. Maybe he was threatening her. Maybe he had dirt on her nobody else did. I'd find out soon enough. Just not tonight.

"Archer," Slade growled in my ear. "What's your issue?"

I rubbed two fingers over my mouth, refocusing on Flick. This was supposed to be a night of celebration, but the old man looked like he was seconds from having a coronary.

"No issue. Just thinking about shit." Shit I had no business thinking about right now.

"We doing Church in the morning?" Hawk jumped in.

Flick nodded. "Yep. Back to the grind." Then he lifted two fingers and motioned Willa over, patting his lap a second later. She was all smiles as she took a seat, her tits pressing against his chest, legs straddled over his lap.

Good. Getting back to the grind meant I didn't have to branch out on my own and take care of shit. I didn't want to do it, but I would without blinking an eye.

"How's Maya?" Flick looked to Slade then. As he asked about his niece, the guy tucked his hands into the back of Willa's skirt. She writhed against his thigh, turning her head to look at me. I saw the hunger there in her eyes, the way her lips parted in a silent moan. It was easier than it probably should've been to ignore her.

"She's good." Slade cleared his throat. "Tat business is going well for her."

Slade's girlfriend had opened up a tattoo parlor across from our main shop a few miles up the road toward downtown Rockford. She'd tatted most of the guys from the club there, and was getting a good client roster outside of just the brothers. Chick was talented as hell. I had several tats on my body proving so, including one on the inside of my right wrist that said, *Self-made or never made.*

"You got plenty of watch on her, yeah?" Flick frowned, nonchalant as he pushed Willa back just enough to start playing with her tits over her skimpy tank.

Loved my pres, but his sexual appetite was worse than mine. Plus, he was more old-school about the women and hang-abouts in the club than any of the rest of us. Taking what he wanted, never really asking… The women always let him, of course. Getting with the sixty-something-year-old man was a prize to most of them—including Willa, apparently.

"Yeah. She's good." Slade nodded. "You gonna go see her tomorrow?"

"Doubt she wants to see me." Flick shrugged.

"The hell you mean by that?" Slade barked. "Hell yes she wants to see you. You're her uncle. You're all the blood she's got left."

Before anyone else could say shit, a loud noise sounded from outside over the bass of the speakers.

"What the fuck was that?" Slade didn't wait for orders, just stood up and took off toward the door, pulling a gun and blade from his jeans while he was at it.

The music shut off, chairs squeaked, men ran to the windows, guns drawn. Hawk dropped his phone on the table and rushed after Slade, one name likely running through his head: *Summer.*

I stood just as the fifty other brothers there tonight followed my best friends outside. Flick got to his feet beside me, a hand on the table keeping him balanced. Old man was more wasted than I thought. Like Slade, he pulled a gun from his waistband, poised to kill and conquer like the rest of us—shitfaced be damned.

"We gotta go," I said. He nodded his agreement. "Crazy?" I yelled to one of the older, original, Red Dragons. "Get Flick where he needs to be."

The old man nodded, then did as asked.

The second I stepped out the front door though, I remembered what I'd left in my room, cursing the fact that I'd almost left her locked in there. She wasn't a prisoner, but I wasn't sure what was going on and whether she was safer out here with us or inside my room, alone.

Realizing what I had to do, I rushed back into the club and headed down the hall toward the dorms, quick feet and hands as I unlocked my door and shoved it open.

"JP, we gotta…"

I looked around, eyes narrowing when I didn't see her.

She wasn't there. The window was open.

She'd left.

Little fucking brat.

My heart raced when I ran back out the front door. *Where the hell has she gone?* I searched the dark, only to spot orange-and-yellow flames flickering up into the sky like a bonfire… directly behind Hawk's place on the other side of the gate.

Shit.

"Go, go, go!" Flick yelled ahead of me, waving his hands, giving prospects their orders.

Brothers rushed right and left, some taking off on bikes, others on foot, all heading in the same direction toward the fire.

"Gonna need outside help," Flick yelled to Crazy over the roar of bike engines.

"On it," Crazy yelled back, pulling out his cell.

We'd need a fire crew for this, but they had to be people not connected to the law. Thankfully Flick had contacts.

I took off toward my bike in the lot, no time to seduce her before a ride this time as all my thoughts were on Emily right then. If she'd made it home or if something had happened to her…

I blinked, pushing the morbid thought away. She was fine. Had to be. Because Hawk would kill me if she wasn't.

Wind rushed over my face and through my hair, bringing with it the smell of smoke the closer I got to the fire. By the time I arrived, a crew of my brothers were already on the other side, standing by as they watched a car burn. My stomach dropped into my toes when I kicked off my engine. But it wasn't the fire that had me all tied up. It was the woman standing next to the lone tree in front of Hawk's house, both her hands on Chop's chest, shoving him back.

Emily.

"Leave me alone," I heard her yell when he didn't move.

Chop put his hands on her waist, holding her steady, and I couldn't help but see red—red not caused by the flames either. Guy just couldn't take a fucking hint.

From over Chop's shoulders, her eyes met mine, going wide, but not for long.

"You're in deep shit," I said to myself, lip curled, vowing to deal with her sneaking out *after* I dealt with Chop.

"Let's go. I'm taking you back to my dorm," Chop said, clutching her wrist.

"Step the hell away from her, Chop," I growled to his back.

His eyes narrowed at the exact moment I grabbed him by the collar of his shirt and shoved him to the ground.

"The fuck, Archer?" he hissed up at me. Two seconds later, he was on his feet, shoving me back. "Don't touch me."

Having six inches—and a hell of a lot more mass—on the former Marine, I didn't budge. "Leave. Go do something useful for once. Emily's off limits."

"Archer, stop. It's fine." Speak of the devil.

Chop ignored her when she stepped in between us, her back to me, facing him. Instead he snarled at me like a rabid wolf. "The hell she is. She's mine. I'm making a claim, right here, right fucking now."

"Yeah, real mature, asshole. Especially since we might've just gotten attacked."

I couldn't fucking stand the man before. But now? I *hated* the motherfucker. If Chop hurt one woman, who's to say he wouldn't hurt another? Willa or Tammy? They didn't deserve that shit. There was nothing wrong with a little kink, believe me. But only when it was done right.

An unmarked truck pulled up outside the gate, distracting the three of us. I turned, finally taking in the scene, eying the fiery car first, which sat about fifteen feet from the other side of the fence. There were no other cars around it, which meant it wasn't an accident but a deliberate fire. By who though? Someone in connection with Pops? And if so, where were they?

Men readied hoses, hooking them up to a nearby hydrant. Water started flowing and it took less than a minute for the flames to die down. If this was an attempt at an attack, it was pretty pitiful.

"She's mine," Chop repeated low in my ear, some sort of a reminder or warning.

Shaking my head, I turned to tell him Hawk wouldn't ever let that happen, especially when he found out what the guy had done to her. But the fucker was already walking toward the fence, where some of the brothers stood with their fingers linked through the metal.

Even in the dark I saw Chop's hands fisting against both thighs. Could almost bet he was imagining what it might be like to deck me upside the head with one, or both, of them.

Bring it, asswipe.

Seconds later, Emily rushed past me, unnoticed by everyone but myself.

"You should've stayed put," I called after her.

She flipped me off but didn't slow as she made it to her door.

"Hey, you hear me?" I followed, grabbed her shoulder as she sank her key in the lock. Spinning her around, I forced her gaze to mine, a hand on her chin, thumb on her neck, stroking where the bruises were.

She winced, shut her eyes too. "Leave me alone. Please."

"You left through the window after I told you not to. Why? What's so hard about listening?"

"I told you. I'm not some dog you can order around." Her eyes popped open again and she shoved my hand away. "I don't even get why you care anyways."

"You leave then just so *happen* to come upon a fire burning in your backyard? This looks really fucking bad for you."

"Are you trying to accuse me of something?" She lifted her chin. "Because I am *not* Pops. I couldn't care less about your club and the people in it."

"Summer's a part of this *club*," I argued.

"Exactly. I lost her. I *lose* everyone. And if I'm not careful, I'm gonna lose my…"

I let her go, frowning. "Lose what?"

"Nothing." Then she turned and headed inside. This time when she locked me out, I didn't grab the spare key in the light fixture that Hawk had told me about. JP could run, but she sure as fuck couldn't hide. And neither could her secrets.

CHAPTER FOUR

Emily

My knees shook as I stepped into my house, panic consuming me like the fire outside. On the other side of the door, I listened, waiting for Archer to walk away, praying the entire time that he hadn't seen the panic in my face or heard it in my words. I hadn't started that fire. But I knew exactly who had and why.

One second.

Two.

Then three…

Finally, his footsteps faded as he moved down the porch, away from me, from my house… I let go of the breath I'd been holding, thinking clearly without fear and adrenaline clouding my mind for the first time in twenty minutes. There would be no forgiveness from the Red Dragons if they found out what I was about to do. Which meant I needed to go. Now.

A younger guy in a leather cut, face hidden by the brim of a black hat, had been waiting for me on my porch when I'd gotten home from the club— more like after I'd snuck out of Archer's window. Still and without fear, he watched me approach, a letter in his hand that now sat burning the inside of my bra. His words had been absent, but his eyes had said what his voice hadn't.

This is it. The last letter. The one you've been waiting for.

Seconds after placing it into my fingers, he'd left like a ghost in the night. I didn't know him. Couldn't pick him out of a lineup either. Without a doubt, this man knew my mom and was also associated with Pops. The scariest part about it? He'd managed to get through the compound gates and over to my house.

Five minutes after he'd walked away, the car had appeared outside the gate. The same man had jumped out of it then run toward the street. Ten seconds after he'd disappeared, the car had erupted like a cannon into the night, bursting flames reaching skyward. It had been stupidly dramatic, but also the perfect distraction for this guy's getaway. For *my* getaway too. If it hadn't been for Chop showing up like he'd done, dragging me off the porch then shoving me against that tree, I would have been long gone by now.

At least he hadn't seen me with the mystery man.

Now that everyone was piled at the gate behind my house, I could finally get out of this place, barring no one was guarding the back entrance of the compound—which was where I planned on going. Now away from both Chop and Archer, I rushed through my house, my palms damp with nerves. From my top drawer, I pulled out the cash I'd been stowing away over the last few months, then grabbed the duffel bag in my closet, stuffing the envelope into the side pocket. Twenty-five hundred. That's all I had. God, I hoped it'd be enough to get me where I needed to go. Through Illinois and Indiana to, finally, Kentucky, which was where Mom was. Where she'd been staying for the last two weeks, according to the letter.

She'd told me they'd be there for a while, and that they were hidden in the forests of Pine Mountain State Resort Park. An abandoned building, she'd said, where Pops was making a home for his new club. Hidden out of sight just enough for privacy, but close to a plethora of towns with all the resources a growing motorcycle club would need.

Was she warning me? I was selfish to not say anything to anyone here on the compound, which was why I grabbed a pen off my dresser then scribbled a quick letter to Summer on a pad of paper. *Be on alert*, I told her. *The rogues are closer than the guys here think.*

That was also the exact second I let myself break down. Quick tears, flushed face, and a guilty conscience most of all. I didn't realize saying goodbye to my best friend would hurt so much. It's probably why I hadn't thought about doing so. But I owed it to Summer to explain, without actual details. So, I told her I loved her; how sorry I was that I had to go. Then I told her to take care of the baby, that I already loved it so much, maybe as much as I loved her.

Voices grew louder from outside my window. I stiffened and held my breath until they passed. I was running out of time and I needed to go, stat. So, I folded the paper and put it on my bed, knowing she'd be over tomorrow to grab the blanket I'd borrowed. Then I got to work gathering my stuff.

Driving a car out of here wasn't smart. Someone would surely see me. Which meant I'd have to leave by foot, walk into town, maybe get a Greyhound ticket or something. A plane ticket would be smarter and quicker, but I needed to save all the money I had for as long as I could.

Once my bag was zipped and ready, I shut off the lights and walked into my living room. There, I stood for a long minute and looked around, marveling at the tiny home I'd made. When I inhaled, it smelled like the homemade chicken soup I'd cooked yesterday afternoon for lunch. As much as I hated to admit it, there was something about this place that I'd miss—though I'd never miss the land it sat upon.

"No regrets," I told myself, grabbing my purse then heading toward the front door. When I peered outside, the first thing I noticed was the lack of men out front. But the noise was loud in the back, which proved they were still by the fire. They wouldn't stay put long. I needed to go, now.

Pushing the door open, I slowly tiptoed outside, holding my breath as I took each creaky porch step down. I looked to my left, noting a light on in Summer and Niyol's house. My best friend's Range Rover wasn't there, but Niyol's bike was. Inside, I could just barely hear the sound of Biker's yipping over the roar of the men out back.

I said a silent goodbye to the pup and snuck to my right, keeping to the dark shadows as I crept through the trees that lined the side of the house. Branches crackled under my feet with every step, and things scurried in the trees. Regardless, I was thankful for the privacy my brother had insisted on keeping when it came to building these two little homes on the compound. Without the woods, my escape wouldn't be possible.

I stayed close to the fence on my right, but not so close I could be seen by anyone who might be along the other side of it. If someone saw me here, they'd shoot at me on sight, thinking I was someone who'd snuck through their gates, meaning harm. How that man had made it through the gates to get to my home without being seen wasn't something I could wrap my head around. No matter, gifts were not meant to be ignored.

I kept going, pushing the fear in my belly aside as I made it further and further away from the fire and my home, and closer to the clubhouse. I'd have to pass the main building then sneak in behind their garages in order to get to the back of the compound. There was a small hole in the fence back there, big enough for my short self to sneak through.

Voices sounded to my left—one voice of a man more specifically. An Irishman.

"What do you mean the cameras are all disabled? Chop said he'd tested them out last week."

I cringed at the anger in Archer's voice. When he was angry, his accent grew thicker, almost incomprehensible. And right now I could just barely make out his words.

"Yeah, well, you better get that shit put back together, otherwise there'll be hell to pay."

His voice was more like a frustrated growl as he hung up the phone. I was pretty sure I was half the reason for his temper tonight. Not that it mattered; I'd be gone soon enough. Which meant *he'd* be out of my life too—good thing. I didn't deal well with men who thought their opinions and needs were superior to my own; Archer, for all his supposed good intentions, drove me insane.

Moving wasn't an option with him so close, so I stayed still, watching him through the dark shadows. His phone beeped in his hands, and I could see his head bow as he looked at the screen.

"Motherfucker," he muttered under his breath. Seconds later, he shoved the phone into his pocket then leaned his head back, hands running through his wavy, blond hair. God, he was tall. The tallest man on this compound. So tall that if he turned even a little bit, he'd easily see through the gap in the trees and likely notice me standing here.

I held my breath, waiting, waiting, waiting some more…

"Flick!" he yelled, moving forward. "We got problems."

And then he was gone, footsteps trudging as he headed toward his club.

That's when I made my escape.

Behind the garage, crawling through the tall grass toward the other side, things bit my hands, my neck too, proof that my cardigan couldn't keep the bugs away. Still, I did what I needed to, eyes widening in relief when I realized there was nobody hovering in the back. Someone upstairs was looking out for me.

Still crawling, my bag heavy and weighing me down, I rushed to the hole in the fence, nudging my bag through first then crawling out like a dog.

Seconds later, I was on the other side. Free. And ready to get the hell out of this place for good.

CHAPTER FIVE

Archer

I hadn't slept in twenty-four hours. None of my brothers had. And the tension around the table in Church was thick with impatience. We were all pissed off and had nowhere to direct it but at each other.

"Why was she out that late? That's all I'm fucking asking." Crazy looked to Hawk, then me. "I don't trust that woman. None of you idiots do."

"She fucking lives there," I murmured, knowing the exact reason why Emily had been outside. She'd been running from my ass, escaping out *my* window. Yeah, it looked bad that the car had caught fire when she'd been outside. But the woman wasn't capable of lighting up some dynamite and then getting back inside without nobody seeing her. If the goddamn cameras had been functioning, then this wouldn't be an issue.

"You accusing my sister of something, asshole?" Hawk pushed away from his seat, snarling. "Because you better think twice about anything else you say from here on out. She's not a fucking prisoner. She has rights. And if she wanted to walk outside at fucking midnight on a Wednesday, then who the hell cares?"

"Knock it off, Hawk." Flick laid his head back and scrubbed his hands over his face. The guy looked like shit, even worse than he had the night before.

"I'll knock it off when your boy here quits accusing Emily of—"

"Shut up," I growled at my best friend, then I looked toward Crazy as I said, "And you." I shook my head. "Jesus Christ, man, you're off your rocker. No way she'd be capable of blowing up that damn car. Nor does she have a reason to." I curled my lip then refocused on the rest of the brothers in Church: Flick, Mute, Talker, Slade, Hawk, then finally Chop. "You all know who was behind this," I snapped. "Don't pretend like you don't."

The room went quiet. Everyone bowed their heads, including Hawk. Of all the brothers, how could he be so stupid? Unlike the rest of them, I leaned forward onto the table with my elbows as I spoke, sure as shit not ready to let this go. "We need to make a move, now. Because if we don't, then we'll lose them again. They're likely close by. Hell, maybe they're here to stay, readying a full-scale attack. Either way, it's time we do something about it."

Pops wasn't dumb enough to stay too close after such a stupid attack like that. One that didn't make sense at all. Blow up a damn car outside the gates—what was the point?

"I'm with Archer. We need a plan." Slade was the only voice of reason at the table. "I'm not sitting around and waiting for more bad shit to happen anymore." He looked to Hawk. "What if that damn car drove through the gate and hit your fucking house when Summer and your unborn kid had been inside, sleeping? You ever think about that?"

Hawk's jaw grew taut, but he stayed wordless because he knew it was true.

Slade kept at it though, the only other brother at the table ready for retaliation like me. "We've been sitting ducks for too long. It's time to hunt. Last night was obviously a warning. It's time we take action."

I nodded, sharing a look with Slade. "Agreed." Then I eyed the room, meeting each of my brothers' gazes from across the table once more. A collective sigh sounded, and I felt us uniting. It'd been a long, long time since that had happened, and I prayed to fucking God that it was just the beginning, especially with Flick back.

"I'm all for taking Pops down, but we got no credible leads," Flick spoke up, folding his hands behind his head. "And we don't got the manpower to make it happen either."

"I sent a few guys out on a run an hour or so ago to see if there's been any movement close by," Slade said.

Flick shook his head, disagreeing. "Thing is, we ain't got nothing concrete. Which is exactly why we need to wait a little longer."

"There wasn't nothing with the car? No notes or anything like that?" Chop asked, the first thing he'd said all of Church.

Motherfucker needed to stand down. Already, I was seconds from telling Hawk what he'd done to Emily. He may have been Flick's favorite, but that didn't mean we couldn't make him quietly disappear one night.

Chop's eyes shot my way, almost like he'd heard my thoughts. I grinned, tapping my pointer fingers together. Maybe I'd sick some rabid animals on him instead. Shove him into a den of wolves so they could chew him to bits.

Scowling, he looked away, squirming a little in his seat.

That's right, asshole. You better watch yourself.

"I don't get it," Talker jumped in. "Why the fuck did our security system catch no one? The cameras we got are everywhere. We should be able to see who drove the car."

My eyes narrowed even more at Chop. He was in charge of that shit. Yet...

"Wires were cut." He scowled at Talker then looked to Flick, avoiding me.

"Boy's right." Flick nodded. "Saw it with my own eyes."

"From the inside?" Talker leaned back in his chair, rubbing at his bare chin. Kid couldn't grow a lick of fucking hair on his skinny little face if he tried.

"Yeah," Chop said, nodding. "Which means it could've been anyone here." A shrug. "Maybe Emily even."

"You motherfucker." Hawk was up and out of his chair before I could blink. Seconds later, he had Chop on the ground beneath him, hands around his throat. Nobody stopped him when his fist flew into Chop's eyes. Probably because we all felt the same way about the pretty-boy suck-ass. I grinned, sure as hell in no rush to stop him myself. Hawk didn't even have a clue what Chop had done to his sister. If he knew, he'd murder him before I did.

"Enough." Flick shoved his chair away from the table and stood. "You assholes are eating at my brains, and I didn't get enough pussy last night to deal with this shit." Then he grabbed the back of Hawk's shirt and tossed him as if he weighed nothing.

"I've made the call." Flick barked at us all then, taking a step closer to the door. "Wasn't gonna tell nobody till they got here, but you're all not making me feel too generous right now."

I frowned, leaning forward in my chair. "Made the call to who?"

Flick looked to me. "Rodent's sending some brothers from the Fallen Order at the end of the month. Once they're here, we'll start to figure out what to do next."

"Hell no." I pushed away from the table and stood, eyes to Slade, whose face had gone pale.

Rodent. The leader of the Fallen Order. The Texas club Flick had been staying with. They sold and traded young girls. We couldn't trust them. And I didn't want to either.

"You don't get an official say in this," Flick said to me, stone-faced.

Who in the hell was this man?

"I sure as hell do. I'm VP." My breathing grew ragged at the thought of those men being here, close to my family. "I told you before you left to go to that fucking place, and I'm telling you again, right now, in front of the brothers. We. Don't. Need. Them."

"I've already made arrangements." Flick stroked his beard, grabbed the door handle.

"The hell you mean you've already made arrangements?" I rushed him at the door, jumping in front of him. He didn't get to fucking leave like that. "They're not even a brother club of ours."

"But they've got the bodies, the weapons, and the guts." Flick shooed me away with his hand.

"Gonna have to stand with Flick on this one," Hawk jumped in from behind.

I shot a look to my best friend over my shoulder; his narrowed eyes were glued to the table. "The hell, man? You want those assholes around Summer?"

Before Hawk could say anything to that, Slade stood up, hands on his face, scrubbing hard. "Not fucking okay, Flick," he mumbled, eyes squeezed shut when he pulled his hands from his face. I'd guess he was probably trying to get the image of those girls in cuffs out of his head like I'd been doing for months now. The Forsaken—an outlaw club located in Texas—had been trading them for drugs, and Slade and I had watched it all go down. We'd seen those girls in that club and, for fuck's sake, Flick likely had too.

Something was wrong with our pres for him to think this was the route we needed to go down. I'd known him going to Texas would mean something in the end, would even mess with his mind. And I was right. This proved it.

"I'm done." Flick shoved me aside, leaving the room, slamming the door shut behind him.

I eyed Hawk from across the room; his gaze was on me. My oldest friend didn't have a clue. None of these men did. But for Flick to know yet not think twice about it? I wasn't sure he was the kind of man I wanted to stand behind after all.

"Open up, JP. We gotta talk." My mind was clouded. I needed a reprieve from Church, the shit that'd gone down, Flick's declaration and walkout most of all. He'd *never* walked out like that before. Which meant he knew something, but didn't have the balls to say what it was.

I also wanted to make sure Chop left Emily alone today. Even if half the club didn't trust her, I was still supposed to be tailing her.

I didn't have a monthly right now, and part of me knew fighting with Emily would get my adrenaline pumping.

"Hey. Open the fucking door." I pounded again with my fist. Maybe she wasn't gonna answer like she'd done yesterday. She hated me. I tolerated her. Our interactions had been rare, up until recently. Now I couldn't seem to stay away. Whatever the hell that meant, I wasn't in the mood to figure it out.

Her car was in the driveway. She wasn't at Hawk's place with Summer—I'd just seen the two of them leave in her Range Rover ten minutes ago.

"Fuck this." I grabbed the spare key in the light, shoved it in the door. Turned the handle too. "JP. What the hell are you doing in here, masturbating?" I frowned and took a few steps into the room. That would have been kind of fun to walk in on, honestly.

But she wasn't in the living room or the kitchen. The lights were off too. I listened for the shower but heard no water. Bedroom it was then. Only, her door was wide open. She wasn't in there either. I looked around, thinking maybe she'd jump out of the closet, ready to karate-chop me in the balls for being here without her permission. But... she didn't.

I frowned, pulled my phone out to call Hawk, but something on her bed caught my eye.

A sheet of paper folded into thirds, the name on the outside saying, *Summer.*

Curious, I swiped it up, sat on her bed, unfolded it, and read the words.

I shook my head, blinked. "What in the actual fuck?"

Be on alert? The rogues are closer than we thought? I'm leaving? I'll miss you?

Red flashed behind my eyes. My upper lip curled. Holy shit. She'd run. She'd actually fucking run. Worst of all, her warnings to Summer made it seem like she'd been in contact with Pops? Probably her ma.

I balled up the paper then flipped on the light switch, breathing heavily, nails digging into my palms. Was she behind last night's ordeal after all?

Goddammit, Emily. Breathing in through my nose, I tried to keep calm, rein in my thoughts, and give her the benefit of the doubt. First things first, I needed proof. Clues that she'd possibly stoop this low.

Where to start? Where to fucking start?

Drawers.

I pulled them out, not knowing what I was looking for. I tossed cotton bras and panties out first, fingers stroking the hems and straps as I did. Even pissed about the possibility that she might be a traitor, I couldn't help but think of how she'd look in the simple things. They were damn plain, but they fit her. Every librarian inch of her.

I hissed, slamming the drawers when I came up empty. Having no idea what I was even looking for, I ran to her closet next. I tossed shit out left and right: shoes, clothes, empty boxes… Still, nothing. Good Christ. The woman wasn't that stupid. She'd be dead if anyone found out about this. Even Hawk might not come back from her betrayal.

I left destruction in my wake, tearing through her house, more closets, her couch, cushions ripped apart… For a good, solid hour I wreaked havoc on her place. Only one more spot left to check: her kitchen. I'd known last night when I'd come over that something didn't feel right. Got a read on her that I'd thought, later, had to do with Chop. But now I wasn't sure what I fucking thought. I'd tie her to my bed, cuff her, hands above her head and…

Shit. I'd enjoy that too much.

The first place I looked in the kitchen were the drawers. Again, I wasn't even sure what I was looking for at this point. Proof that my gut feeling was right? Maybe *this* was why she wanted to be bait? Because she knew things nobody else did and she felt like shit about it.

I tossed towels, bottles, food, and junk like that out of her cupboard and fridge… coming up with nothing. Too many scenarios ran through my head, and by the time I got done ransacking shit, I was sure of only one thing: Emily *had* been keeping secrets. Just not the type of secrets I'd thought.

The last place was under her kitchen sink. I crouched down in front of the open cupboard, ready to give up, call Hawk, tell him what I knew. Until I saw it. A fucking cookie jar.

Slowly, I pulled it out, uncorked it, and…

"Jesus."

Letters. I counted them. Eleven. The name on the return address?

Lisa Lincoln. Emily's mom.

CHAPTER SIX

Emily

I couldn't relax. Not when I was pretty much a sitting duck in the middle of the highway, on a broken-down Greyhound just two hours outside of Rockford. Maybe this was a sign. One that said I was making a huge mistake by running to try and find Mom. Worse yet, maybe my going was a trap. Like, what if Pops had been behind my mom's letters all this time? Maybe he'd been making her write them to trick me. Either way, if I didn't try to go to her and help her escape, I'd never forgive myself.

"Attention everyone," the bus driver called from the front. I sat up, looking down the aisle, thankful for the free seat beside me. Surprisingly, the bus was mostly empty, which was great. The fewer eyes to see me leave, the better.

"I apologize for the inconvenience, but there's an engine problem that's out of my control. Rest assured, a new bus will be here within the hour to get you where you need to be."

Within the hour? Damn it.

On edge, I pulled out my phone. Delays were not on my agenda. I clicked on my phone screen, frowning at the text there from an unknown number. Slowly, I punched in my passcode and opened it, only for my breath to catch at what was written there.

You can run, but you sure as fuck can't hide.

Goosebumps ran over my arms. I sat up, looking at the faces on the bus. When I was certain nobody had stealthily snuck on, I peered out the window, my eyes going impossibly wide at what was there on the other side of the highway.

Oh, God.

Archer was leaning back against his bike, arms folded, looking almost, well, *bored.*

How had he found me? I'd been careful not to draw attention to myself at the bus station. Hadn't seen a single person there who may have known anyone from the club.

My phone pinged again. Without even looking, I knew it was him. And then it dawned on me: he'd found me because of the GPS signal on my iPhone. That had to be it. Ugh. I should've known.

"Focus. You're gonna be fine," I told myself, eyes shut, deep breath in, deep breath out.

Biting my lip, I looked to the right, out the other set of windows across the aisle. Fields of soybeans or corn, something to that effect, covered every bit of land I saw. If I snuck off the bus, I could crawl through them, leave my phone here on the seat. Hide out in the middle of the field until the next bus came and he left, realizing I wasn't on there after all.

Either way, I knew I had to go. Now. Otherwise I was in serious trouble.

Lifting my bag, I slung it onto my shoulder then got to the floor, hands and knees. I shoved my phone under the seat and began to crawl my way down the aisle. Not one of my finest moments.

"Excuse me, pardon me, I'm soooo sorry," I said to whoever I bumped into, sliding my way through, my stupid duffel hitting legs, thighs, feet. At the front, the driver's feet stopped in front of my face. I looked up, wincing when I found his narrowed eyes on me.

"Is there an issue, miss?" he asked.

I chewed on the inside of my cheek, contemplating my answer. *Ignore him, explain… what the* hell *do I say?* "I, um, I need to smoke." I smiled. From the ground. Looking like a complete lunatic.

His lips pursed, but thankfully he didn't question me. Instead, he nodded and opened the door.

"Thanks, I'll, uh, just be a second." Then I turned over onto my butt and scooted down the steps.

Yeah. Graceful, I was not.

The second my feet hit the gravel, I moved in front of a tire, crouching low, praying Archer didn't see my shoes from under the bus. Cars and trucks passed loudly, the crowded interstate definitely distracting. Hiking my bag back over my shoulder, I took off down the ditch, not watching my step, only to slide down into a heap of mud, my shoe getting stuck in what could only be some sort of animal hole.

"No, no, no…" I shut my eyes, yanking at my foot, losing the shoe in the process. On my stomach, I reached down into the hole, shuddering and praying that no little critters came out to get me. Once I grabbed the bow on the flat, I tugged and tugged, my arm soaked in mud as I pulled it out. Sadly, my one success was short-lived as the next second I heard the rustle of feet behind me. Followed by that stupid, sexy, annoying voice.

"And just where do you think you're going, JP?" Arms went around my waist, hiking me up and over his shoulders.

"I'm not going back." I beat my fists against his back, struggling to kick him as my ankles were pinned to his chest. "Not with you or anyone."

A loud laugh echoed from Archer's throat as he walked behind the bus—likely so the driver didn't see me. I could scream, yeah, but I also knew what Archer was capable of doing to me if I tried.

"See? That's where you're wrong. You'll go wherever the fuck I tell you to go from here on out, understood?"

"I can't go back," I tried. "They'll kill me."

"That'd be too easy for what you deserve right now." He chuck-led and started through the lanes of the seventy-five-mile-an-hour traffic like he *wanted* to get hit. Slow turtle mode that had me so terrified I was forced to close my eyes and press my forehead into his shoulders.

"You're pretty stupid, ya know," he continued. "Rule number one of escaping somewhere is never take your phone. Not that I'm complaining. Easier to track you this way."

I rolled my eyes, though I knew he couldn't see it. "And how was I supposed to know I had a stalker on my hands?"

"I'm not a stalker, baby. Just smart." Once we were next to his bike, he set me down on my feet so hard that my entire body rattled. I lost my balance, falling onto my ass with a loud grunt.

"Don't you *ever* call me baby again," I hissed up at his smug face.

"What would you like me to call you then, huh?" He crouched down in front of me and winked.

"My *name* would be nice."

"Talk about predictable." He tutted.

"Go. Away."

"Nah." He curled his nose. "I'm starting to like this little cat-and-mouse game you've got a fetish for."

"I don't have a freaking fetish." I rubbed my eyes and grabbed the side of his bike to help myself up.

Archer reached out and grabbed my arm. "Don't touch my bike unless you get my permission, JP."

I pushed him back and got to my feet the rest of the way on my own. "Same goes for you and me. I don't want to be touched unless I tell you to touch me."

He smirked, eyebrows lifting to mid-forehead. "You plan on doing that?"

"No, God." I shuddered and jumped back. "Not ever."

"Fine." He held his hands up in surrender, that same sly smirk playing on his lips.

"Fine."

"Good." He folded his arms.

I nodded and said back, "Yes. Very good."

He didn't look angry at me anymore. If anything, Archer seemed to be enjoying our little battle alongside the road. Until his eyes narrowed. "You know, I stood up for you in Church today."

"How so?" I frowned.

"Everyone, except for your brother, is saying *you* were the one to start the car fire."

I winced and shook my head. "It wasn't me. I swear." But I knew who it was.

Sort of.

"Yet you took off…" He rubbed at his chin.

"I know it looks bad." I held up my hands. "But you need to know. I'd been planning on leaving for a while and the car fire was—"

"A distraction. I get it." He moved in closer, towering over me, his playfulness erased by the monster I knew he could be. "You working for Pops and your ma? You hiding something for 'em? You're a damn idiot if that's the case. Bigger than I thought you were."

I jerked my head back, blinking when the backs of my legs hit his leather bike seat. "No. I swear."

"Tell me the damn truth, *Emily*." He put his hands on the seat, trapping me between his hard body and the bike. "Are you working for Pops?"

"No!" I shook my head so fast I grew dizzy. Or that could've been the scent of him consuming my senses. The way he smelled, like gasoline and last night's drink. One half soap, and the other half leather. "Please. I'd never put Summer in danger. Or Niyol. That's why I left them a note."

"I might as well just take you back and let Flick deal with ya. How does that sound?" His upper lip curled and a long strand of his blond hair fell over the side of his chiseled jaw. He didn't bother to brush it away.

"Of course you'd take me back there and let *them* deal with it. You're lazy," I hissed out. "Predictable too." More than anything I wanted to get to him and prove I wasn't the meek little sister of Niyol Lattimore. Not anymore.

"How so?" He cocked his head to the side, watching me through hooded eyes.

My palms began to sweat again, so I rubbed them over the front of my jeans. "I knew you'd take me back to that club, that you'd turn me in like a good little Red Dragon instead of handling this on your own."

His eyes narrowed even more, anger rushing through the green hue like sparks of lightning. "You don't know shit about me." Then he pulled back just enough to be able to grab me by the waist and scoop me onto the back of his bike.

"Hey!" I protested, only for him to jump in front of me again. "Let me go or I'll scream."

Ignoring me, he spread my legs over the seat, fingers hot and commanding as they held me in place. His body was flush with my side seconds later, and I could feel something hard growing behind his zipper—that *something* now pressed against my hip.

I swallowed down any further comment I had, taken off guard by the shot of lust that hit me low in the belly. Then when he leaned forward and pushed my hair behind my shoulder in a way that I'd always loved a man to do, I stopped breathing. He knew all the buttons to push on me, as if there was a roadmap of them drawn on my body. Curse this man for being so good when it came to doing something so bad.

Like he knew the effect he had on me, Archer trailed his fingers down my neck, to my shoulder, taking his time down my arm, until he stopped at my elbow and squeezed.

Lowering his face to my ear, he growled out in a whisper, "Don't even fucking try to run, you hear me? Not now. Not ever again."

I licked my lips, unable to stop the seduction in my voice as I said, "And if I do…?"

Slowly he pulled back, his eyes zeroing in on my lips. My heart thumped even harder against my chest and the world spun around me in dizzying circles. I didn't know what was happening or why, but the sudden urge to kiss this man I hated, a man who held my fate in his hands, was so strong that it hurt a little to breathe.

"You won't like the dirty tricks I got up my sleeve, Emily. Trust me."

Instead of taking me back to Rockford, Archer surprised me as he continued to head south on his bike. He didn't know where Pops and my mom were at, but he drove like he did.

Forty minutes later we stopped in a small Illinois town that was comprised of nothing but a single gas station with a tiny diner attached to it. It reminded me of something post-apocalyptic in the sense that none of the pumps worked and there was nobody in the diner besides us, a waitress, and a cook.

"Sit." He pointed to a booth. It wasn't a seat-yourself kind of joint, but Archer commanded a room like nobody's business and the waitress was too busy smoking to care.

"No."

His lips pursed and he jabbed a finger in the air toward the table again. "What'd I tell you about not listening?"

I rolled my eyes but did as he asked, not wanting to look or feel like a chastised child. For now, I'd have to give him credit where credit was due: he hadn't taken me back to the club, which possibly meant he wanted to talk before he did. Maybe if I could reason with him and make him understand what I wanted, he'd let me go. Though I wasn't going to hold my breath.

"Talk. Right now," were the first words out of his mouth as he sat across from me.

My stomach tightened as I stared into the eyes of my new nemesis. "It's not what you think. I swear."

"Then tell me what the fuck it is, JP. Because I'm gonna need a reason as to why I shouldn't take you back to the club right now and lock your ass up until we can figure out what to do with you."

Part of me wondered why—if he was so in love with his stupid club—he hadn't just driven me back to Rockford and turned me over in the first place. What was the point of niceties? Why pretend my opinion mattered when it likely never would? I wouldn't ask him those things though. Not when there might be a chance that he'd hear me out.

Inhaling through my nose, I leaned back in my seat and thought about how I wanted to explain this. Archer could think whatever he wanted about me, but my loyalties lay with my mom, not his stupid club, and definitely *not* with Pops.

I looked at my shaking hands before clasping them together on top of the table. "The first letter came two weeks after she left."

"Fucking hell, woman. All these months you've been keeping this shit a secret?"

I cringed. "You have to understand. That's my mom and—"

"I don't give two shits who she is. That woman is with *Pops*. So, to me and my brothers, she's a traitor to our *club*."

I winced at the hatred there in his gaze. This wasn't the playful man I'd come to know sitting across from me now, not the one who teased me and called me names and threatened me with the dirty thoughts running through his mind.

"I didn't have a choice," I whispered. "She could be in danger."

"Of course you had a choice. So did your damn ma." He slapped a palm on top of the table, rocking the napkin holder against the wall. "We lost two people because of your old man. Imagine what we might've been able to do if you would've given us these earlier." He reached inside his cut, yanking out a set of familiar, white envelopes, all held together by a rubber band. "They got zip codes on 'em for fuck's sake."

I pressed a hand to my throat, trying to stay calm.

"You didn't stop and think about that though, did you?" His Irish accent grew heavier and thicker, making him almost impossible to understand. "All you cared about was yourself."

"I'm sorry." For so many things. "But you've gotta understand. My mom is, and always will be, the most important person in my life. And if she's in trouble, then I'm going to do anything I can to help her."

"So, what then, you just gonna go to wherever the fuck Pops is now? Waltz in there, bat those big brown eyes, and say, 'Please, Daddy, give my mommy back?'"

"That man is *not* my father." I pursed my lips.

"Sure." He laughed. "Tell that to a DNA test."

Suddenly desperate for a reprieve, I tugged the envelope filled with money from my duffel and handed it to him. "Here. Take this."

"What is it?" He looked at the envelope, his nose curling as I set it in front of him.

At this point, if I had to try and bribe the guy, I would. Not sure how I'd actually *get* to Kentucky without money, but I was desperate. So much so that I was willing to do just about anything for him to leave me alone.

"It's the money I've been saving up. Maybe you can, like, I don't know, buy something for your bike or put it in a fund for the club." I took a breath, exhaling through my nose. "I know I messed up by not telling anyone, and I also know people have suffered because of it, but if you take this—"

"No one wants your damn money, Emily. Especially not me. What we want is for Pops to die and for your ma's head to be on a pike right next to him."

"Please." I shook my head, eyes welling with tears. "You can't do that. I know she made a mistake, but she didn't have a choice but to go with him."

"Of course she had a fucking choice," he growled.

"Did you read her letters to me?" I asked.

He folded his arms and leaned back in his seat. "One of them. Couldn't stomach the rest."

"Did you read the *first* letter?"

"Nope."

I motioned for the pile of envelopes, asking without words to pick them up. He nodded, surprisingly, and I took the opportunity to search through the stack to find it. Slowly, I pulled it out from the rubber band, careful not to rip it as I tugged it from its envelope. After I unfolded it, I laid it flat before him, fingers shaking as I pointed to the first few lines.

"See? She was scared."

He leaned forward, read it for a second, then shrugged, disinterest in his eyes when they met mine again.

I huffed out my frustration. "She didn't have a choice. It says right there that Pops was going to hurt both me and Niyol if she didn't get him to safety."

"Yeah. And how the hell would he have done that, huh? We had him captured, for fuck's sake. The woman messed things up for all of us the second she stopped trusting the RDs and helped him escape."

Deep down, I knew he was right. But I'd been trying my best not to think about the choices my mom had made and how she'd gone about making them. I'd been suffering the consequences of her choices with the Red Dragons for almost a year now. Granted nobody had hurt me like they would hurt her, but still. Ninety percent of the men in the Red Dragon club had treated me like garbage—a pariah, really. So excuse me for wanting a fresh start.

"The woman didn't trust *us* to take care of things," Archer continued, shaking his head. "Lisa picked *Pops* over the Red Dragons. You don't do that, not even if you think it's outta loyalty." His square jaw clenched so tightly I was certain he'd crack a molar. It was dangerous to look at, to the point where I shuddered and forced my gaze to the table again.

"She regrets it now." I focused on the letter again, meticulous as I folded it and stuffed it back into the envelope. "It's obvious in her later letters. If you'd just read those—"

"Fuck the letters," he hissed, grabbing the stack from me. I flinched as the words flew angrily from his mouth. "They don't mean shit to me."

My face heated in shame. Archer was right. My mom had made a huge mistake. But I wasn't going to disown her because she'd gotten scared.

"Nobody in the club trusts you anymore," he mumbled this time, staring out the window of the diner.

"I know." I sighed in resolve. "But I also don't care."

Archer dropped his face into his hands. "Have you always been this—"

"Stupid?" I finished for him, chin high.

"I was gonna say stubborn, but you said it first." He shrugged, letting his hands fall away.

"Insult me all you want, Archer, but it's not going to change my mind. She's my mom. And since you only get one of them in your life, I'll do everything I can to protect mine."

He jerked his head up at that, staring at me as if I'd just told him pigs could fly and there was currently one above my head. For a long time he did so, to the point where something rolled through that green gaze of his that I couldn't fully comprehend. He almost looked… sad. Pained.

It didn't last long though.

He stood and reached for something inside his cut, only to pull out a small stack of bills. He tossed the money onto the table then picked up my envelope of cash and shoved it into his cut, replacing what he'd just taken out.

"Did you ever stop and ask yourself why the fuck your ma didn't trust us enough to keep you two safe?"

"All the time actually," I whispered, turning my head away as I gathered my bags.

"She played you like she played us all. You're just too blinded by her to see it." He shook his head, continuing, "She *chose* to go with Pops instead of *choosing* to be with you, the one fucking person who was supposed to matter the most in her life."

I winced. It was true, yes, but I couldn't control my mom's thoughts or feelings. And according to her letters, like I'd just told him, she'd run scared. I loved her enough to believe that she'd run to keep me safe. Archer, obviously, didn't see it that way.

"You realize Pops won't let this happen, right? That he'll either kill her, or you, before ever letting her go?"

I swallowed hard, meeting his eyes again. "The thought has crossed my mind, yes."

He squinted, and a different piece of his hair fell forward, caressing his sharp cheekbone once more. "You got a death wish then. That what this is about?"

"No, of course not. But I have to try and do something. I can't keep sitting around and waiting."

He shook his head. "So damn stupid."

I shrugged, not denying it. "Are you going to turn me in, then?"

Archer studied me from above, the wheels turning in his head—the fight there between what he should and shouldn't do. My question was, why was he hesitating at all?

"Where are they?" he asked.

"Who, my mom and Pops?"

A nod.

"Somewhere south." That's all I'd give him.

He rubbed his jaw, nodded, then grabbed my elbow, guiding me out of the diner. Because I wasn't in a position to argue, I let him.

"When did you get the last letter?" he asked as we stepped outside.

I licked my lips, hesitating before I said, "Last night."

He swung me around, backing me up against the brick wall. "What do you mean, *last night*?"

I took a deep breath, inhaling through my nose. "When I got back from the club, there was a man on my porch. He, um, gave me the letter."

"What fucking *man*?" He seethed. "Someone from the club? A traitor?" His eyes crinkled with anger. Up close like this, I could see several scars along his temples, by his eyes most of all. They were places where he'd probably needed stitches at one point in time but had never bothered to get them.

"No. I didn't recognize him."

He let go of my shoulders, taking a step back, pacing the side-walk, muttering, "Fuck, fuck, *fuck*," under his breath. "You didn't get a single look? Hair color, eye color, dark skin, light skin…?"

"No. I'm sorry. It was dark out and he just… he gave me the letter. I couldn't see his face because he wore a hat that shadowed him. But he wore a hoodie. Blue, I think."

Not looking at me, Archer continued to speak—growl, really. "How did he get in?"

"I don't know. I just… I read the letter, and the next thing I knew he was gone, and then the car was exploding outside the gate."

"You know what that means, right?" He stopped in front of me, teeth bared.

I shook my head slowly, fear in my chest making it hard to breathe.

"It means the club's been compromised. It's un-fucking-protected if anyone can get in like that." He shook his head. "Or worse, we've got a damn rat behind our gates. Someone working for Pops."

"He wasn't from the club, though. I didn't recognize him."

"But you just said you couldn't see him." Archer stopped in front of me, wild eyes searching my face.

"Well, not really. I just… He looked young. I know that. A white guy. But his hair was hidden by a hat like I said, and it was too dark to see his eyes, but he was really tall and super thin."

Archer pulled out his phone, typed something, waited, then typed something again before sticking his phone back into his pocket a moment later. Instead of making a move to grab me or walk away, he continued to stand there and stare at me, merciless eyes filled with hatred capturing me. I didn't know what he wanted, what he wanted to *do* with me either. And because of that, I'd never been more terrified in my life.

Slowly, he crept even closer, trapping me against the wall with his hands along either side of my head. His nostrils flared and a vein jumped in his temple.

"You are so fucking lucky I need something from you," he continued. "Otherwise we'd already be on the back of my bike, headed home, your ass chained up and awaiting punishment right now."

I folded my arms to keep them from shaking, inhaling the scent of cigar smoke on his skin. If he wanted me intimidated, then color me just that.

Archer was a lot more than just the playful, playboy drunk of the club. He was a monster buried beneath a frisky demeanor. A secret weapon, really. Possibly the scariest weapon of all. Maybe that's why he was second in command. The "VP" was the title I'd often heard my brother throw around.

Archer reached behind his back and pulled something out. Cold metal met my belly, and when I looked down to see what it was, I gasped, pulling away just a second too late.

"What're you doing?"

"What does it look like I'm doing?"

He'd handcuffed my wrist.

"This isn't necessary. I'm not going to run. You took my money. I don't have a car either."

"But you got two working feet and a bangin' body. You could get a ride from some lonely idiot in a heartbeat."

Ignoring his "bangin' body" remark, I looked left, then right, then down at the metal cuffs again. "I'm not going to run. I swear. This is totally unnecessary."

"Trust is a hard thing for me to give, JP. And you've fucked it up before I even gave it over, which is why this has to happen."

"I'm not sorry and I won't apologize. And if you think handcuffs are going to make this situation easier, then you're sadly mistaken."

He tugged on the cuffs, not too hard but enough to pull at the skin beneath my wrist. Seconds later, he clipped the other cuff to his wrist, smirking at the view as if the sight excited him.

"You want to see your ma again? Fine. But we're gonna do this my way, not yours."

I blinked, waiting a second, thinking this was some cruel joke. "What?"

"You heard me."

"What's in this for you, huh?" I settled my free hand on my hip, not trusting him.

"When you get me to where you ma is, I'm gonna use *you* as bait to draw Pops out." He pulled me behind him, stopping next to his bike.

He uncuffed himself then quickly attached the free cuff to the side of the bike.

"Y-you're not going to turn me in?"

"Nope. Now, get your ass on the bike." He patted the seat.

I shook my head, confused. Dumbfounded even. Just a minute ago, he was calling me stupid, telling me I was making a mistake, that I wouldn't be getting away with this. Yet here he was agreeing to take me there; to the one place he told me I shouldn't go.

"Why would you do this alone?"

"Got my reasons," he said with a curled lip, nodding me onto the bike with his chin. "Now, you gonna get on or do I have to pick you up again and put you there?"

I blinked at the cuffs. "I can't be cuffed to this bike. What if we get in an accident?"

"We won't."

"How do you know?"

"Because I'm the best rider you'll ever know, JP. That's why."

"I don't trust you." I scowled, wishing I had the power to read his mind.

He smirked at me, patted his seat. "Good. Because I don't trust you either."

CHAPTER SEVEN

Archer

The sun was beginning to set when I felt Emily start squirming behind me. She didn't tap my shoulder or ask me to pull over, but I could tell the woman had to piss by the way her thighs kept squeezing my ass. If I wasn't so damn annoyed by it, I would have kept going.

"Why are we stopping?" she asked after I pulled into a rest stop, parked, and shut off my engine. We were about three hours outside of Rockford now, road construction so damn bad it'd taken us forever just to get here.

"You gotta piss."

"No, I don't."

I lifted my leg off the bike, turned, and poked her in the gut.

"What the hell?" she screeched, her thighs immediately drawing together.

"See?" I smirked.

"You're such a freaking little boy," she muttered, moving one leg off the bike, her arm outstretched from where it was still cuffed. "I don't have to pee, I'm just really ticklish."

"Ticklish, you say?" I grinned, eying her up and down. "That's good to know."

"I will punch you in the balls if you even *think* about tickling me."

"You sure do have an obsession with my nuts, don't you, JP?" I walked around my bike and uncuffed Emily from it. Then I latched the free cuff to my wrist again, not willing to take any chances.

"I do not have an obsession with any piece of you. At all."

"Not yet, anyways." I winked. "Now, come on. Let's use the pisser."

She groaned from behind as I tugged her to the rest-stop door. "For the millionth time, I don't have to pee. My butt's just sore from riding."

"You want me to rub it for ya?" I flexed my fingers, turning to face her as I shoved the door open with my ass.

She rolled her eyes, but I saw her cheeks get pink before she looked away. "I'll pass, thanks."

Inside the brick building, the first thing I smelled was gas, followed closely by the scent of bleach. As far as rest stops went the space was big, with high glass ceilings and walls covered in maps. With me still in front, I pulled her to a row of vending machines then tugged out some dollar bills. "What'll it be, hm? I'd say chocolate, but you're too amped up for that right now."

"Amped up?" I heard the frown in her words.

I slid the money in and pressed a few numbers. "Yeah, I mean, I'm assuming you're horny as fuck. Most women get that way on the back of my bike. And all that squirming you did…" I whistled low, scanning the junk in the machine. Normally I didn't eat this shit. You didn't get a body like mine by junking out on sugar all day. But desperate times called for desperate measures.

"Um, no. I'm not that at all. Trust me."

I grinned at her from over my shoulder, waiting for the chips and cookies I'd picked to fall. "Sure." I winked. "Keep telling yourself that."

She covered her face with her free hand and groaned. "Oh my God, you are so… *weird.*"

I grinned, her words only egging me on. "Just so you know, sexual awakening is common when spending time with me."

"Would you just shut up already?" she hissed.

"No need to be embarrassed. It's a natural thing."

"You're disgusting."

I tugged the food out, tossing it on a bench beside the machine. I grabbed some waters next. When I turned around to hand her one, I said, "Beg to differ there, baby. I'm the most non-disgusting thing to ever grace the earth."

Emily dropped her hand from her face and shoved me against the drink machine with it. I froze, hands in mid-air, wearing an even bigger grin on my lips. What was it about a violent woman that made my cock hard?

"Testy, are we?"

"No. I am not testy. I am *disgusted*," she huffed. "Everything that comes out of your mouth is either degrading to women or chauvinistic, and it makes me want to scream."

I stared down at her face right then. Her nose in particular. There was a small spread of freckles over the slope, dotting out across her cheeks. Nothing big, but enough for me to take notice of. With her severe straight bangs and her long dark hair, she'd always looked like a little girl. Those tiny freckles didn't help matters. But—and fuck if I know why—the sight of them made my chest tighten. To the point where I lost my smile a little.

With other women, I didn't take the time to look at details on their bodies like that, unless it came to their pussy or tits. With Emily, though... being so close to her, and under the bright fluorescent lights, I couldn't help *but* notice. And I wasn't sure if I liked the fact that I noticed either.

"Listen up, asshole," she continued, oblivious to my inner turmoil. "I am not going to spend this entire trip to Kentucky with you teasing me about sex and anything that goes along with it, you hear me? I'm not interested in you, or your penis, so get that thought out of your head."

I lifted both brows at her use of the word *penis*. But that's not what had me snapping out of my thoughts. "Kentucky, huh?"

She blinked, probably realizing what she'd done. Emily had refused to tell me where we were going, other than saying south and which highways to stay on as we rode. Hell, as far as I knew, we could've been going to Florida or something like that. But Kentucky? That was *way* too close to Rockford for comfort.

"Well, we um… I mean, we… uh." She took a step back. "We have to travel through Kentucky is all."

"Can't bullshit a bullshitter, JP. You said Kentucky. Which means that's exactly where Pops is."

She blinked, now as far back as the cuffs would allow. "Maybe I'm a better bullshitter than you—did you ever think about that?"

Despite the fact that she'd just told me the one huge thing the RDs had been wanting to know for over a year now, I couldn't help but throw my head back and laugh. "I'm the master when it comes to telling if someone's lying or not, didn't you know?"

Shaking my head, I pulled my phone out and ignored whatever else she had to say as I scrolled through my contacts. I stopped on Slade's name and punched in a text.

"What're you doing?" Emily asked, her voice filling with panic.

"Doing what needs to be done."

She tried to look around me, over my shoulder, but I held my phone out of arm's reach and gave her my back.

"What needs to be done exactly?"

"None of your concern."

She groaned but stopped being nosy, which gave me a chance to finish my text to Slade.

Pops is closer than we thought. Be on alert. Will send more intel as I find shit out. Going off grid.

Knowing he'd give me hell, I hit send on the text and powered down my phone. I'd texted him earlier from the diner and told him what was up—parts of it anyway. How Emily had run and I'd gone to get her, leaving out the section where I was actually the one to take her in the end. My brothers would kill my ass if they knew what I was really up to. Trying to take down Pops on my own, get shit settled without anyone else going down. If I had to die protecting my brothers and my home, then so be it. I had whiskey and monthlies. They had lives and love.

Slade didn't like the idea of me being on the road alone, but he also knew I had no problem taking care of myself, that I was smart as fuck too. I told him I'd be gone a week, tops, and that if I didn't find Emily, then I'd head home. Hawk wasn't thrilled with the idea of me giving his sister a timeline like that, that I should look for her as long as it takes. He, more than most, knew how badly Emily wanted out of our world in the first place, which is why he didn't see the point in sending anyone else after her. I was the best at tracking people down, so if anyone could find her, it'd be me.

"You're not telling anyone what I just told you, right? About, you know…" Her voice hitched as I finished up my text to Slade. "Kentucky?"

"Don't worry." I pocketed my phone and faced her. "Your secrets are safe with me."

Her dark brown eyes widened in surprise. "So… you'll give me a chance to get my mom out before telling anyone where we are?"

I thought about it for a second, still studying her. It'd be wrong if I didn't let her go, yeah, but it'd be even worse if I did. The thing was, I might not even make it out of there alive so what did it matter either way? Emily was harmless. Her mom, on the other hand, had fucked up, big time. But it wasn't her daughter's fault, and as a former mama's boy, I probably would've done the same thing if I were in her shoes. Still didn't make it okay, but apparently I was feeling generous—had a motive that nobody else needed to know about.

No matter. This all might change come morning, or in the next twenty minutes even. My decisions and choices were like my brain, bouncing around at lightning speed.

"Sure." I shrugged, looking away.

Seconds later, Emily did the last thing I ever expected her to. She lunged at me… then she fucking *hugged* me. Her uncuffed arm went around my waist so tightly it was like she was afraid I'd disappear if she let go. My arms stayed planted at my sides, and instead of cracking a joke about her wanting to feel me up, something lodged in my throat. At the feel of her there, some seriously strange shit happened. It felt like someone had lit a fire in my chest. Good Christ, I hadn't been hugged like this since, well… shit. Since my own ma had hugged me when I was twelve.

"Thank you," she whispered. "You have no idea what this means to me, Archer." Her hair tickled my nose, and I could smell her shampoo. Something sweet, like flowers, which stirred something in my gut as well as my chest.

I winced and tipped my head back at the feeling, eyes to the ceiling of the rest stop, staying wordless. Obviously, I didn't hug her back, but what messed me up was the fact that I didn't push her away either. Memories flooded my mind instead: the scent of cigarettes mixed with the soap ma had always used when I was a kid. The way she would kiss the top of my head then pat my shoulder to soothe me, even as hard as she was. She had told me to have a good day and that she'd be back later. Then her long, brown ponytail was all I could see as she and my old man had ridden away on his bike.

I never saw it again.

It's why I hated brunettes with brown eyes like Emily. Too much of a reminder.

Jesus. Why was I thinking about any of this? It wasn't like I even *liked* Emily. If anything, she was fun to toy with, but she annoyed the piss out of me. I shook my head and stepped out of her space, the fingers of our cuffed hands grazing. I shivered and goosebumps climbed up my arm. The sensation of this woman's hug wasn't something I wanted to feel again. I wanted to tell her that too—*never touch me like that unless you plan on sucking my cock.* But even my normal defense mode didn't work when I saw how damn happy she looked right then. How bright her eyes were, same with her glowing cheeks and her full lips…

Looking at her had me feeling that same shit inside my chest again, so I reached up, put my free hand over my heart, and clutched my shirt, hoping it'd go the fuck away.

"Let's eat," she said, tucking some hair behind her ear, her smile fading but her eyes still bright. "I'm starving, and I'm sure you are too." Then she pointed to the pile of junk I'd bought and yanked me toward the bench.

Wordless, I sat beside her, the food in between our thighs. Our cuffed hands grazed again when she reached over and grabbed a bag of Skittles. "I love these by the way. Good choice." She lifted the bag and opened it with her teeth. "Only the red and green ones though. The purple, orange, and yellow are crap."

The fuck was she talking about? Didn't they all taste the same?

"Do you want some?" She held the bag out to me and I shook my head. "I've used Skittles for various science projects at school," she continued, talking like we were best friends. Like I was Summer or Maya even. "Kids tend to respond better to science when you use materials they're used to seeing or even eating on a daily basis. It's a proven fact. I'm very hands-on with my teaching."

I frowned at the ground, confused. Why was she telling me this?

"I'm gonna miss those kids, honestly. Middle-schoolers get a bad rap. But to me they're just trying to find themselves and—"

"Emily," I cut her off, meeting her eyes. I needed an answer to the shit running through my head, and only she could provide it.

She stopped chewing and frowned.

"Why did you hug me?"

She blinked, obviously not expecting that question. "Um, I…" Her face got red, and she looked to the ground like I'd done. "Sorry. I didn't mean to make you feel uncomfortable."

Did it make me feel uncomfortable? Yeah, but not the actual hug. If anything, that shit was weirdly… *nice*. The thoughts that came with it, on the other hand, were the problem. I didn't like them. It's why I said what I did next.

"Yeah. Don't do it again."

I looked at her just in time to see her nod and bite her bottom lip. The sight of her looking all uncomfortable made *me* uncomfortable though. And I didn't do well with awkward shit. It was rare that anything bugged me when it came to women—I was the master at knowing what they wanted, how they liked to be talked to or touched. But Emily? Damn. I never knew what was going through her head. It's why I teased her so much. She didn't make me bored. Hell, each and every reaction she gave me seemed to make me want to find another and another. I hadn't thought much of it until now. I'd been happy to have something to keep me occupied for once, but I hadn't counted on needing this conversation either.

"Okay, sure. I won't." She nodded too fast. It felt weird.

"At least don't hug me with clothes on." I smirked, relaxing as I grabbed a cereal bar and opened it with my teeth. "Naked hugging might be fun."

Emily sighed and shook her head, but anything she had to say stayed locked inside. For the next fifteen minutes, we ate in silence.

It was what I'd wanted.

But at the same time, it suddenly didn't feel right either.

CHAPTER EIGHT

Archer

"You really want to stay here?" Emily looked around the one-bedroom Airbnb that I'd rented for the night, her nose wrinkled in disgust. It looked more like a storage shed on someone's farm lot somewhere in the middle of Indiana than a place to sleep, but we'd been driving for hours, and I was exhausted. Plus, there was a bed and a shower. That's all we needed anyways. And the fact that the guy had taken cash on sight for payment kept a paper trail off our backs too.

Slade was likely trying to track my every movement regardless of his trust in me, and in order for my plan to work, he'd need to stay the fuck away. All the brothers would.

"It's not so bad." I walked us to the small bed, sat on the end, and bounced. "Plenty of spring to it. Nothing like that SUV bed you got in your room." Then I winked, loving how her face flushed with anger so quickly. It was nice having the power back in my hands—the ability to make her feel weird rather than the other way around.

Emily rolled her eyes but sat beside me... as far away as the cuffs would let our arms stretch, of course. She'd been quiet since the rest stop, not that we could do much talking on my bike. Still, her lack of movement behind me on my bike had me wondering if she was doing more thinking than relaxing. Either that or she was worried I'd comment on her horniness again.

I wondered if she was starting to regret running. I would have felt a hell of a lot better if she'd asked to go back to Rockford at that point, even if there *was* a chance I'd be able to take down Pops myself. Not because I liked her or because I was scared what might happen to her or myself. More so because I knew Hawk and Summer would be damn upset once they figured out she wouldn't be coming back.

"I can't with you, Archer." She sighed heavily.

"What? You can't relax with me?" I laughed. "That much is obvious."

"No, I can relax just fine. I just can't deal with your… your you-ness."

"You've never given my *you-ness* a try, that's why."

She didn't answer, but I knew I'd struck a nerve. That's why I kept digging.

"I don't get it." I lay back on the bed, bringing her with me. She didn't complain or pull back when our shoulders brushed together, surprisingly.

"You don't get what?" she asked the ceiling.

"Chop fucked with you." I gritted my teeth together at the thought then added, "But even before, you ghosted everyone. Shut down and ignored anyone who tried talking to you, including your brother, Summer, everyone who tried getting close to you. I get that you don't like club life, but that doesn't mean every RD is a dumbass."

I dropped my head to the side, studying her. Her lips pursed. A spot by her right eye twitched too. Emily looked like she was thinking about what I'd said, yeah, but also trying not to scream at the same time. I get that I frustrated her, but I wanted a real answer here. No idea why it mattered since she was leaving. Call it curiosity on my part. The Red Dragons were all I had, so to me they were fucking amazing. How people saw them as anything else had always bugged me.

"I didn't *ghost* anyone," she said with another sigh.

"What do you call it then?"

"Self-preservation." She twisted her lips. "I knew from the day I started living on the compound that it wasn't gonna be permanent. So, why should I act like I liked being there and befriend anyone when it was temporary?"

"Then what about Chop?"

"He pushed me." She cringed, lowering her voice a little. "Nobody else did."

"And look what the fuck happened there." I scowled at her. "You women always think you know who the good guys are."

She turned her head and glared at me, our faces just a few inches apart. I could smell her shampoo again and I fought the sudden urge I had to bury my face in her hair.

"This is why I don't talk to you or anyone else besides Summer. Everybody judges me and my choices."

"Just like you judge everyone else, including me." I nudged the back of her hand with my own.

"I don't *judge* anyone. Again, it's self-preservation and prefer-ence. Your *brothers,* as you call them, might be wonderful. But the ones I've interacted with haven't given me the warm and fuzzies."

"The hell you don't judge," I scoffed. "You judged me from the second you came into the club as a teenager with your ma."

"You freaking called me a *hot table*, Archer." She threw her free hand up into the air before letting it smack against the mattress again. "Excuse *me* if that didn't leave a lasting good impression. I *totally* regret it and want us to be *besties*." She mocked me like I'd done earlier.

Weirdly, it made me grin.

"Bygones, baby." I nudged her elbow with my own. "Now, let's go. I'm hungry. Saw a pizza place up the road."

"I am *not* going back on that bike tonight," she huffed. "My legs are like rubber."

I stood, bringing her with me. Sitting still and doing nothing? That shit wasn't me. The only time I liked not moving around was when I was sleeping. It was like I had a wire in me that never stopped snapping.

"We'll walk then."

She shook her head. "It's not safe."

"The hell you mean, *it's not safe*?" I tugged her again, satisfied when she got to her feet. I lifted my cut to show her how *safe* we'd be with my Glock tucked nicely inside my jeans.

She gasped. "You have a gun?"

I nodded.

She covered her face and groaned, sitting back down on the bed.

"Oh no you don't." I pulled her up again by the cuffs. "I'm a man who needs sustenance, which means I'm going to go eat. And where I go, you go."

"You're also in a biker gang with biker guys who might be out there waiting to pounce on us."

I shook my head. "Nah. Slade's got that shit under control. I told him you took off and that I was doing my duty as your bodyguard to come get ya."

"My *bodyguard*?" Her eyes widened.

"Yup." I tugged her behind me toward the door.

"And you really think those men are going to believe you?"

"Of course they will. I'm the VP."

But for the first time since I'd come up with this plan, I wasn't as confident as I should've been. Yes, I had told Slade that I was coming to get Emily, but only after he'd called me in a panic. Apparently, Summer had found Emily's house ransacked and freaked out. Hawk had called Slade when he couldn't get a hold of me—because I'd ignored his ass, not wanting to explain what was up—but with Slade, I'd reassured him that I was fine and on Emily's trail, just about ready to pounce. That would give me enough time to get where we needed to go *and* keep Hawk satisfied… even though Slade didn't seem as easily convinced by my excuses.

If Flick or any of my brothers found out I was going to attempt to take down Pops on my own, they'd either disown my ass or rip me a new one. Either way, I couldn't ignore the opportunity. I'd pay for the consequences later, yeah, by dying at the hands of Pops or his men, or possibly being banished from the club. But if I got rid of the motherfucker once and for all, it'd be worth it.

Emily stopped arguing with me and soon we were outside, walking down a gravel road that led to a town I'd never heard of—probably because there wasn't much to it. Along both sides of the road was nothing but corn, tall and blowing in the wind. It was late May, before the real heat hit. That meant a midnight stroll in the middle of farm-town Indiana wouldn't be so bad, temperature wise.

And I needed to get my mind off my brothers.

"So, tell me, JP. What exactly makes your pussy wet, hmm? What gets your motor humming?"

She groaned, covering her face. "Holy shit. Can you just… *not* with that question?"

"Hey!" I held up my free hand. "I just need to know what makes you wet so I don't do it." I nudged her shoulder. "Wouldn't want you getting any ideas when it comes to me and my amazing body, would we?"

"Seriously. You're like, a ten-year-old boy. The last thing I want or would *ever* want is to be with you like that."

"Fine. Do me a solid though and answer the question anyway."

"Absolutely not. It's none of your business who or what makes my *pussy* anything."

"Say it again." I licked my lips, grinning.

"Say what?"

"*Pussy.*"

She rolled her eyes and folded her arms, bringing my cuffed one along for the ride. Sadly enough, she didn't tell me what I needed to know, which meant I'd have to find out on my own somehow.

"Fine." I sighed dramatically. "Talk to me though. I hate silence and get bored."

"You've obviously got ADHD."

"I do." I shrugged a shoulder. "But the pills fucked me up as a kid. Mom took me off them when I was eight."

She didn't comment, just looked at me funny.

"Come on, gimme a bone here," I continued. "We got half a mile of walking ahead of us."

Our hands smacked together, the cuffs the cause. Unlike me, she clenched her fist, like touching me meant getting burned.

"What about the ex?" I asked. "What was he like?" I was also curious as to why this woman, unlike every other, was so unbothered by me. I get it, she was all prim and proper. But even the godliest of chicks had it bad for me.

Literally. I once fucked a nun outside her church after a run.

"Wasn't he, like, some smart dude? Is that what gets your little whistle wet?"

"I'm not telling you this," she snapped.

"Oh, come on. I need to know all of your dirty little secrets."

"Uh, no. You really don't."

I didn't. But, again, I got bored easily. That's why I loved being part of the club. I was always busy, always doing something. Always had a family member to talk to. Was always working on a bike, fucking a woman, or going on runs. I needed the constants in life. Otherwise I'd think about stuff from my past. Regret things, most of all.

"Hey, you're the one who ran away. We wouldn't be here now if you hadn't. Remember that."

She pursed her lips and stayed quiet as we made it to the main road. Up ahead, I saw the signs in the town all lit up, and my stomach growled at the thought of food. It'd been God only knew how long since I'd put anything in my mouth that wasn't a cigar, coffee, or junk food.

"I am *not* going to tell you about my sexual desires, Archer," she finally said. "But if there's something *else* you want to know or talk about, I *might* be willing to share, depending on what it is."

"Is this gonna be one of those share-all times where you tell me something and I'm gonna have to tell you something too? Or maybe, like, if you can't share it, you have to take off some clothes? Like strip poker, but with words?"

She shook her head, surprisingly not snapping at me about my dirty thoughts. "Nope."

I squinted at her. "You sure? Could be fun."

"Yes." She groaned. "I'm very sure that I do *not* want to play the talking share-all game of strip poker."

I knew very little about this woman, other than the fact that she was Hawk's little sister, a troublemaker, and a certified pain in the ass. It bugged the hell out of me not knowing how she ticked, seeing as how I was a man who could normally read everyone I met.

"Alright. No sex talk, then." I paused, looking around me, trying to think of something non-dirty. Real conversation with a woman, something I wasn't necessarily the best at, made my skin itch. But at the same time, it drove me nuts that I couldn't get a read on her, which was why I'd be stepping out of my comfort zone with this one.

I caught sight of a few trees alongside the road. It wasn't necessarily a forest, but it sheltered us enough to where nobody could see through in the dark. It reminded me a bit of the compound—that and the smell of gas up ahead too. But when I looked up at the sky and saw the moon, my memories pulled me back to another place and time in my life—a time when I'd sit for hours with my ma on wire chairs with rusty feet on top of a stone patio my old man never got around to fixing up.

My backyard as a kid in Ireland wasn't ideal, not like the pictures someone might see on the internet, or how it's portrayed in a movie either. No. My backyard as a kid was nothing but broken stone, rusty chairs, motorcycle parts, and the smell of my old man's favorite whiskey filling the air, accompanied by my ma's perfume. And I wouldn't change it one fucking bit. If I shut my eyes, I could sometimes hear her favorite singer bursting from that record player she never gave up on while she and Dad talked shop and did body work on their bikes. It wasn't often I thought about that time in my life, the stone cottage in the middle of the weed-filled fields with the shitty roof and the even shittier porch, but right then, it hit me like a sucker punch of a memory that wouldn't let go until I talked about it.

Fuck if I knew why.

I frowned then cleared my throat before I asked, "How 'bout this one: if you could be anywhere else right now, where would you be?"

She smiled all wide. It was the first genuine one I'd seen on her in a while. Maybe since I'd known her. "Easy. I'd want to go to Brazil." She skipped a little in place, which was even weirder.

I squinted. "That sounds boring as fuck."

"No way." She shook her head. "Brazil is known for the Rio Carnival and some seriously amazing beaches." Her voice softened a little. "Actually, my mom and I were planning on taking a trip there before my wedding."

Good Christ. Two sore subjects in one statement? I scrambled to try and make a joke. "Well, if there are nudie beaches, count me in."

"Of course you'd bring sexuality back into the conversation when I'm trying to share something personal." She strode ahead of me, but our cuffed hands didn't let her go far.

"Come on, JP. I'm kidding."

"Kidding is your MO in life."

I came to a stop, urging her to face me. She wasn't wrong on that. I wanted to say so too, but by the look on her face, even in the dark, she looked like she wasn't down with me making fun of her or the conversation.

"It's my turn," I told her.

"I don't want to hear it if you're going to be a douchebag."

"Not a douchebag this time." I crossed my chest over my heart in an X with my finger.

Her eyes narrowed like she still didn't trust me, but she also kept her lips sealed. Not many people gave me the benefit of the doubt like that. It was… nice.

I started walking again, keeping her close this time by the cuffs. Not that anyone else could hear what I said when I spoke, I just wasn't used to opening up like this. "You'll be surprised to know, JP, that if I could be anywhere else right now, it'd be back at my childhood home in Ireland."

"Really?" Our eyes met and I saw a flash of something there in her gaze I was pretty sure I wasn't supposed to see. Wonder? Curiosity? Yeah, those were there too, but I was almost positive I saw a bit of respect there as well. I knew what she thought about me; that I was just some idiot biker. But unlike most of my brothers, I had a whole life before I became an RD.

"Yup." My throat burned a little, choking me. I cleared it, trying not to feel weak.

"I bet it's beautiful there, isn't it?"

"In some parts it is." I shrugged. "The sea was pretty badass. It changed colors a lot. Sometimes it was blue, sometimes it almost looked, I dunno, like a light purple, especially when it rained."

"You mean it looked lavender, I'm assuming."

I frowned, guiding us toward the restaurant about fifty feet ahead. "Pizza" was all it said on the outside. Winner fucking advertisement to me.

"What's wrong with just saying light purple?"

"The colors have names for a reason. If you say light purple, you could mean lilac or periwinkle or even orchid." She shrugged. "It's just another scientific fact that's more important to artists than anyone else."

"Shit, JP. That's too complicated."

She followed me in, the smell of grease and bacon hitting us head on. "Only if you make it complicated."

"Touché." I smirked just as the hostess greeted us.

"Two?" she asked, looking between us.

"Yup." I nodded, tugging JP behind me.

Seconds later, we were walking toward the back of the quiet little restaurant, less than a handful of people around to notice us. The waitress, though, she saw our cuffed arms the second Emily slid into the booth first, her gray eyes widening as she glanced between us.

"Newlywed fun," I whispered just softly enough so that Emily didn't hear me. Then I took a seat across from her, our cuffed arms stretched across the table top. Emily's brows lifted in question, and I gave her a soft wink. If she knew I was tormenting this lady, she'd likely yell at me again. I'd already been lectured enough for one day.

"D-drinks?" the waitress stammered.

"Whiskey." I smiled up at her, wondering what she might be like in bed.

Unlike every other time I thought about fucking a woman, though, the image wouldn't come to me. Why? Because all I could see instead was a short little brunette's naked body stretched out on the bed we'd be sharing tonight, my tongue between her legs as I played her body like an instrument. God, what kind of sounds would Emily make when she came? Was she a screamer? A whimperer, maybe? Would she moan my name or—

"Archer."

I blinked, coming out of my fantasy. Turning to Emily, I opened my mouth, but getting a word out was a damn struggle.

Jesus, Archer. Get your shit together.

"Do you know what you want to eat?" she asked, her voice playing like I was a toddler she was trying to punish for not listening.

"No." I frowned, then said, "But JP here would like a margarita on the rocks."

Emily scowled at me, but she didn't say no either.

"You should stop drinking so much." She picked up her menu once the waitress took off, hiding her face as she said, "Liver failure isn't a good way to die."

"And *you* should maybe drink more than you do. Might help your stick slide out a little easier."

"I told you I don't drink."

"Why? Can't handle your liquor?"

"No. I just… It makes me stupid."

I rubbed a finger over my lip, studying her. "Stupid as in drop your panties stupid?"

I waited for a smack to my face, or a punch to my shoulder, but it never came. Instead, she shrugged and said, "Didn't your mom ever tell you to keep your mouth shut?"

Shit. I didn't like that non-answer.

"No, actually. Ma had a bigger mouth than I do."

"Poor woman," she mumbled.

"Yeah. Poor Ma and her big, Irish mouth. That was actually one of the things I loved most about her."

"Oh, um… loved?"

"Yeah." I cleared my throat. "She was murdered back in Ireland."

Emily stiffened, eyeing me from the side of her menu. "I didn't know. I'm sorry."

"What, you didn't know that the police found her body all chopped up and shit? You miss that memo?" I'd meant it to be funny, but her face immediately paled.

"Oh, God." She dropped the menu onto the table and laid her hand on mine. I frowned at the view, not real sure why the sight and the feel of it made my stomach tighten. Still, for some reason, I wanted her to know this. Felt like talking about it for once in my life. Every single day since the day she'd died, I missed my ma. And even all these years later, it hurt holding onto the memories.

"Dad told me it was random. I believed him. They never found the killer."

"That's terrible," she whispered.

I shrugged, finally looking at her face again. I'd let the idea of revenge go a long time ago, though my old man never had. "Eventually he remarried, but it didn't last long. He and my ma were like penguins."

Emily's entire face seemed to light up at my analogy. "Penguins mate for life."

"See? I'm not as dumb as you think."

"I don't think you're dumb," she said with a frown. "I just think you're immature."

"Yeah. So does everyone else." Which was why I did it; why I acted like such a horny douchebag all the time. I wasn't who anyone thought I was. Nor did I tell anyone who I was either. Hell, even Hawk, Slade, and Flick didn't know the whole story when it came to my childhood and all the bad shit that had happened. But it was easier that way. Pretending to be one way to avoid being another.

"Why do it at all though? Why not just let yourself be you?"

"That's the pot calling the kettle black there, JP."

She pursed her lips but kept whatever she was thinking locked inside her head. Good thing too. This was all getting a little too much for me. The sharing shit. I was the one who was supposed to be finding out what made Emily tick, what made her the woman she was. Not the other way around, damn it.

"How'd you wind up in the US?" she asked, running her free hand flat over the menu. It shook a little, almost like she was nervous. "I mean, you don't have to answer that. Niyol told me you don't like talking about your past and I should respect that…"

"Yet you're still asking." I refocused on my own menu and frowned. Emily and I'd be parting ways soon enough though, so what was the harm in sharing my shit in order to get her to share her shit? Wasn't that the point of this whole game? To finally get a read on her?

"Sorry," she whispered and looked out the window, her long hair brushing over my arm as she turned.

A shiver ran up my spine from the way it felt against my skin. I shut my eyes, trying to regain a sense of here and now before I answered. All this damn closeness from the cuffs was beginning to backfire on me. Maybe I needed to rethink them after all.

I scrubbed my free hand over my face then set my elbow on the table. "It's fine. I just don't talk about it for a reason."

She turned to me again. "What reason is that?"

"You're nosy." I nudged her knee under the table with my own.

"It's the scientist in me." A shrug followed her long sigh.

"Fine. I'll tell you. But only on one condition."

"What's that?" Her eyes narrowed in distrust.

"You answer whatever question I want, whenever I ask it."

She leaned back in the seat and huffed. "That's not fair."

I nudged her knee again, grinning as I said, "But the scientist in you won't let it rest until you know everything about me, am I right?"

She stared up at me, all dark eyes and dark brows, pink lips and those motherfucking freckles I was dying to count.

"Fine."

"Yeah?" I lifted my brows in surprise. Hadn't thought it'd be that easy, yet what did I really know about JP?

"Yes." Her word was more of a huff than anything, and I couldn't stop myself from laughing under my breath.

"Well, alright then." I rubbed my free hand over my jeans. "One day Dad got a call from Pops. It was kind of out of the blue actually since they'd only met once, via a mutual biker. Guess they got along real well when they did, enough so that when Pops heard about my ma, he did some digging. Called my dad up and told him he knew a guy who knew another guy who was killing women at random overseas, bragging about it and shit." I looked at Emily again, wishing my story ended a hell of a lot happier than it did.

"It wasn't true, was it?" she asked with a frown.

"Nah. Just Pops being an asshole who needed more bodies to start up his club." I toyed with a napkin, shredding it as I kept going. "I'd told my old man it was stupid to follow up on a lead that made no sense in the first place. Hell, I was twelve and knew it was a fucking farce. But my old man's quest for revenge when it came to his wife led us to the good old U S of A... away from the land I loved."

"I'm so sorry." Emily reached over like before, taking my cuffed hand and linking it with hers.

I frowned, stared down at it for a long moment as I studied the difference between us, the way her tiny fingers looked wrapped around my massive ones. I was pretty sure, as fucked up as it was, that I'd never get over the way holding hands with her made me feel. Maybe it was like the hugging thing because I'd never done it before just for the hell of it.

"It's a part of my life I don't think about much anymore."

She nodded, pulling her hand back to her lap. I hated how I missed it. How I wanted to feel it again. "Yeah. I get it. Mom and I... we went through our own fair share of bad crap." She frowned at her lap. "Sad part about it was things got better when my mother supposedly 'met' Pops for the first time when I was sixteen. We weren't poor anymore, had an amazing home, Mom got to open up her wedding-planning business…"

"You know where all that money came from, right?" I asked, not wanting to burst her little fantasy for the second time in one night. But this time, I had to. Because no part of Pops could ever be good, no matter what anyone thought.

"I do know." Her eyes grew sad, the corners dropping with her lips. "But as much as I hate Pops, it was his appearance in our lives that made things easier for my mom. I was able to go to college, I met Summer, I taught at an incredible school too."

I didn't miss that word—*taught*. Running like this, it meant she'd likely be quitting her job with no warning. Also meant Emily was possibly missing out on a lot of good shit in her life because her ma had been selfish. Because of that, I hated Lisa more than I hated Pops right then. But only because she'd royally fucked things up for her daughter, even if that hadn't been the woman's intention.

"Your dad…" She hesitated, changing the subject. "He was killed too, right?"

"Yeah. Run gone wrong, thanks to Pops."

"Oh." She blinked up at me.

"It's why I'm going with you. I plan on killing the asshole."

Her eyes widened, but, surprisingly enough, she didn't comment.

"You're not gonna tell me it's a dumb idea to go after him on my own?" I asked, curious what was going through her mind.

"Will it make a difference if I do?"

"Nope."

"Then I won't say anything, especially since me going to try and break Mom free is an equally stupid idea."

"You said it."

I wanted to say something else though. That Emily wasn't just stupid for going after her ma—especially when she might not know why the woman ran in the first place—but that she was practically suicidal too. She didn't know what Pops was capable of. Not to the extent me and the RDs did, which was why I was glad to be going with her, only so I could protect her in case something went south. The last thing I wanted was for Hawk and Summer to lose her.

"Not that I'm going to complain, but why are you not telling anyone about what you're planning on doing?"

"Easy." I leaned forward on the table, bringing her cuffed hand along with mine. "If I tell anyone the truth, then I won't be able to go alone. I could lose my best friends. I'm not having that."

Emily didn't respond right away. Just looked at me instead. Nobody ever looked at me like I mattered. Like I was a hero. Why? Because I wasn't anything more than a guy looking to be the best Red Dragon he could be. And Red Dragons did not wear capes.

"You're willing to sacrifice yourself," she stated matter-of-factly.

"I am, yeah." There wasn't anything that could be said beside that. My brothers had lives. I had, well, nothing… other than a few monthlies, my whiskey, and this moment, in this pizza place, with a woman who was looking for something I'd never be able to give her, even if she wanted me to. Even if *I* wanted to.

Stability and friendship. Two things I didn't have with women. Ever.

"Enough about my dumb ass," I told her, smiling, trying to lighten the mood. "I'm boring as fuck to a smart chick like you."

Disappointment flashed through her gaze, but it didn't last long. Come tomorrow, we wouldn't have tonight again. As far as I was concerned, nothing else mattered but the here and now.

CHAPTER NINE

Emily

My stomach fluttered in an odd way when we started back down the road toward the farm-shed-slash-Airbnb. I'm not saying it was happiness, but it was something I hadn't felt in a long while. Contentment? Relaxation? Was it simply the margarita I'd drunk? Or perhaps the company I was keeping? Either way, I was thankful for it tonight.

Archer was definitely different than I'd thought. And I kind of hated myself for not giving him the benefit of the doubt before now. Judging him the way I had was wrong, which left me wondering if I'd judged *all* of the Red Dragons wrong too.

Well, all except Chop.

I rubbed my hand over the mark on my neck, deciding to bring up a new subject. The two of us had talked all through dinner, eaten our crappy deep-dish pizza like it was the best thing since sliced bread. Again, that could've been the alcohol, but I wasn't going to pretend I didn't have a decent time tonight.

"Once this is all over, what will you do?" I asked him, staring up at the night sky. It was starting to rain a little, enough to coat my cheeks and hair. I didn't mind, not like I normally would have. My cardigan was dry-clean only, yeah, but it wasn't like I'd need it again anytime soon. Teaching would sadly be put on the back burner for a while, maybe forever, now that I was running away.

"Easy. Go back to the club and drink whiskey till I puke." He grinned, a dimple forming in his right cheek that I'd never taken the time to notice before.

"Because that's *really* mature." I rolled my eyes.

"I never claimed I was anything else." Unlike every other time he'd joked around like this, he didn't crack a smile.

Had I offended him? I'd feel bad if I had, but I also had a feeling that Archer would never let it go if I had. Either way, I couldn't help but wonder if maybe Archer didn't have a plan when he went back because he didn't expect to survive this.

The thought had my heart racing a little faster. My chest squeezing too. I barely knew this man, but at the same time, he was so different than I'd assumed. I didn't want him to die, not for his stupid club, and certainly not for me either.

Clearing my throat, I asked my question a little differently this time. "Okay. What about this: if you weren't a biker, and didn't work at the club, what would you be doing right now?"

For the first time since meeting Archer, he didn't have an immediate answer for me. It was as if he was almost trying to figure out what to say. It was odd in the sense that if there was one thing I'd come to know about Archer, it was that he loved to talk, if only just to hear his own voice. This quiet, serious version of him made my belly flip a tiny bit.

"Nobody's ever asked me that before." He frowned, staring ahead. We'd just started down the farm road, our footsteps a lot slower than they'd been on our way there. I wasn't sure if it was him or me hesitating more.

"Well, consider me a first."

His eyes narrowed at me then, a dirty little smile lighting up his face. "Oh, trust me. You'd be a first alright. A fun one, actually."

"Stooooop." I shoved him, but instead of being disgusted, I laughed. After only spending a day together, I was pretty sure I was starting to know this man a little more.

As far as my life went, I knew what *I'd* be doing had my mom not run off. I loved being a teacher and had once planned on doing it for the rest of my life. There was something magical about watching kids' eyes light up when they realized how cool science could be. When they looked under a microscope for the first time, or even dissected a frog…

I'd never really decided whether or not I wanted kids of my own, as babies were a bit of a mystery to me. Sam had wanted them. And I'd just assumed we might try someday. But now, if I had to think about it, I wasn't 100 percent sure if having babies was for me. In fact, I once thought I'd foster some kids, maybe adopt an older kid who didn't have much of a chance in life. A troublesome biker even.

A young Archer as my son. All trouble and turmoil. I smiled a little at the thought.

"I'd open a bike repair shop."

"Yeah?" I grinned, imagining him all serious, standing in front of his store, a smile on his face and a red ribbon being cut with a pair of giant scissors as he opened the doors on that first day of work.

"Yep. Kinda a bucket list thing, I guess."

I bumped his hip with mine. I was a little dizzy, to the point where I had to put my free hand on his upper arm for balance. His smile turned into a knowing smirk, which had me rolling my eyes. Regardless, I had to say what was running through my mind. If I didn't, then I'd regret it. Sometimes when it comes to achieving dreams, you do need someone else to acknowledge them for it to feel real.

"You still can, you know. Open a shop."

"Nah." He shook his head. "I'm a lifer for the RDs. I'm good with doing rebuilds on the side."

Was he really though? I wanted to ask but realized it wasn't my place to do so. Just because we'd shared some dinner, some decent conversation, and were currently handcuffed to each other, didn't mean we could become friends. Archer and I were two different people and my opinion of him, his life, was nothing more than a passing day among the 364 others.

He'd said he was taking me to my mom because he wanted to get to Pops. But he was also saying he was my bodyguard. I wasn't drunk, not in the least, but the thought of him wanting to help me at all confused me. Made me wonder if he was being truthful, or simply getting his lies mixed up. I didn't want to not trust him, but the part of me that didn't want to know any of the Red Dragons was still pulling at my thoughts and urging me to put distance between us.

"What about you?" he asked, bumping my hip back—a little too hard for my currently unsteady mind *and* margarita-filled body.

"Whoa." I stumbled and Archer threw his arm around my back, holding me upright, my palm flat on his chest.

I licked my suddenly dry lips as our chests pressed together, meeting his stare beneath my lashes. Under my palm I could feel the beat of his heart, and the more he looked at me, the faster it seemed to go. Archer was all about sex, being with a woman for no more than a month, if that. But right then, he looked not like the man I'd gotten to know, the one who used his lips for things other than kissing. Archer looked, well… a little lost, like my eyes were his sudden compass and he couldn't keep from staring into them to try and find his way.

Pressed so close like we were, though, even in the middle of this sparse field, I'd never been warmer, hotter. Sweat dripped down the back of my neck and into my tank beneath my cardigan. His hips moved closer too, a bulge in his jeans coming between us. I didn't comment on it… and surprisingly neither did Archer.

Something between us shifted though. An unnamed emotion that I'd long turned off. And looking at his lips, then his eyes, the way his hair fell over his face, sticking to his temples… I kind of never wanted to lose that feeling.

"You alright?" His voice was low, tainted with whiskey and lust.

I shuddered, loving how his eyes drifted lower, sliding over my breasts that just peered over the top of my camisole.

"Yeah. Just a little tipsy, I think." My cheeks grew even warmer, and I was thankful for the breeze just then. Slow, just enough to make me shiver for reasons other than his heady look.

Archer shivered too, and as much as I wanted him to be cold, I knew what was really going through his mind. It had been a long time since I'd been with a man, not since Sam. But that look of desire in someone's eyes could never be contained.

Instinct had me gripping the front of his T-shirt a little tighter, pulling him closer—not that we could get much closer. Chest to chest we stood. And soon, I was shutting my eyes, tipping my head back, opening my mouth, waiting, and waiting, and waiting… for what felt like forever, until the crackle of his low voice echoed in my ear.

"Emily," Archer murmured. "What're you…?"

Kiss me.

Make me feel alive, Archer.

Please.

His long sigh blew over my cheek as he dropped his mouth to my ear. But his words… they were nothing like what I was expecting.

"If it's a kiss and a fairy tale you're looking for, JP, then I'm sadly not your guy."

And then he began to laugh.

CHAPTER TEN

Archer

Okay. So, I was kind of an asshole. But what the hell did the woman expect of me? Did she think I'd drop all my rules and give her a ten-at-night-on-a-Thursday farm fantasy in the form of a kiss?

Fuck that shit. Everyone knew I didn't kiss. Emily included. And just because I'd shared a little bit of myself with her that I hadn't shared before didn't mean we were gonna have some whirlwind romance thing.

Either way, I did feel bad that I'd led her on, though that hadn't been my intention. I probably needed to make it up to her. I just wasn't sure how yet. With all the squirming she was doing in the bed next to me—for the past hour that we'd been lying there trying to sleep, damn it—I couldn't think about anything other than how she smelled like fresh flowers, and how her smooth legs kept grazing mine under the covers. It definitely didn't help that my cock was hard as hell. I needed some action.

"Can't you just lie still?" I growled, running a hand over my forehead.

"Can't you just *stop* being a jerk?" she snapped back at me. "I can't sleep with these cuffs on. I haven't showered all day and—"

"Fine, fuck." I sat up, reached over the bed to grab my jeans on the floor. Slowly, I pulled out the key, intending to take the damn cuffs off. Only when I pulled back to sit up, the thing fell out of my fingers, sliding under the bed.

"What're you doing? That hurts. Stop pulling," she hissed at me.

"Move with me then, Christ."

She huffed but did as I asked, adding a smarter step to the mix when she flicked on the bedside light. "There. Now you'll be able to see."

I scowled, pissed I hadn't thought of that.

Seconds before I ducked down to the floor, my gaze latched onto her bare legs. She wasn't wearing pants *or* shorts?

Jesus, Mary, and Joseph.

I'd like to say it was the pale, shapely curve of her thighs drawing me in, but that wasn't it. Instead, my stomach twisted as I looked at her. Tears were in her eyes, dripping at the corners. She wiped them away before they could get far, but I'd seen enough to know she was upset.

Shit. Now, more than ever, I needed to get this key.

Frowning, I got down on the floor, our cuffed hands stretched to the max when I reached under the bed and started searching for it. Once I touched the cold metal, I stood, then got back in bed beside her.

"You promise you won't run?" I asked, studying her profile.

Her eyes narrowed a little. "After tonight, I can't make any promises."

In other words, she wasn't going anywhere.

Slowly, I reached out, undid the cuffs—hers first, mine second. A sigh left her mouth, then seconds later she was up and out of bed, heading toward the bathroom, my guess was to shower.

"Hey," I called to her back.

In the doorway of the bathroom, she stood like a stone, shoulders stiff, hands in fists at her side. "What?"

There were 100 things I probably could've said right then. Starting with, *I'm sorry for being a dick*, followed up with, *Kissing is a curse*, and ending with, *You're fucking sexy as hell, but I don't like attaching myself to people because they always leave me.*

The one thing I did say? "Don't make me regret this, JP."

With that, she left the room, slamming the door shut with a loud *Screw you* from the other side.

I woke to an empty bed. A bed I was lying in the middle of, sprawled out on my stomach… no Emily to be seen. If that woman had run…

"Good Christ."

I jumped up and onto the floor.

Not in bed, not in the bathroom, not in the tiny kitchen…

I ran outside, stopping short at the sight of her there on the little porch, a cup of coffee in hand. I blew out a slow breath, not sure why I'd been panicked. It wasn't like I *cared* if she left. Well, I did care in the sense that I needed a more specific location to find Pops in Kentucky. Maybe that's why I cared. Why my heart was thudding in my temples, my chest, and my throat. Why the sight of her had my knees weakening a little too.

"What're you doing out here?" I frowned. "The fucking sun's not even up."

"I'm enjoying this beautiful morning."

Her voice was chirpy. Too chirpy for Emily, at least. She wasn't Summer. Hadn't ever acted like her perky best friend. Which was why I narrowed my eyes at her. Distrust sat like a knot in my gut as I studied her profile. Was this some sort of act? Maybe she had secret shit planned that wouldn't fare well for me during the rest of our little trip? I wouldn't be surprised.

"We should leave soon, though. It's supposed to rain."

Riding all day in the rain on a damn bike sucked ass. Especially since I didn't have a helmet for myself, just her. "Alright," I said, clearing my throat. "Just gonna shower first."

"Sure. Coffee's ready when you are."

She still wouldn't look at me. I didn't like that, nor did I like the nice-y tone coming out of her mouth. It wasn't like I wanted her snark, but this nice shit didn't feel right.

Was this about her trying to kiss me? My rejection? She *had* to know that kissing me was a really bad idea though, right? Not that the thought hadn't crossed my mind or anything. I mean, she was damn pretty in the moonlight, what with her thick, red lips I wouldn't mind seeing around my cock, especially.

I cleared my throat, pushing those dangerous thoughts away. "I'll be ready in ten."

"Sure." She waved at me from over her shoulder, fingers wiggling, eyes still ahead on the cornfields.

Thunder roared in the distance, and I winced, wondering if we were gonna make it out of here after all. I needed to hurry. God forbid we spent another night in this place.

In the room, I powered on my phone before I went into the shower. Like I expected, I had a shit ton of voicemails and an even bigger stockpile of texts, all from Hawk.

Call me the second you find my sister, asshole.

Don't you touch a hair on her head.

Where the fuck are you?

I'm gonna kill you both the second you come home.

Intending to ignore Hawk, I went to hit the button to power my phone back down, stopping short when I saw a message from Chop come through. The hell was he texting me for?

You think you know her? Because you don't know shit. Her secrets will fuck you up, brother. Be careful.

Her secrets? What the hell did that mean? Before I could question it too much, a phone call came through. Slade. Jesus, all I wanted to do was shower.

"Sup?" I walked into the bathroom and took a quick piss.

"Where are you?"

"Middle of Indiana, three hours outside Rockford. Why?"

"We got problems."

I stiffened, ready to shed my boxers and jump in the tub. "What kind?"

"The Fallen Order's coming tonight."

I froze with my mouth hanging open. *Son of a bitch.* I'd thought I had more damn time.

"Archer," Slade barked. "You hear me?"

"I hear you, damn it." I leaned back against the sink and sighed. "Why the rush? What's changed in twenty-four hours?"

A door slammed on his end, feet thumping over gravel. "Chop went to Flick." He lowered his voice. "Said he had reason to believe you were lying and covering up for Emily. That you knew she was running and it's got everything to do with Pops." He released a low growl as he said, "Tell me that's not fucking true, Arch."

Son of bitch. I'd kill that asshole.

"Tell me, Goddammit," Slade pressed. "Are you with her, and is she hiding something?"

I looked to the bathroom door, eyes narrowing when I heard Emily on the other side, whistling. It was either I come clean now or risk a shit ton of problems if I managed to make it back alive. "Listen. I can't say shit for Hawk's sister. She's on a rampage trying to get to her ma." I paused, exaggerating a little. "Only fucking reason I'm going with her is because she's taking me to Pops."

"The hell you mean she's taking you to Pops?"

I cringed. "You heard me. I don't know a specific location, other than it's in Kentucky. She won't tell me till we get there."

"What the fuck, man? Are you suicidal?"

"Nope. Just done with the runaround. Flick wasn't moving fast enough for me."

"So, what?" Slade growled again. "You plan on taking him down yourself? Go against him and all his rogues? How stupid are you, brother?"

I pushed away from the sink and started to pace the floor. "Look, you can either judge me or help me out if I need you. Keep your cell on, don't give me lip, and if you hear anything else, send word." And then I did what might just get me in deeper shit. I hung up the phone, then turned it off.

"God fucking damn it all to hell!" I kicked the wall, cussing again. Then I pushed open the door, said screw the shower, and found Emily in the kitchen, pouring another cup of coffee.

"Does Chop know?" I moved in behind her, upper lip curled when she stiffened. Against her ear I growled out, "Answer me, damn it. Does Chop know about your letters? Because if he does, then you can bet my brothers are gonna be on our asses like shit on toilet paper."

Emily poured sugar into her cup and laughed. "That's the grossest analogy I've ever heard."

"Hey!" I roared, slamming my palm against the countertop. "Answer me, damn it. This shit ain't funny."

Shaking her head, she turned, facing me, chin all high and mighty. "No. I didn't *tell* Chop. But he seemed to already know and I don't have a clue how."

"He's not an idiot. Guy probably went snooping around your place and found the letters like I did," I hissed, moving back into the bathroom, where I grabbed my phone. Emily hadn't told me everything about her relationship with Chop, what he'd done to her, what she could've done to him. Maybe she was lying about the entire thing. Maybe she was just trying to get under my skin and get me to trust her so she could, I don't know, throw me off. I wasn't sure if I could trust her before, but now? I knew I couldn't.

"Archer, I didn't tell him. I swear."

"It doesn't fucking matter. He told Flick whatever he knows, and now the RDs have asked for help from some seriously dangerous people." I stood and faced her. "People who have done even shittier things than I have, Emily. And now these people are gonna be around my family and your brother, your best friend, and your future niece or nephew."

Her face grew white. "I… I didn't know. I'm sorry."

"Sorry won't cut it this time, JP. You've now not only screwed me and you, but you've screwed anyone and everyone you love."

CHAPTER ELEVEN

Emily

The rain wouldn't let us get far, just sixty miles south of where we'd been, still in Indiana. Every inch of me was soaked, as was Archer, and thunder was echoing over the roar of his bike, following us, promising to get worse.

Archer pulled over into a gas station parking lot, undid my bag at the back of his bike, and led us toward the front door. His hand stayed protectively pressed against my lower back, and I couldn't help but wonder if it was a subconscious thing. For as angry as he was at me, he was still pretending to actually care about my wellbeing. Not that I deserved it. Not that I deserved much of anything at this point. I still wasn't sure how Chop had discovered what I was doing. Either way, I hated the fact that I'd ever spent a moment with him, even more than after he'd hurt me.

Inside, Archer went straight to the clerk, leaving me behind to shake out my wet pants and wring out my hair. This place wasn't as shady as it looked from the outside, but that didn't mean much.

"We went the wrong way," he muttered, walking past me toward the door.

My eyes widened. "What? No, I told you—"

"We're lost, JP. You told me the wrong highway and now we're sixty miles west instead of south."

I chewed on the inside of my cheek then followed him out the front door, stopping just under the overhang. The rain didn't look like it was going to let up anytime soon, yet it was still too early in the day to try and find a hotel. Had I really told him the wrong way? If so, I felt terrible. But at the same time, he'd looked at the same Google map I had, which meant he was just as much as to blame as I was. Regardless, I wasn't in the mood to argue right now. I was wet, hungry, and tired. So, so tired.

"So, what're we gonna do now? It's pouring. We can't keep driving."

"You think I don't know that?" he growled, backing up, running his hands through his hair. "You think I'm that stupid?"

"Why do you keep saying that? I don't think you're stupid at all."

"Yeah, right," he mumbled.

And then the oddest thing happened.

Archer started to smile.

I held my breath, not sure what to make of his sudden mood shift. Maybe this was it. Maybe he was losing his mind. Maybe I'd pushed him over the edge once and for all.

"Hey!" I yelled at him from under the awning still. "Just come back here and wait until the rain dies down, okay? We'll figure this out."

He shook his head, ignoring me. "Ma used to tell me that the rain was good luck, you know."

I frowned. He loved his mom, that much was obvious. I wondered if he'd ever truly grieved her, though.

"Isn't that a wedding-day thing?" I asked, pulling my cardigan up and over my head.

"Fuck weddings, JP." He dropped his head and arms, looking me square in the eye. "Marriage and all that shit? It's not real. It ruins you. Brotherhood is life. Anything else is lies."

I wanted to argue, mostly because I believed what he apparently didn't. His biker world was filled with death and destruction. A world of love, on the other hand? It was filled with things a person could never get enough of. Granted the pain was there too, but the happiness? It outweighed everything. My heart ached for a happily ever after. I just needed everything else in my life to line up first. More so, I needed Mom back with me, guiding me.

"Why are you so bitter?" I yelled over a crackle of thunder.

"Because I've seen what happens." He walked my way, standing a foot in front of me. His rain-soaked hair stuck to his cheeks, while his shirt stuck to his chest and stomach, which outlined the ridges of his muscles I fought against admiring. "You wanna know why I don't kiss lips?"

I shook my head, incredibly confused. From what I'd come to know about Archer, he couldn't stay angry long. It was a trait that might have gotten him in trouble in the biker world, but in my world…? It was endearing. Maybe even a little sweet. And though Archer wasn't perfect by any means, he was different than any of the other RDs. Maybe different than any man I'd ever known. He was a good person, just a little rough around the edges was all.

"Because it's like sealing a curse, that's why."

Reaching up, I pressed both of my hands against his throat—instinct, I called it. A need to help him heal. I held them there, forcing him to look at me.

"You don't have to explain this to me. I get it."

"Yeah." He nodded. "If you got it so much, then you would've never tried to get me to break my rule last night, huh?"

He was baiting me, trying to push me back. I'd bet this was what Archer did to anyone who dared get under his skin. But I wasn't scared of his bark or his bite.

"I warned you what would happen if I drank that drink."

I smiled at him, playful. Light. Needing him to let go of his pain, and whatever made him act this way. Was it me? The revelation about Chop telling Flick? Was he scared what might happen now? The Red Dragons were all he had—he'd made that known from the second I'd met him. If he lost them, what would happen to him? Where would he go? What would he do? It wasn't my place to judge anymore. I was trying to protect my family too.

"Yeah. You did, didn't you?" He shut his eyes, wincing when I stroked my thumb over his pulse. Did my touch repulse him that much? Slowly, I pulled back, letting my hands fall to my side, only for him to stop me, fingers grabbing hold of mine.

Our eyes met again, his holding some unknown emotion there. It was as if he was pleading with me to understand it.

One thing I did know was that over the course of the last twenty-four hours, I'd come to realize that Archer and I were actually after the same things right now, even if the rest of our goals didn't match up in life. We wanted peace for our families. We wanted Pops out of our lives for good. And we wanted it done swiftly, without hurting the people we loved in the process. And because of that, I'd never been more grateful to have someone trust me the way he seemed to.

Decision made, I wrapped my arms around his waist, laying my head on his chest.

He stiffened, like the simple act was terrifying, not to mention unfamiliar too. Because of that, I squeezed him a little tighter, hoping he'd feel what I couldn't say with words. *You're not alone. We're in this together until the end.*

The rain wasn't letting up, and soon my teeth were chattering because of it. But if he wasn't okay yet, then I wouldn't be either. One thing I knew for certain though: I was tired of arguing with this man, but at the same time I never wanted to stop arguing with him.

After a while, I felt one of his arms wrap tentatively around my shoulder.

"Let's go find a place to dry off, okay?" I buried my nose into his chest, exhaustion weighing me down.

"Alright, JP. Let's walk."

It was then that I felt yet another shift between us. This one far more prominent than any others.

We settled inside a tiny grocery store not far from where we'd stood in the street. Soaked to the bone, both of us shivering, our clothes and my back drenched. Archer grabbed a cart and proceeded to walk the length of the aisles, me beside him. It felt oddly domesticated, reminding me of the times Sam and I would go to the store, both knowing what to get, never second-guessing the other's choices.

Neither of us spoke, but our bodies were in sync, as were our minds. Archer got some spare clothes, and I grabbed some gum and Chapstick. After a while, the rain seemed to stop; at least it looked that way through the window. But the sun was also setting, proof that we'd basically wasted a whole day in this town, doing nothing.

"You hungry?" Archer asked, stopping next to the deli counter.

"Sure." I tucked some hair behind my ear and motioned him toward the front of the store to grab a place in line while I picked up some sandwiches and a side salad for us to share.

As I made my way to the checkout, the first thing I noticed was Archer, learning against the cart and smiling at the woman in front of him. She was totally flirting, the whole hair-tuck behind the ear thing, and the batting of her lashes. I grinned, gaze shooting back to Archer's face. The way he leaned into her, the smoothness of his smile, and the dimple on his cheek… He was so much to look at. A pretty boy, yeah. But there was something undoubtedly masculine about him too. I'd be lying if I said I wasn't attracted to him, that I couldn't still feel his skin where I'd brushed it with my fingertips, the way his nose had felt against my neck when he'd spoken into my ear, the way our legs had brushed together under the bedsheets last night in the Airbnb…

Shaking my head to clear the strange sensations, I moved forward to join him in line, only for a baritone voice to call out my name from the left.

"Emily?"

I blinked, lifting my head… losing my smile. Oh, God. Sam? He was here? In this tiny town in Indiana? I thought he'd moved to Des Moines. What were the odds?

"Hey!" I smiled wide, moving closer… only for a woman to approach him from behind. A red-headed woman. Sweet face, green eyes. Tall like him. Pretty and totally *not* wearing a cardigan, but a dress with tiny cherries all over it.

"How are you?" Sam, with his full cheeks and blue eyes, his smile sweet and genuine.

"I'm good." The words felt heavy on my tongue, like thick lies. Because I wasn't good. Not at all. But looking at my ex, seeing him there with his new girlfriend? I understood right away that it wasn't because I missed him. I just missed what we'd had.

He awkwardly introduced me to his new girlfriend. I could tell she was kind by her genuine smile and sweet voice. And because of her softness, I knew she was the perfect counterpart for Sam. She could give him all the things I hadn't been able to.

"What're you doing here?" I asked, glancing back toward the register. Archer had moved out of line and was heading my way, his eyes narrowed.

"Oh, Andy's parents live in town. We came back to visit."

Right then, Andy lifted her left hand, and something sparkly caught my eye. A ring. I wasn't sure if it was an intentional flash or what, but I didn't feel a stab of jealousy. If anything, I felt sadness. Sadness because this life he was leading now was the one he was meant to once live with me.

"Oh, that's cool." I nodded and Archer stepped up next to me, his arm slinging around my shoulder.

"Who's this, JP?" he asked.

I rolled my eyes yet again at the name he'd given me. "This is Sam." I swung a hand toward my ex, then looked to Archer. "Sam, Andy, this is Archer."

"The boyfriend." I stiffened when Archer stuck his hand out to take Andy's, but I didn't correct him either. The last thing I wanted was for Sam to know how miserable I was right now, so this was the next best thing, I supposed.

"Boyfriend?" Sam wrinkled his nose and looked between us, frowning even more when he got a look at Archer's cut. "But you're a motorcycle guy."

"He is." I shrugged and looked to the floor, not really in the mood to see my ex's response.

Sam had never understood why my mom had chosen the life she did. Nor did he really understand the world of a motorcycle club. I was not knowledgeable by any means, but I did know enough to accept my mom's need to be a part of Pops's life. At least once upon a time, I had.

He'd never met Pops. But he had met Niyol. Despite my brother's rough persona, he had always been kind to Sam—as kind as Niyol could be, that was. Sam, on the other hand, had never really reciprocated that kindness. If anything, he'd tended to look down at Niyol, not knowing that he couldn't necessarily help the way he'd been raised. At least my brother *tried* to make decent decisions, especially when it came to the women in his life.

When Sam had suggested not inviting my brother to our wedding because he feared a bunch of bikers would show up with him, I was hurt, maybe a little angry too. I didn't have anyone else but my mom and my friends, so there was no way I'd *not* invite Niyol. We'd bickered over this multiple times and, to me, that had been the beginning of the end for us. Nobody knew that, of course. Not even Summer or my mom. I may have despised the life Niyol lived, but he was my brother. Always and forever.

Archer bent over, surprising me again when he kissed the top of my head. "JP loves living the life as my old lady. Trust me."

I shut my eyes and blew out a slow breath. For the love of God… Just when I was starting to tolerate Archer…

"Oh." Sam cleared his throat, clearly confused—not to mention uncomfortable. "How's your, uh, mom by the way? Did she ever grow up and come home? Or is she still on the run with that fugitive?"

My eyes popped wide at his words. The odd smirk on my ex's face was… off. Sam wasn't this callous asshole. What was his deal?

"Mom's… um—"

"We're on our way to get her right now, actually," Archer jumped in, squeezing me closer. "Lisa's doing well."

My throat closed off when I realized what Archer was doing.

Rescuing me from embarrassment.

He didn't have to do this and I'd never ask him to, yet there he was, being the endearing man I didn't know existed under all of his snark.

"I guess that's good then." Sam laughed sarcastically. "But I'm betting she's in trouble with the law, am I right? Hiding out with your criminal father and all that." He tutted and shook his head, catching me completely off guard.

Archer spoke before I could again, his laughter filled with mirth and anger though. "The law? Are you fucking seriously trying to throw your nerdy, tough-boy words in? You're a goddamn—"

"Archer." I touched his arm, squeezed his hand in mine. He stopped talking and stared down at our now intertwined fingers, inquisitive eyes watching my thumb stroke the outside of his. Can you go check out the groceries so we can go?" I batted my eyelashes at him, hoping to get through his angry state of mind. I just wanted to go. This was already uncomfortable as it was. Having him verbally sparring with my ex was not high on my agenda today. Or ever. Especially when said ex was wasting our time.

Andy looked like she'd swallowed rat poison; her face was white and her sympathetic gaze was on me in a *what do we do* sort of way. Honestly? I kind of didn't know myself, which was why I took Sam's gaping mouth as a cue for us to leave.

"Hey, it was good to meet you," I told Andy."

"You too." She smiled.

Sam's gaze was like stone as he studied Archer a second longer, melting a little when it met mine, into something that resembled pity. "If you need anything, you still have my number, right?" He lowered his voice, though I'm not sure why. "I worry about you and…" His eyes flickered to Archer, who's body grew stiff next to mine.

"I'll be fine, don't worry about me." And I would be, just as long as I got to my mom.

The memory of the last time Sam and I had been together flashed through my mind as I looked at my ex's face for one second longer—Sam on his knees before me, crying and begging for another chance. Only now, that same guilt I'd felt had gone away. Not just because he seemed happy, but because I realized now, just how much he had judged me and my family. I would have never wanted to spend the rest of my life with someone who always thought I held baggage.

Before I could turn to Archer, grab his arm and urge him to leave, he bit out his own opinion, not holding anything back.

"Listen, bud, I'm gonna say what my girl here won't." He pointed a finger at Sam's chest, stabbing it against the center. "It really wasn't good to see you *or* meet you. And if I have to again, it'll be too damn soon." Then with those parting words, Archer turned his back to us all and headed toward the cash register again, staying there this time.

I looked after him, followed him too, feeling my lips turn up into a small smile. Archer was just so… so bad. So rough around the edges. But he was also an unexpected surprise I kind of couldn't get enough of right now.

CHAPTER TWELVE

Archer

We were on borrowed time and possibly hours from being tracked by my brothers. Yet the second we left the grocery store, Emily took me by the hand and started leading me across the street toward a park.

"Bike's that way." I tugged her in the opposite direction.

"Ten minutes, please?" She glanced over her shoulder, tugging me back. "That's all I'm asking."

I groaned, eyes to the people on the street walking around us. A few people glanced at my cut, my long hair pulled back in a ponytail now too, otherwise we were all but invisible. For now. At least it'd stopped raining, which meant we should've gotten back on the road ahead of the next storm. But Emily was being stubborn, insisting we fucking eat in the park across the road from the store while we had some dry time. I was finding it hard to tell her no, and that was a problem. A big one I'd be dealing with. Just... not right now.

"This ain't a good idea, JP. We don't know who's lurking. Staying in one place too long isn't smart."

"I know. But we can't starve ourselves either. And since we haven't eaten at all today, I think we owe it to our stomachs to put some *sustenance* in there." She smirked at me. "You know, since *men need to eat* and all."

I frowned at her mocking, smart mouth, surprised she could be this fluffy and perky after just running into her ex. That guy was a total dickface, and spending five minutes with him was too long. How had she dealt with it for as long as she had? However long that was.

She slowed to keep my pace, bumping her shoulder against mine. "What were you saying about *me* having a stick up my ass?"

"There's a difference between us. My stick has everything to do with the fact that getting our asses to Kentucky means not meeting up with enemies. Yours means you're boring."

"Point made, though not appreciated." She sighed and continued walking in the direction of a picnic table that sat just up ahead. "We can't exactly eat on a bike, though, am I right?"

"No. But we could've waited until we got to the next town over, where we weren't out in the middle of everything."

She grabbed my wrist this time, forcing me to sit on the wooden seat. Standing above me with her hands on her hips, she said, "Stop worrying, alright? Ten minutes won't make or break us."

"Yeah, right. Tell that to any of Pops's men who might be out there lurking. Or even one of my brothers looking to take you down now that they think you're a traitor like your ma because of those damn letters." I grabbed the bag from her hand and slammed it onto the table.

Surprising me, Emily still kept up the perk. "Did anyone ever tell you what a smart-ass you are?" She took a seat across from me and opened the bag, taking out the food.

"I've been told that a time or two."

"It's annoying, but I also get it now."

"Get what?"

She unwrapped her pre-made sandwich. "Why you are the way you are."

"And what *way* am I?" I narrowed my eyes and put my elbows on the table, studying her. The last thing I wanted was to hear her psychoanalyze me, but at the same time it was interesting to watch someone try to figure *me* out rather than the other way around. Not that I'd ever admit it to her.

"You're like my middle-school kids, actually. Pretending to be a badass on the outside, while on the inside, you don't know what you want out of life."

I blinked. What in the actual…? "I ain't some pubescent teenage kid, JP. Got the major cajones to prove it."

She rolled her eyes. "Not on the outside, no."

"Or in my jeans."

"Yes. I suppose that too." She covered her face, lowering her hands just enough to where I could see her eyes as she spoke again. "But inside, I know you long for the same things I do."

"Sex and whiskey?" I winked.

"Just… ugh. Never mind. I'm tired of trying to have a serious conversation with you only for you to bring up body parts or sex in the end." She huffed and turned away from me as she finished up the rest of her food, eyes everywhere but on me.

I waited for her to continue playing this game we were so good at, but even after she finished chewing the last bite of her sandwich, Emily didn't speak. It was like she'd sunk back into whatever hole she'd once hid inside and was planning on staying there until I forced her out again.

I gritted my teeth. Did she get off on this? The *I'm gonna ignore Archer until I can get under his skin* angle? Yes, I knew it was my fault for her shift in mood, but I didn't want to apologize because I was fucking terrified of what would happen if I did. If I let her in, let her stay under my skin as someone other than Hawk's annoying little sister, then I had a real bad feeling I wouldn't be able to get her out.

That was why I pushed this back into the safe zone, the back and forth I could handle. My hope was she would take the bait, otherwise this was gonna be one long-ass trip to Kentucky.

"Anyone ever tell you you're cute when you're pissed? Especially with all those freckles across your cheeks. They get darker whenever your skin gets red."

Her eyes narrowed, staying glued to whatever thing she was looking at across the park. "Actually, yes." She picked up her yogurt this time and slurped in a mouthful between her lips, pointing the end of her spoon at me. "People have said, 'You're cute, Emily,' my entire life."

"And that's a bad thing?" I scratched at my jaw, frowning.

Emily finished another two spoonfuls before she spoke again. "No. It's not. But I'd much rather be sophisticated and beautiful. Not *cute*."

"But you *are* cute." This was why women confused me so damn much.

"Yeah. I was also the *cute* kid growing up. The girl people looked at for a minute and thought, *She's sweet*, then tended to forget what I looked like or who I even was come the next time we met up." She shrugged, and I could tell by the tone of her voice this wasn't a subject she wanted to talk about, but I did. Because, well, shit like this fascinated me.

"Saying someone's cute is a compliment," I told her.

"It also means that someone is forgettable."

Forgettable? Is that what she thought? What the hell kind of dude was that Sam guy to make her feel like she was forgettable? I opened my mouth to tell her she wasn't *just* cute, but also goddamn stunning. That whenever she came into a room, people looked, especially me, but I couldn't get the words out. And from the slump of her shoulders when she looked away again, I could tell she was disappointed.

I'd teased her once about looking like a table when she was sixteen because that was the first thought that had come to my mind when we'd met. But as a guy whose only compliments to women had ever been, *You've got some fantastic tits*, or, *Your pussy tastes like sweet honey*, I wasn't really sure what to say when I saw her. She'd reminded me of ma. A shit ton. So much so that it'd royally fucked me up inside for a few minutes when our eyes had first met. My mouth had blurted out words my brain and heart had known wouldn't be too nice.

I cleared my throat and grabbed the other half of my sandwich, taking it down in three bites. Wasn't even hungry, but anything was better than the thoughts currently running through my mind.

She quirked an eyebrow at me, smiling a little more. "Not hungry, huh?"

"I'm a man. You put food in front of me, I eat it."

She laughed and tucked some hair behind her ear at the same time, which immediately drew my eyes to her neck. The scratches there were fading, yeah, but I could still see them clearly. Deep down I knew she was lying to me about what Chop had done to her that night. In turn, that had me wondering again what the hell else she might be keeping from me. Like, what if I got to Kentucky only to get ambushed? Fuck, though. Em wouldn't do that. Would never side with her old man.

Or would she? If it meant getting her ma free.

It should have been easy to trust my best friend's sister. But Emily wasn't a Lattimore. She was a Lincoln through and through, just like her mother.

She took a drink of her water and cleared her throat, folding her hands on the table like a businesswoman ready to go to war. "So. I wanted to say thank you by the way."

I frowned. "For what?"

"For what you did back in the store with Sam." She lifted her bottle and took another drink. Tiny wet droplets spilled down her chin, too quickly for her to wipe them away. My mind went south the second that tiny bit of water did. What would her skin taste like if I lapped up those drops with my tongue?

I shuddered at the image forming in my mind then pushed it away to refocus on her face.

"Are you listening to me?" She laughed a little, but her brows were all pushed together like she was confused.

So am I, JP. So am I.

"Yeah. I'm listening."

"Anyways, I feel like I should clarify things a little when it comes to Sam. You see, he was good to me the entire time we were together. And there's no denying the fact that we were in love."

There was that word: *love*. Who the hell loved someone who judged them for who their parents were? If love meant dealing with that kind of backlash, then it was all the more reason for me to *not* ever fall for someone.

"He was never okay with my mom or the biker club though," she continued.

"You're not a fan of the club either," I challenged.

"Touché," she said with a shrug. "Buuuut I dealt with it because I love my mom, you know? Sam was constantly ragging on me about how we should just stop going to see her because you never knew when we'd run into trouble." She rolled her eyes and played with the plastic wrap from her sandwich, her cheeks going a little red. Almost like she was ashamed to admit it out loud. I just wasn't sure which part made her feel that shame. Was it Sam? Or the club? This was about the time I wished I had a manual on women and what their words actually meant.

I decided right then that I didn't like it when JP looked ashamed. It made my chest tighten. My hands clench under the table too. No idea why that was the thing, but it was. It so, so was, and it sucked.

"We need to go." I pushed myself up from the table.

"Wait." She blinked up at me, stood too, then rushed to my side, where she touched my upper arm. Held her hand there was more like it. "Why did you tell Sam you were my boyfriend?"

My jaw clenched. Was she that oblivious? The guy was looking at her like she was the scum on the bottom of his shoe. The shit he forgot to wipe off. It could've been because he was still in love with her and was fighting it, or it could've been because he wasn't the prince she probably thought he was. Either way, I wasn't in the mood to tell her the truth—that I didn't feel like she should have to stand there and explain herself to that fucker when it was none of his business what was going on in her life now.

"It was fun. That's why. Anything to get under your skin." I gathered the crap we needed to take with us and stuffed it under my arm. The things we'd be throwing away, I shoved into the empty bag.

"But you could've just said you were my friend. Or a ride."

I gritted my teeth, ignoring her question as I headed back toward my bike across the grassy park. "Let's go. It's gonna storm."

A loud clap of thunder sounded in the distance, taunting us.

"Archer, stop. Please," she called after me.

I wouldn't stop. Not this time. I was so engrossed with her today that whenever she said or did something, I forgot I was sitting in one place listening to her. I also forgot what we were doing. And that, to me, was more dangerous than anything else. It meant that I was feeling something. *For* her. Not lust either. Because lust could be dealt with—there was a remedy to lust: sex.

At my bike, I re-tied her duffel bag a little tighter to the seat, then unlocked the helmet from the handles. Once I sat down, I held an arm out with the helmet, waiting for her to approach.

"Hey, what's going on? Did I say something to upset you? Do something wrong? Archer," she tried again. "Answer me. Please."

My jaw clenched… and I still ignored her. Maybe I really was like the middle-school kids she taught.

"Fine. Never mind then." She tore the helmet out of my hands and sat on the back of the bike.

While I waited for her to get ready, I wondered if that douchebag ex of hers had ever gotten this worked up over her for no reason. Guy was smart enough not to, right? He seemed like the type, all well-dressed and decent-looking, if not a little dorky. The type who preferred nothing but a missionary fuck. I could almost betcha he didn't ever have thoughts about spanking her ass like I currently was. No reason for the image in my mind either, other than the fact that I wanted to see the white curves turn pink by my hand, only so I could soothe the heated skin with my mouth.

Screw that shit.

It was bad enough feeling the pain in my chest. Getting my dick more involved with this woman was… well… shit.

Who was I kidding? My dick had been involved since the second I'd laid eyes on her bright-red cardigan that night in the club—probably long before that if I was being honest with myself.

"Hey!" she hollered at my back and snapped her fingers in front of my face. "I need help. I can't get this stupid thing on." And now she sounded pissed at me. Great. A pissed-off Emily was a sexy Emily.

I turned to straddle my bike the other way, which wasn't too smart. Because my dick was currently like steel, which made it really fucking hard—no pun intended—to move and be just inches from the glorious spot my big guy was intrigued with between her thighs.

"Goddamn cardigans," I mumbled under my breath, and I shut my eyes for a second, trying to check myself.

"What'd you just say?"

"Nothing. Come here." I opened my eyes again and leaned forward to toy with the strap beneath her chin. She didn't argue or bother asking me what was wrong again, which I was thanking Christ for. But I could still feel her gaze on me the whole time. I wanted to ask what she was looking at, but what if I didn't like her answer?

I scowled and patted the side of her helmet when I finished, eyes up, zeroing in on her face. She was smiling a little, relaxed again. And there went that thud in my heart like before.

"Thanks. Guess you gotta be a genius to figure this thing out."

I wasn't good or smart, nowhere near a genius. But I didn't correct her. "You ready?"

She nodded. "As I can be knowing I'll be straddling this bike again for God only knows how long."

I opened my mouth, ready to say, *I got something else you can straddle instead,* but the fact that my insides were all weirded out over this woman right now kept me from saying shit.

"You get tired, tell me."

"I will."

I turned around, fighting the urge to look at her as I did. I started the engine, revved it loud. Then like she was meant to be there, Emily wrapped her arms around my waist and set her chin on my shoulder, like she'd been riding behind me for years, not days. Normally, you didn't put a chick on the back of your bike unless she was old lady material. And Emily? She was about as far from old lady material as a man could ask for.

Yet the thought of anyone else on the back of my bike suddenly didn't feel right. Emily, with her arms wrapped around my waist and her head to my back? It almost felt like she was meant to be there.

Whatever the fuck that meant.

"This is a train caboose," Emily nearly squealed in excitement the second she jumped off the back of my bike. She unbuckled her helmet and handed it over, not even looking at me as she headed toward the door.

"Yeah, no shit," I muttered.

I untied her bag and threw it over my shoulder before following her. We'd wound up at some wildlife preservation park. Not an ideal location to lay our heads, but we were much closer to Pops now, so I couldn't complain. What I did like about the setup was the fact that we were surrounded by woods. Sheltered from the outside highways and roads. Nobody would ever expect to find us here, honestly. Not my brothers or anyone out there who could be associated with Pops. Plus, it was the cheapest place I could find in a 100-mile radius that wasn't booked. Apparently, it was the beginning of fair season or something. I hadn't figured we'd be forced to stop and sleep as much as we had been, but the rain had been relentless.

"The man said there might be buffalo outside our door in the morning, did you hear him?" Emily smiled from over her shoulder, sliding the key into the lock.

"Yippee." I smirked, thankful that my bad mood wasn't as crappy as it had been. Thanks to the last few hours on my bike, I was calmer with a clearer head and my goals locked in place once more. Get Emily to her mom, take Pops down, and hopefully stay alive while I was doing it.

"I need the shower first," she told me. More like *ordered*.

"Whatever." I couldn't even muster up a dirty joke about sharing the shower to conserve water. Regardless, her taking a shower might give me time to jerk one out too. That'd help even more. Not that it was ideal. If anything, it was kind of sick that I'd have to do it. But something had to give now that we'd be spending the night together in the same space again.

I flicked the light on as we stepped up a short, narrow staircase. The caboose was skinny, to the point where I had to turn sideways to get through the aisle. There was a bathroom first thing up front, then a kitchen, and two twin beds set up across from one another toward the back.

"I call the one on the right," Emily said.

I sat across from her, bouncing, or trying to. There was a serious lack of spring in the mattress. "I won't fit here," I muttered, more to myself, as I looked at the length. This was a bed made for a freaking toddler. Well, more like a person under six foot.

"Yes, you will." Emily rolled her eyes then grabbed something from her bag. "It's only for a night, remember?" She pointed her shampoo bottle at me.

"Whatever," I mumbled, leaning back on the bed.

The floor rocked as she moved toward the bathroom; the entire place was unstable. I wasn't high maintenance by any means, but damn… I wasn't feeling this place.

The second I heard the water start up, along with Emily's humming, I relaxed against a pillow and shut my eyes. My feet hung over the end, boot laces catching on the metal. I kicked the damn things off, prepping to do what was necessary to get me out of this fucked-up mess that was my head. These walls were like paper, though, so I needed to keep it down.

Licking my lips, I shut my eyes and unzipped my pants. I hadn't jerked off in months, mostly because I'd had a steady diet of women to keep me busy. The thing was, even if one of my monthlies magically popped up offering their services, I didn't think I could take them up on it.

Why? Because the only image I could conjure in my mind right then was one of a brunette. The one currently humming in the shower.

I listened for a minute, frowning as she hit a low note. The sultry sound sent a wave of heated energy through my gut and straight to my dick, sounding more like whispers and moans than music.

I shuddered, sliding my hand into my pants. With a hard squeeze, I gripped my cock, stroked it once, lips parting as her singing stopped altogether. The shower continued though, and in my mind I could imagine her in there, fingers sliding over her breasts, down her belly, settling in between her thighs, where she'd be wet because, well, she'd be thinking about me.

Yeah. I was a dirty son of a bitch, but it didn't take a rocket scientist to figure out what my problem was either. It wasn't just the fact that I was horny. Nor was it the fact that I hadn't put a drop of whiskey in my mouth all day. I was pissed because at some point within the last twenty-four hours, Emily taking that stick out of her ass had made me want to do something else down there instead.

Sweet, tight, wet heat… I jerked faster, biting on my lip. I mumbled her name under my breath, jerking faster, up, down, the friction almost enough to get me there. Just another minute…

"Hey, I need your help. I couldn't get the water to shut off because… Oh, God."

I jerked my head back, cringing when I saw Emily. She was crouched on the floor, her face buried in her hands.

"Good Christ, JP. What're you doing down there?" I chuckled, despite the fact that she was ten feet away, had just caught me jerking off, and was now hiding her face like a kid.

"I'm sorry. I didn't…" She lifted her head, eyes zeroing in on my crotch. Seconds later she stood and spun around, facing the bathroom again.

I wasn't the least bit embarrassed about being caught. If anything, things had just got a hell of a lot more intriguing.

"Already in the cardigan?" I smirked, tucking my cock back inside my jeans but leaving the button undone. He was angry and hard, deprived as hell, too. I'd just have to pay him special attention later in the shower.

"Did you, um…?" She cracked her neck from side to side.

"Did I put my dick away?"

"Uh huh. Yup."

"I did. You're safe."

Slowly, she turned back around and made her way over to her bag, making sure to keep her eyes everywhere but on me.

"What, you scared of me now? Afraid of what you might see?"

"No. I'm not scared." She rummaged through her duffel but didn't actually pull anything out.

I moved in, unable to stop myself, and leaned against the side of her bed just so I could get closer to her. I knew I should've just left well enough alone. But the sight of her flustered and not so in control? It messed with my reality, to the point where forgetting what had just happened wasn't gonna be easy.

"You interrupted me." I frowned, licking my lips as her cardigan slid off her shoulder nearest to me. I had the urge to lean closer and slide it up, but my greedy eyes were desperate to see if the rest of her pale skin matched the polka dots on her nose.

"To be fair, I didn't know what you were, um, doing." She huffed and turned around to face me. Wet hair slid over her cheeks, down her chest. The ends dampened the material of her sweater right above her tits and that was damn unfortunate.

Careful with my touch, I lifted my hand, sliding it to the buttons. With surprisingly steady fingers, I toyed with the top one, swirling a finger over the smoothness… chuckling to myself when I noticed her chest rise and fall a little faster.

Finally, I was affecting the sober-version her. She'd been like a vault and I was desperate to find the key to open her.

"What are you doing?" she whispered.

Fuck if I know.

I tapped the first button. "Mind if I…?" I made a popping noise with my mouth.

Her eyes widened. "Um, yes. I do mind."

I frowned, pushing my bottom lip out. "Pity. You're soaked."

"What?" she gasped. "I'm not… No."

I shook my head. What a dirty little mind she had. "Your *cardigan*, I meant."

"My *cardigan* is fine."

I shrugged one shoulder. "What's with these sweater things, by the way?" I ran my finger down to the next button, circling the outside, careful not to push too far.

She pursed her lips.

"Not complaining." I met her eyes, holding them for a moment. Then I eyed the curve of her tits again, grin widening when I noticed something poking out the front of said cardigan. Nipples. Both of them were hard, which could've meant she was cold, or possibly turned on. I'd bet my left nut on the latter because, so close to me, I could feel the heat of her body.

"Hot for teacher, hot for librarian… What other fantasies can you provide for me, JP?"

Emily rolled her eyes. She turned, giving me her back as she bent over to mess with her bag again. I didn't miss the way her hands shook when she did. How she opened and closed her fists as she hovered over her duffel for a second before she started actually looking through it again. Like before, she still didn't pull anything out. Instead of asking what she was looking for, I rolled with the moment and took the time to study her ass beneath those fancy khakis she wore.

"Anyone ever tell you that you got a fine little ass, JP?" Not only did I want to look at it, I also wanted to touch it. Both sides, one side… preferably if she was naked on top of me, her hot pussy gliding up and down over my throbbing dick.

Man. How I ever thought she was unfuckable was pretty damn stupid. I was in deep shit if I didn't get to finish jerking off soon.

She huffed.

"Don't be ashamed." I stepped up to her side, bent down a little, and let my lips slide against her ear as I whispered, "It's a fantastic ass. I'll gladly help you wash it next time you're in the shower."

She shivered.

She also didn't tell me no.

Hell. Yes.

Was I *finally* getting to her? What was the key, though, the turning point, really? Did I keep pushing, did I not push at all? Jesus, I didn't know what to do. This wasn't normal for us. Not that I'd complain. The thing was, though, she never acted this way with me. She always called me out on my BS. I wasn't sure if I hated or liked this more, mostly because I was a horny bastard and resisting the little letter-writing runaway and possible traitor was proving more difficult as each minute passed. I wanted to see just how far she'd let me push her. Tomorrow I'd regret being an ass, but right now? I couldn't find it in me to be anything else.

"Here's what's gonna happen." I pulled her around to face me, my hands on her elbows. "I'm gonna sit on the bed, like I was before, and finish what I started."

She whipped her head up, eyes widening, lips parting too.

"You're welcome to go wait in the shower or outside, or, if you're interested, you can join me."

"Join you?" she choked.

I nodded. "Yeah. Have you never watched a man jerk off before?"

Slowly, she shook her head, which didn't surprise me. That little ex of hers was likely all vanilla in bed.

"I'd be happy to show you how to do it."

Her lips parted like the no was on her tongue. But something flashed through her eyes at the same time, something I sure as hell could relate to.

Determination.

"Fine," she said with a huff.

I lifted my eyebrows. "Fine, what?"

"I'm gonna prove you wrong, Archer Benedict, *and* I'll one-up you while I'm at it." With that little snapback, Emily sat on the side of the bed, nearly missing it. Even clumsy and obviously nervous, I wanted her to keep going. Step outside of her comfort zone and prove me wrong. I had no idea why, but I rolled with it anyway.

"How're you planning on proving me wrong?" I dared her with my eyes, sitting across from her on the bed I'd picked. The space between us was so small our knees touched. The thing was, she didn't bother moving away like I thought she would.

"I'm going to get undressed."

"Yeah, right." I laughed and shook my head.

"You think you know me," she said, sliding her hands up her thighs, stopping along the base of her cardigan. Her pink-nailed fingers messed with the hem as she kept talking. "But you don't. Probably never will either."

"Sure." I smirked.

"I'm being serious," she argued. Then she shrugged, sliding her hands up to the top button of her cardigan and doing the unthinkable—the last thing I'd ever expected. She started undoing the first button. The one I'd been toying with. Then the second and the third…

My throat grew hot, almost painful. "Is that so?"

"Yes. It *is* so. I'm not the girl with a stick up her ass like you think I am. I can have fun and relax. I just choose not to. In fact, when I was in college…"

I tuned the rest of her story out. Not because I didn't want to hear it, but because she was down to the last button and… Holy. Shit.

She took it off, sliding the cotton off one shoulder, then the other…

"… and if you think that I'm—"

"Shh." I studied her tits beneath her tank. The nipples pressed against the silk. I shuddered at the thought of putting my mouth over them. But I also knew better than to cross that line.

"Archer?" she whispered. "Did you hear me?"

Only then did I lift my gaze to meet hers.

And what I saw there? It scared me even more than the idea of crossing lines.

CHAPTER THIRTEEN

Emily

Was I losing my mind? Possibly.

Did I care? Less than I probably should have.

The thing was, the longer I was around Archer, the more I realized that life wasn't about planning for future moments. It was about living in the ones given to you in the here and now.

I may or may not make it out of Kentucky alive when this was all said and done. But I was sure of one thing right then and there: I loved how Archer was looking at me, like I was so much more than just cute. And because of that, I knew exactly what I wanted—what I needed—to do to prove to this man, and myself, that I wasn't afraid of letting go.

"Good Christ, Emily, what're you doing?" he murmured, licking his lips when I began to unbutton my khakis.

I didn't want him to know how nervous I was, but if he looked hard enough, he'd see my hands shaking. "I'm getting comfortable."

"Correction." He laughed. "You're taking your damn clothes off is what you're doing."

"I am," I said, pulling in a shaky breath. "But *you're* not."

He pressed his lips together then reached behind his neck to grab his shirt, no second thoughts. Once it was in his hands, he dropped it onto the floor between us, displaying a body I'd only ever seen in magazines.

I bit my lip, allowing myself a selfish moment to look at him. Perfect abs, so many lines, and two glorious pecs that were quite possibly the most beautiful things I'd ever seen. What surprised me the most, though, was that there was only one tattoo on his chest. As far as I knew, the majority of the Red Dragons were covered in ink, including my brother.

Archer's gaze did an eager sweep of my body too when he started to unzip his jeans. He lay on his back and arched his hips, tugging his jeans down with his fingers. A minute later he was in nothing but his boxers.

"Now what?" He wiggled his brows and propped himself up on his hand.

I swallowed hard, not quite sure what to say. I'd put on quite the show a minute ago but that was *before*. *Before* I realized how perfect his body was. *Before* I realized that there was a reason he was so loved by women. *Before* I realized he was actually calling my bluff, which wasn't supposed to be a bluff.

"You tell me. This was your idea."

"Nope." He shook his head. "My idea was to show you how to jerk off. This getting-half-naked thing?" He waved a hand up and down my body. "That's on you."

"I'm not naked." But I kind of wanted to be. The problem was, I was clueless as to what I wanted to do once I did get naked. Archer may have been super comfortable with sex and all the stuff that went along with it, but I wasn't. I really hadn't experienced anything beyond what Sam and I had shared, and our intimacy could only be described as lukewarm. Never bold. Satisfying, but not exhilarating either.

"Hey," he said, his voice no longer teasing. "Don't do that."

"Do what?"

"Hide yourself from me."

Looking down, I noticed my arms folded over my chest. I must have done so subconsciously. It wasn't like I wasn't actually *going* to get naked here, this was just me trying to prove to Archer that I was in control.

"Your body, Emily." He lowered his voice, sounding more serious than I'd ever heard him. "Let me look at it."

Slowly, I let go of a long breath at the same time I dropped my arms, feeling naked when I wasn't even close to being so.

Archer's green eyes darkened as he whispered, "Why you hide that beautiful body under a sweater all the time is beyond me."

His words emboldened me. I lifted my chin and said, "Show me."

"Show you what?" His lips tilted on one side.

I swallowed the last of my nerves and finally let my inhibitions go. "How you touch yourself."

He touched his chest, rubbing a palm over his heart. "Like this?"

I rolled my eyes. "You know what I mean."

"No. I don't think I do."

Why was he such a tease? And why the hell did I like it so much when just two days ago, he was the most annoying man on this entire planet to me?

And then he said words I would never forget. "Sit there and watch me, Emily. Don't look away."

I shuddered at the order and control in his tone, loving it so much more than I should have. Then when he slid his hand into his boxers and pulled out his erection, I couldn't help but gasp.

More than anything else, I wanted to see his expression. My body burned even hotter at the thought of our eyes meeting and holding as he stroked himself over the edge. So, despite his warnings, I did lift my gaze, heart lurching into my throat when I found his eyes on my face.

"You make me crazy," Archer murmured. "You and those damn freckles and your inability to listen…"

I reached up and touched my nose, my cheeks where the freckles were most prominent. As I did, he bit his bottom lip and released a low groan, the sound making my belly twist in delicious circles. I didn't know what to do or say. But my body sure had plans. And for once in my life, I let it take the lead and began to rock my hips a little, the pressure rubbing me all wrong against the mattress.

"You feel it too, don't you?" The slide of his palm slowed, the wrap of his fist easing.

I looked him in the eyes again, my face warming as badly as the space between my thighs.

He grinned. "Are you wet for me, Emily?"

Was I? Likely. But did I want to admit it out loud? Not really. Thankfully, Archer didn't push the subject.

"You want to ease the ache? You wanna come like I'm gonna?"

I blinked, chest heaving. Speaking was impossible, so I nodded just once.

"Do it, then. Put your fingers in your panties. Tug 'em aside. Feel how wet I make you, because I can guarantee you are fucking soaked right now."

My neck was hotter than my face; my ears rang too. "I-I don't…"

"It's okay. Don't be shy," he murmured, never losing that cocky grin.

This was happening. And I couldn't stop myself either. Archer had made it so all I could focus on was my desire, and if I didn't get to chase my release soon, I might just lose my mind.

I slid my hand down like he ordered, slowly tugging my panties to the side.

"That's beautiful," he whispered, watching my fingers work. "Spread your legs." I did. "A little wider so I can see," he whispered, eyes locking with mine. "Because your pussy is gorgeous. Just like the rest of you."

His words made me smile a little, relax too. "Nobody's ever…" I shrugged.

"Fucking bastards. All of 'em. Your pussy is the prettiest I've ever seen."

Feeling brazen from his words, his encouragement too, I slid a finger over my clit, circling, rubbing… "Oh, God."

Archer's tongue darted out over his bottom lip, a growl deep in his throat. "Just like that, baby. Pretend it's me." He stroked faster again. "Pretend it's my fingers, sliding around. Pretend I'm between your thighs right now. My mouth right there over the pretty pussy."

Archer moved his hand faster, our knees touching a little, but nothing else.

"Archer," I whimpered, already feeling the beginning of my orgasm take over. My fingers were soaked. I was sure I looked a mess down there, but I suddenly didn't care. For the first time in my entire life I let myself enjoy something without worrying about the consequences.

Faster and faster, I rocked my hips back and forth, looking at him and imagining it was his tongue there instead of my own hand like he said.

I moaned loudly, louder than I'd ever done before. And then I was coming, a blissful electric snap of nerves and tension and a beautiful ache of pleasure that I couldn't get enough of.

"Fuck, Emily," Archer growled low, and when I looked at him, his bowed head, his squeezing, stroking hand, I shuddered through the aftershocks of my orgasm as he found a release of his own.

Seconds passed.

I panted and tried to catch my breath, unable to take my eyes off his flushed face when he lifted his head back up. His eyes were closed, his shoulders relaxing.

Archer didn't look at me. But he did open his eyes and stand. Methodically, he tucked himself back into his boxers then slid on his jeans, avoiding my gaze even still.

I froze, inside and out. Coldness like I'd never known raced through me. Disappointment not far behind.

"Archer?" I whispered, grabbing a blanket to cover my legs.

He stood in front of me then, our knees touching like before, though he'd never felt further away from me. Hair fell over one of his eyes like an animal, uncaged. Rabid.

He curled his lip, a smirk overtaking his face. "Lesson over, JP."

Turning away from me, he grabbed his shirt and slid on his boots. Then he left the small sleeping area, not going to the bathroom to shower or wash his hands.

He left *me*.

And he didn't bother coming back.

CHAPTER FOURTEEN

Archer

Midnight came and went before I finally felt able to face the music and go back inside. I was sure Emily thought I'd taken off, despite the fact that my bike was still in the same spot it'd been in since we'd gotten here earlier. I wasn't stupid enough to leave her alone like she probably thought. The woman was my ticket to Pops. No way would I risk the chance of letting her run off because I'd had a momentary loss of sanity and thought, for a second, that I might actually have *feelings* for a woman I'd just jerked off in front of.

No, scratch that. Not a woman. *Emily.* My best friend's little sister. Someone who was getting under my skin and making me feel too much. A beautiful, sassy, smart as fuck woman who'd just spread her legs and shown me a piece of herself that I was pretty sure she'd never been generous enough to share with anyone else.

My chest tightened right then and not from my cigar either.

It didn't matter though. I could not cross that line again, damn it. Not now. Or ever. Not when I had plans to end her old man's life and *she* had plans to run away with a traitor and become one to my club too.

I was sated now. *That's* what mattered. I'd had my release, my fun, scratched a little itch…

Except I wasn't. Sated, that is. Not at all, actually. If anything, I was more on edge than I had been before. And I didn't have a damn clue why either. Or I did have a clue, and wasn't in the mood to admit it.

I gritted my teeth and headed toward the door, slowly pulling it open. I probably should apologize for running out. But it wasn't like she'd run after *me*. If anything, I was guessing she was relieved I'd left, pretended like what had happened wasn't worth a second thought. She had a type and it wasn't a biker. She'd made that known to everyone she encountered at the club.

Even with that thought in my head, my heart skipped a little when I stepped inside the caboose. Instead of wanting to touch her, I just wanted to look into her eyes again. Wanted to brush her bangs away and trace her freckles with the tips of my fingers.

I stopped between the beds and sat down, eyes to the floor, elbows on my knees. The second I heard her mumble something in her sleep though, I lifted my chin and allowed myself to look. My gut hardened the second I laid eyes on her. Moonlight from the window above her bunk shadowed her cheek, and my weird mood got only weirder right then. It was like someone had sucker-punched me in the chest and stolen all the air from my lungs at the same time. It hurt to breathe, really.

Long hair hung over her cheeks and her shoulder as she lay curled in a ball, no blanket, hands beneath her chin like she was praying in her sleep. Emily looked so innocent and sweet. No way could a person tell by her sleeping face that she had the mouth of a witch and had put a spell on me with her inability to stand down from a challenge.

Without taking my eyes off her, I lay down on my side over my elbow. Like that, I studied her until my eyes got heavy. Studied her lashes against her cheeks, memorized the purse of her lips—lips that were more tempting than any other set before.

That alone should've been a warning. But I was too blinded for once to see.

*

"Archer. Archer, please. Wake up. Please." Hands shook me later that night. That morning. Whatever the fuck time it was.

I opened one lid, wondering if I was dreaming, eyes widening when I realized Emily was on the floor between the beds, shaking in panic and fear.

"What the hell?" Disoriented, I sat up, wondering if she'd had a bad dream.

She opened her mouth to say something, only for two pops to fill the air outside the caboose. Gunfire?

"What the hell?" I tackled her to the floor, my arm over her head, my body on hers as another three filled the air outside. Emily screeched but didn't shove me away, and I held her there, sucking in a sharp breath when a crash came from outside—metal upon metal. Two minutes later, the roar of a bike engine filled the air, echoing in the distance as whoever the driver was took off.

We'd been ambushed.

Or warned off, I was guessing, since they'd done a shitty job of trying to off us.

"You okay?" I whispered into Emily's ear.

"Yes. I… I tried to wake you when I heard the bike pull up."

"It's fine. You did good." I leaned back, taking in her wide, terrified eyes.

"Who was that?"

I shrugged and sat up. "Don't know. But I need to make sure nobody else is out there."

She tugged on my arm when I got on all fours to crawl to the table.

"I'm going with you."

"The hell you are," I hissed and reached up to grab my gun off the wood.

"Archer. Please. Don't leave without me."

"I'm not leaving you." I lowered my voice, my throat closing at the vulnerability in her words, her face.

"But you're…" She trailed off when she spotted the gun on my lap, bottom lip tugged between her teeth.

At least she didn't freak out at the sight of it this time, but she did keep quiet.

"Emily." I stuffed it into the front of my jeans then set a hand on her shoulder. I took her face in my other hand and urged her eyes to stay on me while I spoke. "I'm not leaving. I just need to go look and see if there's anyone else out there we gotta worry about."

"And if there is?"

I pointed to my gun. "Then this will take care of them."

Surprisingly, she didn't flinch. Instead she nodded and launched herself at me, hugging me again. Trusting me most of all, it seemed.

"Please be careful."

My throat grew tight. I didn't wrap my arms around her back in return though. "I'll be fine."

She nodded against my neck, sniffling. "You have to be."

I shut my eyes, wondering why she seemed to trust me so much when it was obvious I still didn't trust her… even if it was getting harder not to.

"Just tell me if you need me, alright?" she asked, pulling back.

Despite everything, I couldn't stop the slow grin from spreading on my mouth as I crawled to the front door. She couldn't do shit for me if something went down. But the sentiment meant more than any other I'd heard before.

Once I was by the front door, I pushed to my feet and snuck a look out of the glass pane.

"Get under the table till I give the all clear," I told her, our eyes locked across the space.

She nodded and did as I asked for once. I took her in, the panic in her wide eyes, my chest tightening and squeezing at the same time. She wasn't in the mood for dying this morning, apparently, and honestly? Neither was I.

Slowly, I slid open the door, heart racing with adrenaline, not nerves. *Never* nerves. Fighting didn't scare me. Protecting didn't either. It's what I did as a Red Dragon. As a man. Made no difference who they were. An old lady, a brother's niece, or a woman who I couldn't keep from thinking about.

The sun was just rising and the first thing I noticed was a shit ton of buffalo outside strolling the field. The second: my bike.

Or what was left of it.

"Shit," I hissed.

"What's wrong?" Emily called out.

I held a hand up to keep her quiet, eyes scanning the almost lighted field. We were so far removed from any other cabin or caboose that I was sure the gunshots could've been blown off as hunters. They had grounds set up for hunting nearby. Fucked up if you asked me. A wildlife preservation park close to hunting grounds.

"Archer?"

"It's all clear," I told her.

My shoulders slumped as I opened the door and stepped outside. Tire marks led away from the scene, and mud was splattered everywhere along the caboose and covering my damn bike. Whoever had done this didn't want to hurt us. They wanted us to stay put. A warning for sure that said, *Stay away.* But from who?

My first instinct was to call or text Slade, ask if any of the RDs had been sent our direction. But my brothers weren't stupid enough to mess with my bike. And if they knew where we were, they'd have our asses back on the road toward Rockford in no time.

A gasp sounded from the doorway behind me. I didn't look to see what was wrong because I already knew. My bike was fucking wrecked. Tires blown out, seat smashed, chrome pipes dented in…

If I was a crier, I'd be bawling right now.

My precious fucking bike.

"Archer, look!" Emily said, the creak of the steps proving she was coming out.

I turned to look at her, spotted the black leather cut on the ground a few feet away.

"Is that…?" she asked.

"Sure the hell is." I walked toward it and pulled it from the mud, frowning at the emblem on the back as I lifted it in the air.

A red dragon.

"Shit."

"Is there a name on it?" She crouched next to me, pointing at it.

I turned it over to look, but whoever it belonged to had ripped the name patch off the front. It was all the proof I needed to know that whoever had done this was too chickenshit to say who they were, but *big enough* to say they were done with the RDs.

It looked like we had ourselves an official rogue in the mix.

A rogue that I could almost bet was now working for Pops.

Bags on our shoulders, one mutual goal in mind, Emily and I set off twenty minutes later. We needed to find another bike or vehicle even. I didn't want questions from the law when they found the caboose shot up, which meant I was walking my bike to the closest town, hoping someone might buy the parts, or work through a trade with us. Fat chance of that happening, seeing how this was farm-town Indiana. But I had names and contacts all over the state. Someone had to know somebody, right?

"You don't have as many tattoos on your body as your brothers. I noticed last night." It was the first thing Emily'd said since we'd left. Weird thing to bring up right now, but maybe this was how she handled stress. By talking about random stuff, ignoring the tension between us, what had happened and the fact that I'd run away…

"I only tat myself with shit that means something."

"Oh. I gotcha. Makes sense, I suppose."

I nodded and continued through the fields, one hand on my bike handle and the other on the seat. Sweat dripped down my temples, the side of my face too. It was humid, muddy as hell. But it wasn't raining at least.

"The one on your chest," she continued. "Is that a raven?"

"Yup."

A beat passed. "What does it mean?"

I didn't hesitate to say, "Bad luck."

"Really?"

I nodded. "I lost a lot in the span of three years. From the time I was twelve to fifteen. My ma first, then my old man…" I shrugged, thankful when we finally made it to a road.

With a grunt, I pushed the bike up the hill, only for it to drive deeper into the mud and get stuck. "Damn it."

Without me asking for help, Emily hustled up to the other side, taking the same position as me—one hand on the bike seat, the other on the handlebar.

"On three?" she asked.

I nodded.

Emily counted.

With the both of us grunting and groaning, we pushed until we got it to the road. Our eyes met from over my bike, holding longer than I wanted to. She smiled shyly at me. I couldn't stop myself from smiling back.

When the shared stare got to be too much, I cleared my throat and looked down the road. "Thanks." Then I nodded toward a sign listing the nearest towns. "Five miles. You good with that?"

"Yeah. I'll be fine," she said, keeping pace as we started walking again.

For some reason, I wanted to keep the tat conversation going. Like bikes, I loved talking tattoos.

"First tat I ever got was the raven," I told her.

"Oh yeah?"

"I wanted to remind myself never to be too comfortable with one thing, ya know? That it's best to just move on with shit, otherwise bad luck is gonna strike." It was how I'd lived my life, especially when it came to women.

Emily hummed thoughtfully and hiked her duffel up higher onto her shoulder. I'd been calling it a duffel because that's what it was to me, but the damn thing had fancy-ass Ds and Bs covering the surface, so I was sure it was expensive.

"You think loving someone is a curse, then?" she asked a second later. "Including your family, right?"

"I do."

Another minute passed. "And the one on your arm, under the barbed wire. What does that mean?"

I didn't have to look to know which tat she was referring to. Written in old Gaelic, a tribute to my Irish heritage, the memories of losing my ma so early on, too.

Pain becomes strength.

Too personal. Too real. I didn't do real unless it was within my own head. And God knew that was a scary place to be in.

"That, JP, is for me to know and for you to never find out."

She didn't push. Didn't give me snark either. I looked at her for a second, curious what she was thinking, not that I was good at reading her. Emily's eyes were locked ahead, but there was tension at the corners. I knew she was trying to distract herself here. So, for her help with my bike, I'd throw her a bone.

"You got any tats?"

She shook her head. "No."

"Why not?"

"I wouldn't know what to get." She shrugged. "And, like you, I'm not going to throw random things on my body either."

"Not even a tramp stamp?"

She laughed. "Not even one of those."

Her words made me grin a little. Smart girl, she was. "You ever do *anything* reckless?"

She looked at me from out of the corner of her eye. "Is that a trick question?" She was clearly remembering last night.

I looked at her mouth. The way it twitched a little as if she was fighting another grin. "Nope. Not this time."

She lost her smile, looked at me full on. Her face was serious now. There was no light in her eyes, not a twitch to her lips either.

"If you're reckless you don't have a plan." She shuddered. "It's scary. And it's also why the last several months of my life have been nothing but miserable because every day I never knew what to expect."

"Because of the club?"

The RDs weren't reckless *or* unknown. We ran on control and order. People saw cuts and assumed we were outlaws, but that wasn't the case anymore. We were good men and wanted order and peace. Happiness and a brotherhood. Hell, we'd been trying to get that exact thing for over a year now. The thing was, in order to find peace, we'd likely have to do some really bad shit—me especially. But in the end, I'd be doing the world a favor by offing that man and his little crew. Doing my brothers a good deed most of all.

"No. Not the club…" She trailed off, shaking her head. "More so because my mom lied to me all those years about who my father was, and now I don't know if I can trust her anymore."

"Then why the hell are you going to her at all?"

"Because I don't have another choice. She's my mom, and even though she's not who I thought she was, I can't help but think that she needs me, despite her never asking me for help."

It was stupid of her to go, thinking she could fix things without knowing it was possible. But that was also exactly what I was trying to do, but for my brothers and the club, nobody else.

Emily pursed her lips, continuing. "Do you know what it's like to not be able to trust the one person in your life who's supposed to be your solid ground to walk on?"

"No. I don't, actually." Because my brothers didn't lie to me. My own ma and dad never held back their truths either. That was also why I kept my trust circle small. Letting people get close to me, only so they could turn on me in the end—or worse, die... No. I wasn't having it.

"You're lucky." She sighed.

I didn't deny it. But I didn't agree with her either. I *was* a lucky bastard in the sense that the people I did love and trust had been true and real, but an unlucky bastard because I'd lost some of those people in the end.

"So, everything's been about your ma, then?" I asked, steering the question back to her. "You being cold to everyone was because you didn't want to let anyone in?"

"Yep."

In other words, Emily was me.

Jesus, that was... weird.

She looked to the road as she spoke this time. "Could you, maybe, tell everyone that when you go home? Apologize for me?"

"Why?" I frowned, not sure if I'd even make it home myself. I didn't say that though.

She shrugged. And I didn't push for once.

"Fine. I'll try to. But I'm not sure it'll help." Plus, if my brothers didn't hate her before, then they sure as hell would after finding out what she'd done. What *I'd* done, most of all.

Emily cringed and looked the other way. I didn't say sorry. She needed to know what was to come if she did get her ma away from Pops in the end. If she or Lisa ever crossed paths with any of my brothers, they'd end them without blinking an eye. Her *and* her mom.

"Running's only one part of this equation, Emily. You know that, right?"

"I do," she whispered.

I cleared my throat. "I get it, though." More than she probably knew.

She looked at me and frowned a little. "What do you get?"

"I *get* what it's like to have to start over when it's the last thing you want."

Her eyes widened. "You do?"

"Yep." I looked ahead, tensing when a car grew closer, releasing a deep breath when they passed without interest. "Change is good. Letting go of the past to rebuild a future isn't so bad either. It's dangerous and scary as fuck. But it's doable if it's done the right way. Just be smart about this. Make sure you know what you're doing."

Emily went quiet. So much so that I wanted to look at her, but I couldn't bring myself to do it because I was scared of what I might see. Her words when she did speak, though? They messed with me, with my head.

"You're a beautiful soul, Archer, despite the playboy mentality you choose to live by. I just want you to know that."

"There's not a thing about me that's beautiful." My throat tightened. "Except for my dick maybe."

"You're the king of deflection." She laughed. "Why is that?"

"Not deflecting. I'm just the kinda man who hates serious shit."

Emily stopped moving then. Stopped talking too. I stopped myself, hands tensing around my broken machine. Frowning, I turned to look at her, but she was already on the move around the front of my bike until she stood in front of me five seconds later.

"What are you doing?" I asked, tensing when she lifted her hand to put it over my heart.

"I'm sorry," she whispered, searching my face.

"What the hell do you have to be sorry about now? We're in the middle of a road and—"

"Stop talking." She covered my mouth with her free palm. "Seriously. Let me get this out."

I rolled my eyes, pretending that my heart wasn't racing like a fucking bandit in my chest.

She lowered her hand. "I'm sorry for not believing you're more than this." She gestured at my body. Then she smoothed her palm down the front of my shirt, in between my pecs.

"What, that I'm more than a hot piece of ass you can never have?" I only half joked. Because right then, I didn't think I'd ever wanted to give my body to a woman more than I did Emily. Fuck if I knew what that meant.

Despite everything that might be ahead of us, being real with this woman in any shape or form, even if it was alongside some random farm road, scared me more than death itself.

CHAPTER FIFTEEN

Emily

We made it to a gas station an hour or so later, neither of us really speaking words that weren't grunts, yeses, or noes. I think I'd officially freaked Archer out with my confession. He finally had nothing to say.

When I needed to let go of my emotions, I tended to turn into a waterfall. Archer, on the other hand, was like a drip from a faucet. He would take forever to fill up a sink, but it would happen at its own pace.

I grinned at the thought, losing it a second later when realization hit me in the belly, the chest too, in the form of a deep and longing ache. Archer had been asking me for two days what made my body hum for a man, and I'd finally figured out what my answer was.

It wasn't a hot body or a smart brain.

Not even a man who knew how to make a woman come.

It was simply a man who opened himself up to the world and the people in it, unknowingly giving them pieces of his heart when he wasn't trying to. And Archer had done exactly that. Not that I'd tell him. Not that I'd make an actual move on him either. I'd already made that mistake when I'd tried to kiss him. Oh, and don't *even* get me started on the other thing we'd done, though technically our hands had never done any actual touching.

Plain and simple, Archer and I would never work. I could tell he knew that too. Our lives would go in different directions once I got to my mom, and any sort of cushion I had back in Rockford with the Red Dragons would be ending.

"There are showers here." Archer pointed to a sign at the rest stop that was hanging next to the front door.

"Oh, thank God." I was just desperate enough to risk what might be waiting for me inside the stalls for a chance to get the mud and sweat off my body right now.

"You're good with taking your clothes off inside a place like this?" he asked, lifting his brows.

"Yes, I'm not a prissy princess." I rolled my eyes, despite my revelation just minutes ago. This back and forth we shared? It was easy, and I needed to refocus on that path with him, staying there once and for all.

"Can you be quick?" He settled his bike against the side of the building then rubbed a hand through his hair as he took me in.

"I can be very quick."

His lips twisted like a dirty joke was on the tip of his tongue. But, to my surprise, Archer didn't make one. "Alright. Let me see if I can't get some intel on where to get a new bike or transportation first. Then I'll go in with you and shower too."

"Into the shower?" I held my breath for a second too long, nearly choking.

"The *bathroom*, not the shower itself. They got walls in those things, I'm sure, so it's not like I'll be able to sneak a look at ya." He winked.

"Yeah." I paused, studying him. "I don't think I can trust you."

"I'm serious." He grinned, despite his words. "Scout's honor, I won't look at your tits."

"I doubt you were ever even a scout."

"No. I wasn't." Archer shrugged one shoulder. "But it sounds better than saying *biker's* honor, don't you think?" He wrapped a loose arm around my neck, guiding me to the front of the building.

Unable to help myself, I inhaled his all-consuming scent—cigars and spices. My body heated at the thought of burying my nose further into his neck.

So much for refocusing.

Twenty minutes later, after I'd consumed a cinnamon roll and read through a trashy celebrity magazine in an attached McDonald's, Archer crouched down in front of the chair I was sitting in and dangled a key in my face that said *Bathroom 32.*

"You ready for this?" A blond lock of hair fell over his mischievous eyes, and I could imagine him right then as a toddler getting into all sorts of trouble. Not that he'd changed all that much, I was sure.

Nervous for some reason, I swiped the key from his hand and stood at the same time he did, not willing to move away when our chests bumped together. "I'm as ready as I'll ever be, I suppose."

He reached down, taking my wrist in one of his hands. Calloused fingers grazed my pulse point, back and forth, before he winked at me and said, "Come on." Then he pulled me behind him down a long hall to the left.

Ignoring his attempts to control me, I said, "Did you figure something out with your bike?"

"Yep."

I waited for him to explain, but he didn't. The closest town was forty miles away, and unless we wanted to hitch a ride with a trucker—which I was adamantly against—we were kind of screwed as far as what to do travel-wise. Archer had been on the phone with someone from a tow shop while I ate. He absolutely refused to get picked up by a Lyft or an Uber, like I suggested, claiming he had it handled. But *his* handled and *my* handled were very different things.

Regardless, I was too tired and dirty to argue right now.

We found bathroom thirty-two easily enough. A family room, it said on the outside of the door. Supposedly it was big enough for more than one person, but private enough so we didn't have to share the same facility with strangers. Fraternization was against the rules, according to a mile-long list of them that sat outside the door on the wall. From the smirk on Archer's face, I could tell he'd just seen that rule himself. Still, he didn't make any comments or jokes. Now that I thought about it, since last night he'd kept his sex jokes on lockdown, even when I'd opened myself up for one earlier. I should have appreciated it. But deep down, I kind of missed them. Whatever that said about me, I didn't really care right now.

We were sweaty and muddy, in desperate need of transportation, and with his reaction last night I shouldn't have even been thinking those thoughts anyways. But when he'd left I hadn't felt hurt or embarrassed; I'd just wanted him to come back. Sometimes my brain worked in mysterious ways, and when it decided it wanted something, it didn't tend to let go of that want until I followed through with whatever it was.

It was the scientist in me, I supposed.

I jumped in front of him, ready to fight for the first shower, but the sight of the space before me left my mouth agape and my throat drying up. It was so… so *nice* in there. Nicer than the bathrooms at the club. Nicer than the one in my own *house*, actually. Tiled walls, dark browns and light tans… a tall shower on the right, a wall in between that and a small lounge area with a leather couch accompanied by a sink.

"What is this place?" I asked in wonder.

Archer stepped up behind me and lowered his mouth to my ear. "An expensive-ass bathroom is what this is."

I shivered from the sensation of his lips pressed to my ear but ultimately turned around to face him, putting a foot between us. "I thought the shower is free for travelers?"

He shoved his hands into his pockets and shrugged. "It is. But all the private rooms were taken. I had to pay a dude a hundred and fifty to trade. Otherwise we wouldn't have been able to be in the room together."

"Why would you do that?" I frowned. "You could've just stood outside the door while I showered."

"And risk you running when *I'm* taking a shower?" He quirked a brow then pushed around me to go to the sink. "Don't think so."

"You still think I'm going to run?" I scowled at the back of his head.

"Maybe."

It shouldn't have bothered me as much as it did, Archer not trusting me. We were likely—hopefully—never going to see each other again after we got to Kentucky. But for some reason, I was hurt that he still thought I was going to ditch him. Yes, I'd been tempted to run when he'd found me on the bus, but now I couldn't imagine *not* having him with me for the remainder of this trip. It's strange how quickly your priorities can change.

Shaking my head, I grabbed my bag and set it down in front of the shower. I heard Archer's footsteps on the other side of the wall, then his heavy sigh followed when he sat on the couch.

I slid into the stall and undressed, tossing my stuff back out onto my bag a moment later. My thoughts grew heavy as I turned on the water, my mind spinning in directions it shouldn't have been, only to land on the night before.

The beds.

My hand between my legs and Archer's hand on his erection as he spoke those dirty words to me that had been running through my mind since he'd left me alone afterwards. I'd thought for sure he'd taken off on me when he'd left through that door. Up until I'd looked outside a half hour later and found him sitting on the picnic table, his cigar lighting up the night sky.

I shut my eyes at the thought then leaned my head back into the heated water. After lathering up my hair, then rinsing it out, I went to work on my body, rubbing at the caked-mud spots on my arms and ankles most of all.

Before I even realized what I was doing, I settled one palm on the stone wall under the shower head and slowly ran the fingers of my other hand between my breasts, over my stomach, landing just below. God, he'd turned me into a great big ball of lust. The temptation to touch myself was so strong it nearly hurt.

Knowing Archer was on the other side of the wall had me shivering—wondering what exactly he might do if I asked him to forget his worries and fears and to join me in this shower he'd paid an obscene amount of money for. I wanted so much to touch him with my mouth or my hand, for him to touch me too.

God, I wanted that. So much. No matter how angry or frustrated he made me, or how confused my head was whenever we were in the same room together. I wanted to experience the rush of Archer losing control because of me. Even more than that, I wanted to lose control too.

"You alright in there?"

I stiffened at his voice. He sounded close. When I looked down and over my shoulder, I noticed the shadow of his boots beneath the curtain. I licked my lips, inhaling through my nose as I prepped the words on my tongue. I must have lost track of time because the water was already getting cold.

I wanted to tell him: *No, I'm not okay.* I also wanted to rip open the curtain and grab his leather cut and say straight to his face as I climbed his hard body, *I want you. I want you so much it hurts just thinking that I can't have you.*

But I didn't. More like I couldn't. Me and him? We were not meant to be.

"Yeah," my voice cracked. "I'm great."

Our luck changed for the better a half hour later when we were both clean and exiting the bathroom. A stranger in a motorcycle cut was standing at the other end of the hall.

At the sight of him I stiffened, grabbing the back of Archer's arm.

"It's fine," he told me, squeezing my wrist. "Give me a sec?"

I wanted to go with him, but his eyes urged me to stay put. And from the sight of the big man down the hall with the burly beard, I wasn't sure if I wanted to argue.

So, I didn't.

"Heard you need a new ride," the stranger mumbled as Archer approached.

My lips parted in shock when Archer shook his hand and said, "You heard right."

They spoke in low tones after that for a good few minutes, exchanging things. Keys, from what I could see, and possibly money too. Five minutes later, the stranger gave me a curt nod and left the hall, while Archer approached me with a wide smile.

"Let's go, JP. Time's a wastin'." He picked my bag up off the floor then headed in the same direction as the stranger.

"Who was that?" I rushed to keep up with him.

He was moving even quicker now, like he couldn't wait to get out of here—more importantly, away from me.

"Don't worry about it," he said, first dropping off the bathroom key, then leading me out into the parking lot.

I frowned, not liking the secrets, his change in mood neither.

"Are you sure you can trust him?" I asked, needing to make sure.

"Yes," he said as we came to a stop beside the bike.

I frowned at it, wondering whose it was. Worse yet, wondering if it was stolen or something like that. "Whose bike is this?" I questioned.

He tied my bag to the side this time, using a leather strap. "This bad boy here belonged to my old man."

"What?" I jerked my head back. "Your dad's bike?"

He nodded, tying the bag up with another rope. "You know how some people hoard shit in their houses?"

"Yes."

"Well, my good ol' dad hoarded bikes all over the country for safekeeping." He shrugged. "When he died, they all went to me and an old MC buddy of his. Every once in a while, I need one if I'm somewhere without my bike. Sometimes it's hours away, sometimes minutes."

I gasped. "How many bikes are there?"

"Fifty or so. All in the Midwest though, so don't worry."

"So you knew there was one close by all along then."

"No, not at first." He scrubbed at his jaw, avoiding my eyes. "But I made some calls, like I said."

"To who?"

"My old man's friend. He has codes and locations for half of them, and I have the other. My old man was weird as shit." He laughed though, a fond sound that sent warm shivers up my spine and made me smile. It was obvious he loved his parents a lot.

"Are you always this lucky?" I smiled and looked over the seat. It was wider, which my backside would most definitely appreciate. My thighs, on the other hand, would not enjoy being spread for that long… even if they liked the feel of Archer between them.

"No." He cleared his throat.

I looked up, expecting to find him smirking at me. But his expression was sober and blank once more. Maybe even a little sad if I looked hard enough.

"No?"

He moved in closer then tucked some wayward, wet hair behind my ear as he whispered, "I'd say that my luck has never been shittier, actually."

CHAPTER SIXTEEN

Emily

We made it to the Kentucky border sometime around seven that night. A thunderstorm had chased us over the state line, catching on just now like some kind of ominous warning that said, *Run away, don't look back.* Maybe I should have taken nature's advice and done just that because a trifecta of indecision, fear, and sadness was currently brewing around inside of me.

Come tomorrow, we'd make our way to where my mom was. The problem was, I wasn't 100 percent convinced I was doing the right thing anymore. Call it nerves. Call it distraction by way of Archer Benedict too. But since we'd left that truck stop, something was bothering me. Big time. And something between me and Archer? It had shifted immensely as well.

After only stopping twice—once to use the bathroom, the other to get some gas and food—I was more than ready to stretch my legs and get off the bike for the night. It was too stormy to head into the mountains for my mom and Pops, but to be honest, I was fine with that. I wanted to stall. Not just because I was nervous, but because I also wasn't ready to say goodbye to Archer yet.

There was something weighing on him too. I wanted him to trust me like I did him and tell me what it was. I also wanted him to realize that we were the same in so many more ways than either of us ever imagined.

What I wanted, most of all, was to be closer to him.

Archer had grown quiet after we'd left the rest stop. Not that we could talk much while driving. But even during the two times we stopped, he was jumpier than usual, tensing whenever I wrapped my arms around him on the bike too. Maybe he was just getting nervous about finding Pops on his own. Honestly, the idea of trying to take that man down scared me just as much, if not more, than it did him. He was alone. Probably had only one weapon too. Which meant there was more of a chance that he'd die than me.

I blinked at the thought, feeling my eyes warm with tears. Was that what he wanted? To die? Because I wouldn't let him. He had to go back, even if I never would. Which was why I made my decision when I did, vowing it was the right one. For him.

The town close to where my mom's last letter had come from was nothing more than a gas station, a couple of houses, and a post office that was closed for the night. There were no hotels, nowhere to stay overnight at all, from the looks of it. It was a ghost town that shouldn't have been considered a town at all.

With no place to take cover from the impending rain, Archer drove over a small, mostly stable bridge and headed toward what looked to be an abandoned barn on miles upon miles of empty farmland. It was the only shelter we had from the storm, and as the bike began to be overtaken by wind, we both knew we were limited in our choices of where to go.

There were no people in sight, and the homes that *were* there looked abandoned. The name of the town had been scratched out on the small, green sign—other than a C—and a sudden feeling of unease washed over me. It felt post-apocalyptic here.

The rain began, increasing in speed as Archer drove us down a small, gravel road. It fell on our heads like cold sheets of glass, soaking my shirt, my cardigan, and jeans. I could feel it all, each droplet stinging my skin like liquid fire. It came so quickly I almost forgot about our issues with one another, and wanted nothing more than to find shelter in the tiny barn we were headed toward.

He cut the engine and yelled over the sound of the thunder, "Get off!"

I did just that, following him as he walked the bike toward the back of the barn. There, he propped it up just as lightning unfolded in the sky.

I jumped, automatically reaching for his hand. He let me take it, interlocking our fingers as we rushed back toward the front of the barn, our feet sinking into the muddy field. Without words, we shoved the barn door open together and headed inside as the evening sky seemed to turn black. The wind angrily blew against the boarded-up windows, making whistling noises as the water battled for a way inside.

"Just till the storm passes!" Archer yelled over the increasing rain.

I nodded, shivering as I stood in the middle of the barn, unsure about so many things. Too many to count. The weather, where my mother was, and Archer and me most of all.

With my arms wrapped around my waist, I sat down in the middle of the barn's floor, only for the rap of thunder to clap harder above us. I shuddered, pulling my knees to my chest. Archer didn't hesitate to walk over.

"You alright?" he asked, and I swear his voice sounded like he was seconds from crying, but Archer didn't get emotional. Certainly not over me.

"Yeah. Are you?" I brushed my bangs out of my face and looked up at him, surprised when he took a seat in front of me.

Instead of answering, instead of keeping his distance even, he reached for me, tugging me up then setting me on his lap, legs tucked around his waist.

"I'm sorry, Emily," he whispered, wet hair brushing my face.

I shut my eyes, feeling his hot breath against my cheek.

"For what?"

His arms tightened, squeezing desperately. I didn't expect him to say anything, but he did, and it nearly sent me over the edge of no return. "For everything I'm about to do and say to you."

CHAPTER SEVENTEEN

Archer

"I'm cursed, Emily. Shit like this doesn't happen in my life because if it did, then I'd likely lose it all."

I felt like a pussy saying what I did out loud. But instead of looking at me like I was stupid, Emily frowned in confusion. She had to know this though. I was tired of holding it in. The woman had messed with my heart and my head and everything I had to offer. She'd taken my world and split it in half, my RD side separate from her, and only her. She'd been the only person to do this to me, and other than stripping her naked and fucking her on this barn floor, I didn't know what else to do about it other than spill my guts as to *why* it would never be a good idea for me to want her the way I did.

Tension had been building inside me all day. Since last night when she'd nearly sent me over the edge and I'd almost lost control. Seeing her so open and trusting of me, doing what we'd done? No woman had ever been that way with me, and I liked it, not just because it was so hot. But because I liked *her.* Probably since the second I'd met her, if I was being honest with myself. And now that I had her here, I didn't want to let her go. Didn't want to take her to her mom, most of all. I just didn't know what else to do. She couldn't go back to Rockford and the club now. But I couldn't leave the club.

So, there it was.

Emily leaned in closer and settled her forehead into the crook of my neck. This time when she wrapped her arms around my waist, I did the same, hugging her so tight I was sure she couldn't breathe.

"I don't understand. Why are you telling me this?"

"It's better if you don't know." I slid my fingers up the back of her wet shirt and tangled one hand into the back of her hair. That's also when I noticed how bad she was shaking. How cold the skin on her neck was too.

"You're freezing," I said.

"A little bit." She tightened her hand into the back of my shirt like she was afraid I'd run. "But I'm fine."

I squeezed her even tighter to me, finding a benefit to this hugging thing after all. Not just to keep her warm, but because I liked the way she felt against me. Liked even more that she didn't seem to want to let me go either.

Emily Lincoln really had cursed me. Just like my ma had cursed my dad. But instead of ignoring it, I wanted to go with it. Just this one time. Because who the hell knew what tomorrow would bring.

"Body heat is an amazing way to warm up, you know," she whispered out of the blue, lips against my neck as she spoke.

I stiffened. Then pulled back, blinking down at her in surprise. "That so?"

She batted her dark lashes, smiling coyly. Was she trying to seduce me?

And was I gonna let her do it?

Yeah. I think I fucking was.

I lifted my arms, inviting her to take off my soaked shirt. She bit her lip, hesitating, but not for long.

As she tossed it to the barn floor, Emily took in a deep breath and studied my tats for a second, a gleam in her eye I wouldn't ever forget. On my chest and over my heart, there was an empty space with no ink. I'd been wanting to get something tatted there for a while now. And if I got back to Rockford alive, the first place I'd go would be Maya's tattoo shop. There, I'd ask her to ink two letters on me.

E and L.

I went for her purple cardigan next, taking my time to unbutton it, grinning when I got to the shirt beneath.

"You really love purple, don't you?"

She pursed her lips as another bout of thunder roared above us.

"I really love *lavender*."

I shook my head, tugging that *lavender* shirt up and over her body, losing my smirk at the sight of her bright, white bra. There was a bow in the middle. A purple one. And I suddenly decided that the letters I'd ink into my skin would be that particular color of purple.

Lavender to be specific.

For so long, I'd been focused on playing a game, bedding as many women as I could get. But then this lady came along and changed me—*wrecked* me.

I really was cursed. Tomorrow might be a different story, but for tonight, I wasn't scared of what that meant.

"Don't think." She held my face between her hands then, our eyes clashing like night and day. "I want this, Archer. And I know you do too. It doesn't have to mean anything. But I can't go to my mother tomorrow without giving into this thing with you."

I shut my eyes, trying to tame the erratic beats in my chest. Then I leaned forward and brushed my nose against hers, breathing her in, just as droplets of rain began falling on our heads.

I looked to the ceiling. Emily did too.

Not thinking twice about it, I hiked her legs up and around my waist and walked us backward and into a dark corner. The light from the nearby highway lit up the barn, along with the lightning flashes, so it wasn't pitch-black in there. Still, the only thing I wanted to see right then was Emily.

Her body trembled as I trailed my tongue and lips up and down her throat. She tasted like rain and salt, smelled like roses in a storm too. Soon, her fingers dipped into the back of my hair, forcing my gaze to meet hers. I knew she wanted to kiss me. I could tell by the way she licked her mouth. But I wasn't going to break that rule tonight. Not because I didn't want to for once. But because I was pretty sure I'd never be able to let her go if I did.

I pulled her hair out from behind her instead, squeezing to wring the water out. She shivered more, and I finally put her on her feet, only so I could tug her pants down, crouch before her, and nip at her bare hips.

"Archer," she gasped, digging her fingers into my hair.

I pressed my lips over her panties, humming against her gorgeous pussy, whispering a word I'd never used before with a woman.

"Mine."

I knew she couldn't hear it over the thunder and the rain. But I had to say it because in my fucked-up, cursed world, she was the only woman I wanted as mine. If things had been different, if we didn't want separate things, I'd bet the two of us together could've been brilliant.

Taking her panties aside, I didn't waste a second of time as I licked a line up her clit and nuzzled my nose against her soft skin. It was hard not to rush, but without whiskey to dull my senses, I was a mess of feelings and needs with this woman. And with a few strokes of my tongue against her, I knew I couldn't hold back if she asked me for more.

Her hips bucked. A moan slid from her throat.

I grinned, lifting one of her legs to drape it over my shoulder. "Put your other hand on the wall," I ordered.

She moaned again, thrusting her hips faster this time.

Another crack of thunder sounded. And right then, all I wanted was to make her come until the sun rose, and all the bad shit in our lives was nothing but a distant nightmare.

I hummed at the thought, trailing my tongue up her clit again.

I buried my nose deeper, sucked her more.

"Can't seem to get enough of you," I said, tasting every inch of her pussy. "Don't got a damn clue why." Or I did, and couldn't actually get it out.

"Archer, please."

I shook my head, eyes shut. "You're dangerous, woman."

She pushed me back on a gasp, forcing me away. I waited there, licking her taste off my lips as I stared up into her wide eyes.

"Fucking love your tits," I said, smiling, feeling like a teenage boy as I stood.

She laughed low and reached for my hand, pressing it over the top of her tank. "Show me how much."

Grinning, I did just that, cupping them, squeezing each one until I had her crying out my name, until her face was buried in my neck and she was begging.

"Please, Archer. I-I need you inside of me."

Goddamn did I love the sound of those words on her lips.

I looked around, taking stock of the place. The barn was old and worn down, but clean, like someone had been taking care of it. Folded over a haystack to my left was a blanket. Green-and-blue plaid—fucking convenient if you ask me. Reaching over, I grabbed it and threw it down on the ground, thankful it was clean enough.

Emily was eager to help—even more eager to lie on the ground. I stood above her for a second, wondering if this was some sort of dream. I wanted this woman like I'd never wanted anyone else, and though it scared me, I wasn't willing to walk away. Not this time.

She took me by the hand and led me down on top of her, hips meeting mine as she arched up against me. I kissed her neck, tasted her sweet skin, then brought my mouth to her tits, where I sucked on her nipples over her shirt. She shook all over—from the cold or the sensation, I wasn't sure. Either way, I was more than ready to warm her up.

Until I realized what I was missing. "Shit." I dropped my head to her forehead.

"Wh-what?"

"I don't have a condom."

"Oh." She grinned.

"Don't look so smug."

"I'm not smug." She reached behind her and slid her fancy duffel closer. "I'm just prepared."

Seconds later, she was pulling out a box of rubbers and… I think I fell in love with her a little right then.

The thought was a gut punch. Fuck curses.

Fuck everything that was even remotely wrong with being with this woman.

I, Archer Benedict, had feelings. The big kind. The scariest kind there was.

Taking a deep breath, I grabbed the condom from her hand. Tugging my jeans and boxers down, I let my cock free and pulled the rubber on, smiling a little. Feeling like a smitten teenage fool.

"What are you smiling about?" she asked, moving closer, a hand on my shoulder.

I looked into her eyes and shook my head. "Don't have a damn clue." I did though, that's the thing. But Emily would never, *ever* know.

Distracting her, I rolled over onto my back and pulled her on top of me, tugging her panties aside. "Ride me, baby," I whispered, watching in awe as her dark hair fell over her shoulders and onto the ground. "Wanna feel you come."

She shuddered, eyes hazy, cheeks flushed. Seconds later, she slid down my cock, and one single word flashed through my mind as she did.

Home. She was my fucking home. And I'd be leaving her.

She'd be leaving *me.*

"Emily," I hissed at the thought, stomach twisting with both fear and rage. But she distracted me again, her hands on my chest as she began to ride me like I'd asked, hips sliding, hair back…

If there ever was a time in my life when I should've been thinking with my head instead of my dick, it was now. But Emily Lincoln had fucked me up and I didn't know which way was up or down anymore.

I was a goddamn mess for this woman.

"Tell me no." I yanked her closer, biting her neck, hoping the pain would change her mind. "Tell me you don't want me."

"Never!" she cried out instead of pulling away, wrapping both arms around my neck as she increased the speed of her hips.

"Emily, Goddammit," I hissed, so close already I could feel her wet heat soaking me. "You don't want me. You don't."

"I do." She stopped grinding long enough to put her hands on either side of my face against the barn floor. "No matter how hard I tried to tell myself I didn't, I realize now that I've never in my life wanted anything more than you."

I pulled her face to my neck, digging my hands into her hair. The rain echoed above, leaking through the roof on either side of us now. It didn't matter. This was right. *She* was right. And come tomorrow, I'd figure out what to do. How to keep her safe. How to take her home—get her mom away from Pops too, if I had to.

My body shook. This felt so damn right that I couldn't tell her no if I tried. Which was why *she* needed to be the smart one here. The resister.

But she wasn't.

I shook my head, allowing her to take me. All of me. She rode me slow, that hot, wet heat of her pussy making it impossible for me to not feel amazing. I wanted this to suck. I wanted to feel bored. But I didn't.

I'm pretty sure feeling Emily's writhing body wasn't something any man would ever tire of.

Losing her would be my undoing. Losing my heart to her, though? It'd hurt me even more than Pops or his rogues ever could.

So, when she said, "Please. I need you on top of me," I didn't hesitate to give her just that, slowly rolling her over. I knew being with her like this, me in control, *me* setting the speed, was the only way I would ever be able to ignore these fucking emotions inside of me.

I'd put her on a pedestal. But for her safety, and my ugly, ass heart, I'd have to knock her down, even if it meant hating myself in the end because of it.

I moved hard, rode *her* fast. Our hips slapped, her body still moving and writhing beneath mine.

"Yes," she pleaded, nails digging into my back, the pain so goddamn pleasurable, I couldn't see straight.

I hissed into her hair, biting at her lobe.

Her response was to lift her hips even higher, which forced me to match her pace. I thrusted, unforgiving and fast, just like she wanted. One of my hands dug into the wooden barn floor, the other gripping the back of her head. I tilted her chin, lingering over her lips as I looked into her eyes.

"I'm not yours, you hear me?"

She nodded fast, her tongue darting out as she said, "Then I'm not yours either."

Ugly lies. Two of them. And I gritted my teeth, wanting to fight back. To tell her she'd been mine since she was sixteen, when she'd brought me to my goddamn knees with her sassy, smart mouth, her pretty eyes, her flushed cheek.

"This is all you'll ever get from me." Another punishing thrust, and her body was moving against the wood. I was sure there would be marks and scratches, bruises all over us, but her eyes stayed wide and sure, face riddled with pleasure, not pain.

"Oh, God," she murmured.

"Fuck, Emily." I pumped harder, faster, squeezed my eyes shut tight so I didn't have to keep torturing myself. "Fuck, fuck, fuck."

Her answer was a cry, clawing fingers moving over my shoulders, down my back, to my ass… And then I felt it, the pulse of her pussy clenching my cock; her orgasm running through her body in the form of a shudder. The rain against the barn faded to nothing but the sound of her throaty moans, and it was the most beautiful, agonizing storm I'd ever experienced.

Thrust after thrust, a hand on her hip, lifting it… "Emily," I growled, coming hard, knowing that my thoughts of never doing this again were traitorous, because I was pretty sure I never *ever* wanted to stop.

Out of everything I'd experienced in life—near death, murder, losing my family—that was the most dangerous thing.

CHAPTER EIGHTEEN

Emily

By the time the sun had set, Archer and I were dressed—him sitting on a haystack by the door, attempting to keep watch, only to fall asleep within minutes of pulling me back against his chest. Neither of us said a word before he dozed off, and I was okay with that. Why? Because my thoughts were terrifying enough as it was, consuming me to the point where I didn't think sleep would ever come.

I'd fallen in love with a man who was incapable of loving.

And it was singlehandedly the stupidest, most reckless, bittersweet thing I'd ever done.

I wasn't sure what time I actually fell asleep, but it was the kiss on my temple that woke me, a hand in my hair, stroking.

"It's time to go," Archer whispered. His tall, muscular arms squeezed me even more as he said the words. He was there, yes, yet his mind was a million miles away, like my own.

We rose to our feet. I'd remember Archer, and the last two nights, for the rest of my life. Those wild green eyes would burn through my memories forever. But for now, I would continue to let that side lie dormant, pushing all of my emotions there to rest until we were apart.

Archer was nothing like I'd thought. He was also the only man who'd ever truly understood me. But I couldn't, in good conscience, choose between him and my mother. I wouldn't.

This afternoon, or later today, whenever I found my mom, he would go one way, and I the other. But thanks to the text message I'd sent to Niyol, via Archer's phone after he'd fallen asleep last night, he wouldn't be going at this alone anymore.

I'd told my brother where we were. Where Pops would be. I'd told him what was happening, what my plans were, and I'd told him that Archer had only been doing what he thought was right, and that if they were going to hate someone, then it sure as hell better be me, not him.

I also told my brother I was sorry. That I loved him and Summer so much. As those three little dots danced across the screen signaling his incoming reply, I'd turned off the phone and hidden it under a pile of hay, not wanting Archer to see what I'd done. Not wanting to see Niyol's response either.

At least now I knew he'd be safe.

I just hoped the Red Dragons would get here in time to help Archer, but not too soon to see me leaving with my mom.

Using the sleeve of his T-shirt, Archer wiped the wet seat of the bike down the best he could, then straddled it, inviting me on with a small pat to the leather.

I licked my lips, wondering what he would think or say if I told him what I'd done. Would he hate me? Thank me? It didn't matter. He thought he could go at this alone. But he didn't have to.

"What's wrong?" He frowned.

"Nothing." I tried to smile, but it didn't work. Archer could see through me now.

"You don't gotta do this, Em."

My belly swooped at his statement, the nickname most of all.

Em. I think I liked it when he called me Em. I liked the sound of it, the way it looked on his mouth when he spoke it out loud.

"Say that again," I whispered, ignoring him.

"Say what?"

"That nickname."

"JP?" He scowled.

"No," I laughed. "Say 'Em'."

His eyes grew tender and serious. Lifting his hand, he cradled my cheek and traced my jaw with his thumb. "Em."

I smiled. "I like that."

He leaned forward, closer, pressed our foreheads together. His voice shook as he said the words, "Don't do this."

I stiffened.

"Come home with me. Back to Rockford. Please. Don't fucking leave."

My eyes burned with unshed tears. I shut my lids, though, because I didn't want them to fall. I didn't want Archer to see them. And most of all, I didn't want to make this choice.

"It won't work," I said, pulling away. "You know what will happen if I try to bring my mom back—"

"Then don't bring her." His eyes narrowed. "Your mom left you, Emily. What part of that don't you get?"

I shook my head. "She did it because she had to. Mom was trying to save me and Niyol."

He growled and shook his head. "Fuck that."

I touched his arm, squeezed his elbow tight. "Please, Archer. You have to know there's no choice for me here. I can't stay. My mom needs me."

"And what if she doesn't, huh?" He laughed bitterly. The noise made my skin crawl and had me taking a small step back again. "What if you get there and she's all fucking happy with her life? What if she doesn't want you around? What if she's lying to you again? You know she's capable of it."

A knot formed in my throat, but I lifted my chin, not willing to back down. "I'll convince her otherwise."

"Stupid, stupid girl." He gripped his bike handles so hard his knuckles turned white.

I winced and got behind him, trying my best to hold back the tears as I pressed my forehead against the middle of his back.

Surprisingly, though, Archer didn't start the engine. Instead, he spun around on the seat, facing me, his eyes pained. Tortured, even. "Listen to me, Em. Your mom? She's a wanted woman. If my brothers ever find you two together…"

My heart throbbed in my chest when I realized what this was about. Archer was scared for me.

As far as I know, nobody had *ever* been scared for me before.

Not my brother. Not Sam. Maybe not even my mom.

"It's gonna be okay." I cupped his face between my palms. "I know it is." For him, yes. But not me. My life was over. Getting my mom to go with me was just one step. Everything after that? I was clueless about.

I really was stupid.

"You don't know that," Archer barked, dropping his hands. "I want you safe, Emily. But you can't side with traitors and expect everything to be fine. Even if I do take care of Pops, your mom has pissed off a lot of people, and you being on the run with her is gonna make you a target too. I'm only one person in a club with hundreds."

"I'm not asking for your protection. I'd never expect for you to choose sides," I whispered.

Fingers glided through my hair, a palm cupping my cheek this time. Our eyes met, an impending explosion just waiting between us. "You're crazier than I am, you know that?"

I tried to smile but couldn't. Everything hurt when we were so close like this. Everything pulled at me in a direction opposite to my mom. I was torn. And it killed me because I knew that the decision I wanted to make—be with Archer—wasn't the decision I was destined for.

"If you want to come home, I'll make it happen," he continued. "I'll keep you safe, make some shit up about Pops threatening you or something. Hell, we can turn around right now. But if you go with your ma, I can't do shit for you. And that…"

"That what?" I whispered.

"That will kill me."

My bottom lip trembled, and my heart ached with crushed hopes and stupid dreams forever laid to rest. "It's a good thing I'm not asking you for help then, right?"

Archer hesitated, studying me with furrowed brows. And just when I thought he'd argue with me some more, he nodded and did the opposite, turning back around in his seat, forcing my arms around his waist as we left the barn.

After multiple dips and divots taken through the fields, and a layer of thick mud coating our shoes and pants, we finally made it up to the main road that led back to the two places of business. We weren't on the road long when it began to rain again, though, making the blacktop slick for the tires. As we approached the bridge from yesterday, I found myself on edge, struggling to slow my frantic heartbeats. Just before the bridge was rushing water, faster than it probably should have been going. The base of the bridge could still be seen, but getting to it would be an issue. Regardless,

Archer kept going, his speed slow, his legs and feet glued so tightly to the bike that no force of nature would tear him off of this thing.

But my body, on the other hand…

I continued to peek over his shoulder, a total control freak by nature. My chin was so close to his neck that my breathing had to be hot against his skin. He shuddered a little, and I worried for a second that maybe I was distracting him… until I heard him say, "Fucking hell, we got a tail."

I looked over my shoulder this time, eyes widening at the sight of the dark car drawing close. "Who is it?" I yelled, feeling my heart beat faster, my stomach tighten.

Archer shrugged, kicked the speed of his bike up too.

"We need to find somewhere to pull over and hide!" I shouted into his ear.

He shook his head then veered right, taking an unmarked path that I hadn't seen.

Quickly, I glanced back over my shoulder, still spying the car. The road we were on narrowed ahead, but the black car kept going, speeding faster, the rain splashing harder against the windshield.

Archer took a quick left then, followed by an even sharper right a few minutes later. My arms tightened around his waist. This time when I turned to look at the car, I didn't see a single thing but the trees around us and the falling rain.

"We lost them!" I yelled over the roar of the thunder.

He nodded, but instead of going faster, he slowed the bike, cursing loudly. Slashes of water became like buckets against not only our faces but our calves as the rain fell faster and the water grew higher beneath us.

Crap. We were in flood waters now.

"Hold on tighter."

I buried my helmeted face against his back, praying for a chance.

A chance we never got.

The water increased in speed below us and above us, my heart racing so fast it was as though it knew it needed to escape as much as my body did. Eventually, Archer was forced to stop. He pulled over to a patch of land beneath a tree, which sat up on a small hill that was quickly getting surrounded by water.

He turned off the bike just as a flash of lightning filled the sky above. I jumped, as did he, and the fierceness in his gaze as he slid off the bike and reached for my hand was something so dangerous.

Archer, for the first time since I'd known him, looked terrified. "We gotta move."

I nodded, rushing after him, feet sliding as I followed. I officially hated the rain—all bodies of water really—and if I *ever* had to be outside in a thunderstorm again, it would be too soon.

The rumble of a car engine sounded somewhere below. I looked, finding that same black car trying to get to the path we were on. "Archer!" I yelled, motioning a hand toward it.

"We gotta go. Now." We raced through the mud, me falling to my knees once when my foot sank into the ground.

"Emily!" he shouted.

I yanked at my pant leg, my ankle too, looking back at the car, then the hole again, which only seemed to grow deeper by the second. Unable to see through the steam filling my helmet, I whipped it off just as Archer dropped down beside me. He yanked at my leg, pulling my foot loose, minus the shoe.

A loud crunch sounded from behind. The two of us turned just in time to see Archer's new bike being overtaken by the rush of water.

"Fuck!" he cursed loudly, bending over to scoop me up into his arms.

My eyes burned with tears as the water grew higher below. When it got to be too much, I buried my face in his cold neck, saying another silent prayer that we could get up and over the hill to the field on the other side before the water overtook us completely. Before the black car found us too.

"Can you climb it?" His hair stuck to his face and mud coated every inch of him.

I looked to where he was pointing. A tree just ahead.

"Yes, I can climb it."

"Alright. You go first." He set me on my feet then urged me ahead, pointing at a low tree branch. "Step there," he ordered.

As a child, we'd mostly lived in apartments, so the tree-climbing thing had never been a part of my world. But thankfully my legs were strong and my body was in shape from the gym, so it didn't take me long to figure out how to make up for my lost childhood.

Once I made it up as far as I could go, I turned, eyes widening when I noticed Archer was still at the bottom, watching the water, his back braced against the tree. I screamed his name and begged him to come up. But when he tilted his head back and glanced my way, I realized two things.

Number one: he wasn't going to climb up here.

And number two: he was sacrificing himself for me.

"No!" I yelled, not thinking twice as I moved back along the creaky branch and slid to the trunk, beginning my descent.

"Emily, what the hell are you doing?"

By the time I got down beside him, there was absolutely nothing that could stop me. "You asshole." I flung my arms around his waist, gasping as I stepped into the cold water that now hit mid-calf.

Another crash of lightning hit, and the thunder followed within seconds.

"You're so stupid," he yelled back, pulling me closer, his lips on my head, his arms encased around my body. "Why the fuck—?"

I cut him off, yanking his face to mine. Then I did what he'd told me not to.

I kissed him.

CHAPTER NINETEEN

Archer

I wasn't scared of dying. Never thought about it. I didn't believe in God and all that shit, and I'd always been fine with the logic of life ending and there being nothing beyond.

But beneath that tree, for the first time in my life, I was terrified of what was next. Not for myself but because of the woman in my arms. The woman who was breaking all my rules.

My old man once told me kissing was the curse that started it all, and I'd be fit not to do it. Ever. Other than a couple of times when I was eighteen, then again at twenty, I'd taken his advice and kept my lips to myself. But Emily... sweet, sassy, stubborn Em. She'd ruined my mind and my rules.

Hell, I was pretty sure she'd ruined me for *every* woman now. Either way I looked at it, I was going to die, whether it was at the hands of Pops or this water, it didn't matter. All I wanted was to get Emily to her mom and away from Pops and his rogues. Then I'd die a man worthy of death.

To think that the woman I'd always thought was a spoiled pain in the ass was now the one thing I couldn't live without. A woman who wanted her family safe, just like me. How the fuck could I have ever resisted that?

I gripped the base of Emily's hair, pulling her head back. Water filled my shoes, covered my weakening knees, but Goddammit,

I wasn't about to die without feeling every inch of her mouth against mine. Slow but fierce, I parted her lips with my tongue, running it over the surface of those red lips that had been teasing me for days—years, really.

Her fingers tightened along the back of my shirt—whether it was fear or lust, a combination of both, I wouldn't know. But I took it all, let it happen, devouring her. Loving her.

The water rose higher, hitting my thighs. Emily fell against me, and I slammed a hand back against the tree, keeping the other locked in her hair. My balance was shit, felt like I was seconds from being pulled under the water, but if I was gonna die, then I wasn't about to go down without making sure Emily Lincoln remembered who I was and what it was like to be kissed by a man who'd sworn to never do it again.

The tips of our tongues barely touched before she started falling away. Our lips disconnected, foreheads pressed together…

"Archer!" she screamed, losing her balance too.

"Hold on, damn it. Don't you fucking let me go, you hear? I'm going to get us out of here."

She nodded against me, wrapped her legs around my waist beneath the water. We began to float, my hands slipping, her legs sliding away.

"Emily!"

Her eyes widened in panic. I reached out, grabbing her sleeve, only for my body to be thrust back… and for hers to disappear beneath the rising waters.

CHAPTER TWENTY

Emily

My head throbbed. Water choked me, but the land beneath my body was dry, and when I blinked, I found myself being lifted in the air, something holding me tight. I coughed before I could scream, eyes blurring through tears. A familiar face was there… until it wasn't.

The second time I woke, I was in a hospital, a nurse hovering over me and taking my vitals. My ears were buzzing like they were both filled with water, yet I knew the nurse was speaking to me because I could see her lips moving.

Panic clawed at my throat, and I immediately sat up straighter in the bed, my gaze frantic as I searched the room and tried to yell, "Archer! Archer!"

Our kiss.

His panic-stricken eyes.

His fingers clinging to the sleeve of my cardigan just before the water swept us apart.

I shuddered. My bottom lip began to tremble too. Oh, God. Where was he? Why wasn't he here? Why hadn't he even tried to climb that stupid tree? Why was he so stubborn?

Had the men in the car found him? Found *me*?

I ripped the blanket off my lap, going for my IV next, but a hand settled against my shoulder. The nurse. I looked at her, blinking through my haze and tears and panic.

"Where is he? Where's the man I was with? His name is Archer Benedict. He's blond and tall and… and…" A sob let loose, strangling me. I should have told him not to come. I should have run away. I was selfish and stupid for letting him come with me, and I hated myself. So much.

He wasn't there.

He was gone.

The nurse's words grew clearer, but her face was filled with confusion as she looked over her shoulder toward something—or I should say some*one*. A figure moved into the room, standing beside the nurse.

Short body, long hair, eyes that matched mine… I gasped, a hand flying over my mouth when I finally realized who it was. Instead of happiness or relief, the only emotions waging war inside of me were confusion and anger.

So. Much. Anger.

It was her fault we were here.

Her fault Archer might be gone.

Her fault that my life had fallen apart because she'd lied to me about it all.

No longer did I want to reach out and hug her. Instead, I wanted to reach out and wrap my hands around her neck and shake.

My mother.

My mom.

Why was she here?

Where had she *been*?

She smiled at me, giving me a small wave. In her hands was a cup of coffee. Always freaking coffee, always in a Styrofoam cup.

She looked healthy. She'd put on a little weight even. She looked…
good. She wasn't supposed to look good. She was supposed to be
Pops's prisoner. Bruised and battered and skinny and imprisoned.
I'd been so worried about how I was going to get her away from
him, yet there she was, this well-dressed and *happy* woman standing before me.

My hearing grew clearer just in time for the nurse to say, "You're
so lucky your mom was able to get to you in time."

I whipped my head her way, eyes narrowed. "What?"

"Your mom. She said she had been following your car, but the
two of you got separated."

The black car. Mom had been in that black car.

CHAPTER TWENTY-ONE

Archer

I woke up cuffed to a wall. Go figure. Kinky toys and sex would never mean the same to me now. Not after my time with Emily. With *Em.*

At the thought of her, I yanked on the cuffs, needing to get out of here. To find her and make sure she was okay. God, if only I'd held on a little tighter or forced her ass to stay in that tree...

Think now, Archer. Regret later.

Breathing in deep, I looked around the room, trying to figure out where the hell I was. Four white walls, no windows, and an old black table with folding chairs sat surrounding it. I didn't know who'd gotten me because I'd been knocked out—the bump on the back of my head proof. But I wasn't dumb. We'd been close enough to wherever Pops was that it was likely him. Who else would it be?

My stomach grew hot and hard at the thought, while my brain waffled between images of Emily and the water, the black car too. If she hadn't drowned, then there was no doubt that whoever had me also had her.

"No," I growled to myself, yanking at the cuffs even more. Still, I got nowhere.

I laid my head back against the wall, sweat dripping down the back of my neck. Damn it, she had to be okay. Emily was my fighter. The woman who'd broken my walls down and figured me out when nobody else could. She was also the only person in my life that I was pretty fucking sure I'd break every rule for if I ever saw her again.

God… let me see her again, please, if you're real at all, you owe me this.

Fear and desperation had me yanking my arms once again, harder this time. I grunted as the chains dug into my wrist and burned my skin, but the pain was nothing in comparison to what it'd be like if she hadn't made it.

My adrenaline rushed fierce as the image of her being tied up like me flashed through my head. I needed to get up. Get out of here. But when I tried to stand, my knees gave way, too weak to keep me upright.

My stomach churned. Good Christ, I was gonna hurl.

And I did, turning to the left and puking all over.

I groaned, falling to my ass once more. It was as if I'd been drugged.

Sweat coated my temples now. I tipped my head to the side, trying to dry them with my shoulder. My vision blurred in and out of focus even more under the bright lights, and I blinked, struggling to see.

That's when the door opened, and a familiar voice sounded ahead. "You look like shit."

I froze, lifting my head just in time to see the last man I'd ever imagine being there.

"Chop?"

He moved closer and crouched down in front of me, elbows on his knees. "Out of all the brothers, I should've known you'd be the one." His lip curled. I knew right away what his issue was with me. Emily. "But I didn't think *she'd* be stupid enough to let you into her panties, that's the thing."

"I don't know what you're talking about." It was a lie, a lie to protect Emily in case he'd somehow gotten her too. Because if I told him how I was really feeling about her, how we'd spent last night in that barn, fucking like there was no tomorrow, then who knew what kind of psychopathic rampage he'd go on?

"She was mine, did you know that? I was gonna make a claim. She was going to be *my* old lady." Veins bulged out by his eyes, eyes that were red and menacing. Nothing like the smart brother I'd gotten to know over the last year, the techy nerd of the club. "We could've been fucking amazing together. Then your ass had to step in and take her away from me."

"She never wanted you, asshole," I hissed, nails digging into my palms. "You pressured her. You *hurt* her."

He shook his head and stood. "Because she wouldn't listen. I had to make her listen. Control her. Show her who the is the king."

Psycho bastard. "She never wanted you. Ever. You put your filthy hands on her and—"

"Lies." He took a step back. "All of you are liars just like he warned me."

I stiffened. "Who the fuck are you talking about?"

He didn't answer, just started pacing, raging, words coming out like vomit. "You bang Summer and Maya too? You guys pass those women around like a buffet?" He stopped in front of me again, hovering. "You're all pieces of shit." Then he spit in my face. "I should've gone in that caboose and shot a bullet through your skull like I wanted to. But noooo," he whined. "You're the bait we need to end this feud once and for all."

I blinked, wetness pooling down my forehead from his saliva. I couldn't stop to care was the thing, not when my mind was running wild with all the shit he'd just said.

That had been Chop's cut.

Chop had been the one to fuck with my bike.

And now he was using *me* as bait.

Chop was a rogue. An RD traitor.

"Who are you working with?" I snarled, already knowing the answer. Pops.

"You'll find out soon enough." He sneered.

My tongue grew thick and dry. "Where is she? Where's Emily?"

He smirked at the mention of her. "You don't gotta worry about her now, she's safe." Then he held a finger up and said, "Actually, you made my job a hell of a lot easier by getting her here too, so thanks for that."

"Leave her… the fuck… alone," I managed, somehow getting to my feet, only to fall back against the wall.

"I mean, you can't blame me for this, can ya?" He rubbed a finger over his mouth. "I've wanted between her legs for months now, but she'd never spread them for me. Now that she knows you're here, I'll bet she'll do anything I want just to see you set free."

"Don't… touch her.." I groaned as a shot of pain ran through my temples, almost blinding me. Chop blurred in and out of focus again, but I knew he was moving closer. I could practically feel his hot breath against my face as he spoke.

"I'll touch her if I *want* to touch her."

Without thinking, I jerked forward and headbutted him. Blood started pouring down between my brows, which didn't help with my dizziness, but who the fuck cared? I'd kill him before he ever got his hands on her again.

"You motherfucker." He leaped at me, grabbed the back of my hair. After yanking a handful out, he slammed me onto the floor, face down.

I barely blinked when my forehead collided with the floor, but my focus was shot to shit regardless, and when I turned my head to look at him, he was two people, not one.

Not willing to give up, I growled again, slurring when I tried to speak, but couldn't. Instead, blood and sweat dripped over my lips as the cold cement floor rubbed my cheek nearly raw.

"I was gonna be nice. Beg for mercy for you." He stuck his knee into my lower back, digging it in. "Not now though." Then he stood up and kicked my ribs with the toe of his boot.

Once. Twice. Three times.

I grunted, agonizing pain shooting up my body, into my back, my stomach, even my chest. Chop stood tall and moved away, laughing, just in time for the door behind him to open. Somehow, I could see enough to notice the new person, more so his black boots thudding against the floor as they stopped just inches in front of my face.

When the new guy crouched down, it took only the scent of him to know who it was. The smell of his mint Skoal. Just to make sure I wasn't hallucinating, which I could've been, I re-opened my eye, seeing the dark face of my best friend Hawk… only with thirty or so years on him. Black hair to his shoulders. Dark eyes, pale cheeks tinged with red…

Pops.

I knew it. I fucking knew it.

Bile formed in my throat. I lifted my head enough to dry heave on his boots. This man had killed so many, ruined lives, including my father's.

"It's been a while, *Benedict*," Charles Lattimore mumbled down at me, a hint of humor in his words. "You've looked better, that's for damn sure."

I wasn't sure who I hated more right then: the man who'd hurt my woman, or the man who'd been a part of giving her life. Either way, I vowed right then that I *would* kill them both… or die trying.

I curled my lip, trying to mumble those words, but nothing came out.

Something I managed must've pissed the guy off because Pops grabbed my throat a second later and squeezed with one hand. I didn't even have the energy to push him away. My arms were too numb, body practically limp.

"Fight me, boy." He squeezed tighter, and I shut my eyes, relaxing, imagining Emily.

Her lips. Her body. Her smile. Her laugh.

"Fight me!" Pops yelled louder, my vision going black, then brightening, then black again.

Time went by—minutes, seconds, hours—and somehow, throughout it all, I stayed conscious, even though I couldn't breathe. Pretty sure my jaw was broken, my nose too. I couldn't feel shit in my arms, and all my ribs were practically bursting from my gut. But somehow, when he shoved my head back against the wall and got down in my face even further, I looked that motherfucker in the eye. And I smiled.

"Crazy son of a bitch," he said. "I warned that man." Pops let go of my hair, or what was left of it, but continued to hover. "He made you all weak, especially my son. And look at you… All pussy-whipped for my slutty little kid."

I spat in his face, like Chop had done mine. Nobody said shit about Emily.

The door opened a minute later, then I heard Chop say, "She's on her way."

Pops held my gaze, a hidden message there. He wanted secrets. He thought I'd crack. He thought a little shit-kicking would break me to the point where I'd give up my club.

Well, too bad for him I wasn't a snitch.

I'd *die* before I ever let anything happen to my brothers.

More feet moved around the room. I had to shut my eyes, though, because I needed sleep. Or I was passing out. I didn't know. Didn't care.

"Charles?" a woman's voice rang out. Like bells. The bells back home at the church. Not in Rockford. In Ireland.

"What's going on in here?" she asked.

My bottom lip started shaking. I was hallucinating, that had to be it. Because I swear, I knew that voice.

I tried to open my eyes. Tried to blink. Tried to see if it was real or just my mind playing tricks on me. Blood poured over my lids, my mouth, out my nose. I was losing a lot of it. But I had to know.

"*A leanbh?*" she whispered the old Gaelic words. Words I'd heard countless times as a kid.

No fucking way.

CHAPTER TWENTY-TWO

Emily

I refused to look at her. Refused to speak to her. I couldn't. Not after what she'd just said to me.

I love Charles.

I had to get him away from Flick and those men.

If I hadn't, he would've been killed, and he's a good man who deserves so much more than what he's been given.

I didn't want to hurt you though. That's the last thing I ever wanted to do.

I sat back in the hospital bed, shaking my head in both disbelief and disgust. Mom was a good actress. But even this was above her abilities. That was how I knew she was telling me the truth.

I'd thought she was in danger when I'd read her letters, that she'd been taken and that if I found her, I could help her escape. But I'd been wrong. She *had* chosen him over the club. Over her own daughter and son. Which meant my biggest fears were coming true. The one thing that had niggled at the back of my mind since the day she'd run away.

I was too angry to care now though. Too worried about Archer and where he might be to raise hell. Because if there was even the slightest chance that he was still alive, he too would be with Pops— wherever Pops was. If I wanted to get him out of there, if I ever wanted to see him again, then I needed to cooperate as best as I could.

My one saving grace was knowing that Niyol and the rest of the Red Dragons were likely on their way here.

A face peered into the room from the hall then, the leather on his jacket crinkling as he moved. His hair was a bright-red color, and his eyes were an even brighter green, achingly familiar. He was tall and thin, with a square jaw. Model-worthy, but so young still, with that boyish face, red cheeks.

The second he pulled a hat from his back pocket and tugged it on over his messy hair, I couldn't help but gasp.

Oh my God. I *knew* him. This was the person who'd been on my front porch the other night. The person who'd hand-delivered my last letter from Mom, then started the fire.

Curiosity lit his face as he studied me for a moment, and I could tell from the gentleness in his gaze that he wasn't a killing machine. Not one of Pops's rogues either. Still, if he knew my mom, then I had a feeling he was part of the rogues now under Pops's command.

"Please, Emily. Just talk to me," Mom continued, drawing my attention away. "I'm here now, which means we can finally be together as a family. Doesn't that sound wonderful? You, me, your da—"

"He's not, nor will he ever be, *my father*." I looked to the window and sucked in my cheeks, refusing to let myself lose control. Deep down, though, I was raging, thinking back to a time when things between me and Mom had been simple and real.

"You don't even know him. Please, Emily, don't push him away before giving him a chance. Not this time." She took a heavy breath, continuing to string her web of lies.

"No. You can't ask me that, Mother."

"Please." She took my hands in hers. "Don't be angry at me, honey. You know what it's like to love someone that much, don't you? Isn't that how it was for you and Sam?"

I blinked, taken aback by where my mind went.

An Irish accent, strong masculine fingers. I could almost feel him naked against me, sliding inside of my body in that barn last night…

God, could he make me laugh too. Even if he had a tendency to anger me, there was nobody who could drive my emotions wild like Archer Benedict.

"Emily?"

Tears built in my eyes. *Please, Archer. You have to be okay.* Wherever he was, I just hoped he was safe, that Slade or my brother would come for him, find him, help him. That their army was rallying and, together, the Red Dragons would take Pops down once and for all.

When Mom quieted, I grew braver, needing to find out if she knew where Archer might be. "There was someone with me. We got separated in the water. Is he…?" I swallowed hard, tears forming in my eyes. "Is he okay? Is he here?"

I wasn't selfish enough to ask for a chance at happiness or survival myself. Not when everything was so messed up—when I'd been so dumb. I'd put Archer at risk by coming here and now I wanted him to be okay. *Needed* him to be, was more like it.

"Archer, you mean?" my mom asked, her eyes narrowing a little.

I forgot she knew who he was. "Y-yes. He brought me here so I could find you."

Her face softened, and she set her coffee down to come closer to my bed. "Honey, Archer's fine. He's with Charles now. He'll take care of him. Charles always takes care of his men."

"That man is a *murderer!*" I hissed. "How could you side with him?"

"It has always been unintentional," she whispered, "and always for the boys in the club too." Movement near the door caught my eye as my messenger slipped inside. His eyes narrowed between us, likely because of the noise. Not once did he smile or speak. Instead, his face was stoic and serious, making him look way beyond his young years.

"Most of the boys Charles has recruited are so young and sweet. Just like this young man here." Mom stood and approached the quiet teenager.

"Yeah, I doubt that." I snort-laughed. "Are you even aware of how much terror and destruction that man you claim to love has caused since you left?" I continued. "People have died because of him, Mother. Maya and Slade were both nearly killed, and Archer's..."

My throat closed off. A choked sob built up in it. I didn't want to cry. I wanted to be brave. But my worry for Archer consumed me.

"Hush now," Mom cooed as she sat down beside me on the bed. "Everything's going to be okay. I promise you."

Pops had so obviously brainwashed her—turned her into this shell of a woman that she was now. It was too much to take—and we'd only just been reunited.

I sat up in the bed and hit the nurse's call button. "I need to go. Can you take me to him? To Archer?"

Mom frowned. "Honey, that's not really possible right now. But soon. I promise you'll see him."

"No. I want to see him now." I shook my head. "I need to be released," I told the woman over the speaker. "I'm fine and now I'd like to go."

My hands shook as I reached for my IV and yanked it out. Blood squirted over me, dripping down my arm, but I didn't care. The longer I stayed here, the more danger Archer could be in.

"Emily, stop. You're going to hurt yourself. Why are you so upset?"

"Because I need to see Archer!"

Mom grabbed my arm, yanking it away when I reached for my sack of clothing on the floor. "No. What you need to do is calm down."

I shoved her back against the bed, wired and angry. "I won't calm down until I see him alive with my own eyes, so take me to wherever he is. Right now."

The boy moved closer, hesitant. If he was supposed to be some sort of bodyguard for my mom, then he sucked at it.

"Angel, it's okay," Mom said, holding a hand up to stop him.

I whipped my head toward the boy, scowling. "Your name is Angel?"

Mom set her hand on my forearm. "It is, sweetie."

I shoved her away, and she immediately cringed. Good.

"Angel," she continued, her gaze never leaving my face, "can you grab the rest of Emily's things for her? We'll be leaving now."

My knees grew weak at the thought of going with her—to where she and Pops were staying. Even if she hadn't been lying, I'd been stupid to think I could get her away from Pops at all. Archer had been right yet again on that one. Why hadn't I listened? Why had I thought I'd ever be able to do this? Be a hero, find my old life, then run with it like nothing had changed since before she left?

"I'm so stupid," I whispered under my breath, taking a seat again.

Mom sat on the bed beside me, wrapping my arm up with a towel to stave off the bleeding. "You're not stupid." She sighed. "You're just naive."

I blinked. "Naive? Really?"

"You don't understand the club and its name. What it means. Did you know that your father was one of the Red Dragons' original founders?"

"No." And I didn't care either.

Mom squeezed my arm. "You don't understand what it's like for him. He lost everything."

"It's not just our lives we need to protect anymore, Mother. Summer is pregnant, damn it!" I blurted out.

I looked up, wincing the second I saw Mom's tear-filled gaze widen. She covered her mouth, blinking through her tears.

"Summer is pregnant?"

"Yes. She and Niyol are going to be parents." And I might never see my niece or nephew. Or my best friend again. I shut my eyes, fighting another wave of tears.

Mom latched her hand around my wrist again, squeezing. This time when I looked back at her, I saw a smile touching her lips. I held my breath, praying the old mom was in there, that she cared enough to at least try and leave with me. Or help me get Archer free, even.

"I'm really going to be a grandma?"

"You are." *Come back to me, Mom. Please, come back.*

She took my hand in hers, sniffling. Her dark hair, when I looked down between us, was almost as long as mine now, peppered with gray streaks that hadn't been there last summer.

Breath held, I waited for her to speak. And when she finally did, it nearly broke me.

"Your father is going to be so thrilled to hear this."

That's when I realized I'd lost her forever.

The doctor came and left my room in a matter of minutes, ordering me to rest for the next few days. I dressed in a pair of old navy sweats and a T-shirt with green stripes running up and down the center, and we left the hospital—me, Mom, and Angel.

Mom hovered and fussed at my side the entire time, and I let her, turning off my mind.

All this time, I'd built up an image inside my head, a plan that was supposed to include me and Mom running *away* from Pops instead of running *toward* him. Everything seemed to be falling apart, and the only place I wanted to be again was in Archer's arms. I'd take to being one of his monthlies at this point instead of living under Pops's lock and key.

We climbed into the backseat of a worn-down Chevy that smelled like stale beer and mint gum outside the ER doors. Mom moved in beside me while Angel, who barely looked old enough to drive, stayed quiet in the driver's seat. Our eyes met in the rearview mirror, and instead of a normal, broody biker, I saw an insecure, mysterious boy—barely a man.

I peered over at Mom, taking in her thin cheekbones, the new wrinkles by her eyes too. She wasn't the same, no. But neither was I.

Fifteen minutes later, after taking several long, winding streets through the town I'd yet to figure out the name of, we took a left toward the mountains and were soon driving up a gravel road. My ears popped continuously the further up we went. I looked out my window, trying to get a sense of direction, but I was still so out of it that nothing seemed clear to me. Still, wherever we were, it had to be where Archer was, right? That thought had me sitting up straighter.

Ten minutes we drove through gravel, the car dipping in crevices, rocks banging against the side and windows. We stayed beneath a canopy of oaks, so much so I couldn't see the sky above. I was *so* over being in the middle of nowhere—I felt like the next time I saw a highway, I'd fall to my knees and kiss it.

At the thought, another image of Archer ran through my mind. His smart mouth, his hair falling over one eye, his sweet green eyes lighting up whenever he teased me. Without a doubt, I knew what he'd say. *I can think of a lot better things for you to kiss while you're down there, JP.*

JP. What did that nickname even mean? Chills broke out over my skin. What if I never found out? What if I never heard him call me it again?

"We're here." Mom squeezed my hand, and something in her eyes softened. I wasn't foolish enough to believe that she was feeling sorry for me though. The woman truly thought that my being here meant we'd be a family. And for that, I felt sorry for her.

The doors were unlocked, then opened. When Angel stood over mine, I barely spared him a glance, instead choosing to look up at the abandoned building. Was this where they'd been all this time? Mom had said just two weeks, but this looked more permanent than not.

"Come on." Mom took my hand in hers, squeezing it again. "He'll be waiting for us."

I quickly took a breath and followed her out, my entire body trembling. Angel followed us up the long cement walkway, and I realized right then that I'd never heard him speak.

"Does he talk?" I asked, jerking my head back at him.

Mom winced, then whispered, "Only to his mom and occasionally me, but otherwise, no. Charles… doesn't let him speak."

I frowned, glancing at the boy once more. He looked so empty and sad.

"The last letter you sent," I said, pulling my mom to a stop. "Did he deliver it?"

She smiled, nodding once. "He did. He's a messenger for the club. Does a lot of runs for them." Mom was fond of this kid, I could tell. But why? "Anyways, he was doing some recon for us in Rockford and I asked him to leave it for you instead of sending it."

"He snuck onto the compound, Mother."

"Yes. I'm aware." She smiled tightly but didn't comment further.

A door opened ahead of us, pulling my gaze up to the front of the building. I stopped in my tracks when three older men came out, forming a V around a man who I knew, right away.

"Daughter." He nodded, still staying behind his group. Then he looked at my mom, who was clinging to my left arm as if I was there to protect her. It was obvious my mom was also terrified of the man she was so desperately in love with.

Good thing for her, I wasn't.

I lifted my chin. "*Asshole.*"

He tossed his head back and laughed.

Angel, I noticed, had moved further away.

Pops moved out from behind his men and stood a few feet in front of us. His eyes, though, were only on me. "You're quite the little bitch, ain't ya? Might have to break you like I did your mom here."

I flinched, looking behind him to try and keep it together.

His little group of three men had turned into ten. They ranged in age. I'd heard, at one time through the grapevine back in Rockford, that the majority of Pops's rogues had been young, but these men were mostly older. It could have been just a show for me, a power thing. His young crew could be inside, shaking in their tiny boots. But their ages didn't matter. They were all enemies to me.

"Got a friend of yours here. You're gonna be happy to see him." Pops winked.

My heart skipped. Archer… he *was* here.

"But we'll save the reunion for later." Then he grabbed the back of my hair, yanking me in behind him.

Mom gasped and yelled, "Stop! You promised you wouldn't hurt her."

I fell to my knees, gasping when the cement scraped my palms.

"Shut your mouth, woman, before I shut it for you," Pops roared at my mom.

I winced when he tugged me from behind, and my eyes began to burn the second he tried to drag me on my butt. Somehow, I got to my feet and followed him, stumbling in both pain and rage, his men laughing around me, a few of them catcalling too. My throat clogged up with a sob, but I refused to let it out; he seemed to get off on others' pain. Pops hadn't changed one bit since I'd last seen him, though there was an urgency to his steps and movements now that I didn't remember from before.

We walked at a pace that was a step before running, and I barely had a chance to look around once we were inside. It reminded me of an office building, with little rooms and cubbies on my left and right as we passed by. We wound up at the end of a hall, where he finally let go of my hair.

"Open it," Pops yelled at Angel, who I'd somehow missed.

When I turned around to look for my mom, I realized she hadn't come in after us.

"Wait…" I grabbed Pops's arm, using my other hand to rub the now balding spot where he'd ripped my hair from my scalp. "Where'd my mom go?"

"Don't ask questions. Just shut your mouth and do what you're told."

He shoved me into the room with a desk and two chairs, wooden with broken legs. Then he pushed me into one and took a seat behind the desk across from me, ordering Angel to shut and lock the door behind him once he left.

Shaking, I turned, catching the boy's eyes. I swear, he almost looked regretful, but it wasn't long before his face grew blank again, and he did what was asked of him.

The door slammed shut seconds later, and I heard the telltale sound of a lock being clicked from the other side. I stiffened, only looking at Pops when I heard the flick of a lighter.

"Listen, bitch. We're gonna make this quick. If you don't answer what I'm about to ask, then bad shit's gonna happen. If you do, then I'll let you see your friend."

"I won't tell you anything," I hissed.

He laughed then knocked on the wall behind him. "Guess we'll be doing this the hard way then."

A curtain rose up, revealing a window and another room next door. Wooden walls surrounded a wooden floor, a table, chairs— and there in the middle of it all was… "Archer!"

I jumped up from the chair and headed straight to the window, pounding on it. He looked like he was asleep, but the longer I pounded on the window, the more I realized he was unconscious.

"What have you done?" I screamed, facing Pops.

"I've got a doc nearby who'd love to help him. I mean, he's got some internal bleeding, and a huge list of other shit wrong with him that might cause irreversible damage if he doesn't get help soon."

My eyes burned. I knew what he was trying to do. I *knew* it. But if I told him anything about the club, then more people would be in danger. Still, I could never let Archer die.

"What do you want to know?"

"For starters, why don't you tell me what the hell Flick's been up to in Texas?" His brows lifted and he leaned back in his seat, kicking his boots up on the desk.

I could just barely see the rise and fall of Archer's chest. *Tell him, Emily. Tell him now.*

"He's…" I swallowed.

For Archer. Do it for Archer.

Taking a deep breath, I turned to Pops and said, "Flick is building an army."

CHAPTER TWENTY-THREE

Archer

I woke up to the voice I'd gone to sleep hearing. Her voice. Ma's voice. Only instead of being rough and tough like she once was, she was holding my hand, hovering over me as I lay sprawled out on the floor. Next to her stood Lisa Lincoln.

"Emily…" I managed to get out, but it hurt too much to speak. Hell, everything hurt, my chest most of all. It felt like I'd had a ton of bricks dropped on me, all in the form of boots and fists and who knew what the fuck else.

"Nicholas," Ma crooned. "Can you hear me *a leanbh*?"

My eyes shut again.

Damn, what I wouldn't have given for some whiskey right then.

CHAPTER TWENTY-FOUR

Emily

I sat in the same office that Pops had just left from. I'd been alone in there for an hour and a half, locked away and waiting for whatever came next.

They'd taken Archer away the second I'd spilled the truth, his body lifeless and hanging in the men's hold. I'd sobbed at the sight of it, stood, and pounded on the window too. After demanding to know what they were doing with him, Pops had laughed and called me an impatient bitch.

The second that man left the room, I'd let the numbness inside of me take over, followed close with an undeniable hatred for myself I'm pretty sure would never go away.

I'd been weak and spilled secrets that were not mine to share. I just prayed Pops kept his end of the deal and got Archer the medical help he'd promised.

My only comfort had been Angel. He'd crouched down in front of me, soft-green eyes searching my face before he spoke. When he finally did, his voice sounded so odd and I couldn't help but cringe. I wondered if someone, Pops perhaps, had done something to him. Forced chemicals down his throat or something worse than that.

He'll be okay, he'd told me, so brave and kind, ignoring my reaction to him as he spoke.

Despite his demeanor though, I knew better. I couldn't see a way out of this. Not after everything Pops had done. Even if the Red Dragons did arrive, Archer might not be here for them to save.

I covered my mouth at the thought, a sob of fear and pain lodged in my throat. He had to be okay. I couldn't live with myself if he wasn't.

Back and forth I rocked to try and keep my body from freezing in place, from locking down in case I needed to fight. Where was my mom? Why hadn't she come to me again?

It was cold, like an icebox. Still dressed in those sweats and the striped shirt from the hospital, I felt like my body wasn't my own. The room eventually lost its light as the sun began to set. There were no lamps or ceiling lights, nothing but the light from under the door and the shadow of someone pacing outside.

"Go away!" I screamed at whoever was there. I guessed it was Angel. I hadn't heard him walk away, hadn't even heard him lock the door. But trying to run and escape? It wasn't possible.

Not even five minutes later, the door handle twisted. A tall, wide man stood in the entryway, staring back at me, a hood over his face, hiding it in the shadows. I jerked back against the wall, turned my face away…

Until I heard his voice.

"Emily."

My eyes popped wide. I had to be hallucinating because that couldn't be…

"Chop?" Slowly, I stood, disbelief clouding my mind. Why was he here?

Never had I wanted to be rescued by a prince, but a biker with a dragon tat, on the other hand, might just be okay. Even if said biker had hurt me in the past.

"You're here," I whispered, walking toward him, slow and steady, knees knocking together with both nerves and relief.

"Where's Niyol and Slade? Flick?" I bit my lip, wincing. "I'm so sorry. I had to tell Pops things, but they have Archer."

Chop didn't smile at me in reassurance. In fact, he didn't move a single muscle in his face.

I blinked, thinking maybe he still held a grudge about the fact that I'd left with Archer. But this was life or death. Or maybe they were all here, but none of them wanted to rescue me because of who I was.

"Where's Niyol?" I looked behind him. "We need to tell them that Archer's hurt and—"

"Come on." He took my wrist, yanking me behind him. "You're my responsibility now, so you'll follow me."

Pain shot up my arm. "You're hurting me."

Ignoring me, Chop moved faster, leading us down another hall, this one with flickering lights above, reminding me of a horror film. The walls were all made of bricks and nothing hung on them, like at the Red Dragon compound. No cuts, no old photos of former bikers, no dragon pictures either. But the thing that was most obvious as we moved throughout the building was the absence of actual bikers. There was no sense of brotherhood or friendship in the air. In fact, whenever we walked by someone, they stayed quiet, looking at me as though I were a leper. Fear pushed my heart into overdrive while panic stole my voice. The sneers and gazes back in Rockford were nothing in comparison to the men looking at me here.

"Where are we going?" I asked, tripping over a door frame, down another hall, and toward the front door.

"Just shut up, would you?"

Uncertain terror ran through my veins, and with all the strength I could muster, I yanked out of his hold, freezing just before he could lead us outside. "Where. Are we. Going?"

He turned to face me, backing me against the closest wall, a sneer on his lips, his hand to my throat. "To my room."

"No." I shook my head, my face going cold. "Y-you…" He wasn't here to rescue me. Chop was a part of this.

Chop was a rogue. He dropped his hand from my neck and ran it through his mussed blond hair, taking a step back, calming just enough to where he almost looked like the man I thought I once could be friends with.

"How could you do this?" I whispered, placing a hand over my mouth.

The front door whipped open before he could answer me. A woman walked in, wearing a green dress that hit her knees; she had dark-brown hair that hung just below her chin, and friendly brown eyes. She also looked entirely too familiar.

At the sight of Angel behind her, I froze. There was no doubt in my mind that this was his mom. The similarities they shared were uncanny, down to the freckles across their noses.

Angel's mom's gaze was hesitant as she looked at me. She seemed like she wanted to smile but wasn't sure how. "Good evening," she said, and my heart lurched at the sound. She was Irish, like Archer. Their voices the same, hers just a little less pronounced. What were the odds?

Before I could say anything Chop grabbed my upper arm and tugged me outside.

"Hurry up, would you?" he asked, rushing us through a grassy front yard.

I looked back over my shoulder at Angel, whose mom had her hand out in front of his chest. My heart jumped a beat when I realized he wanted to protect me. I lost sight of them both as Chop tore through a grassy field and forced me to the back of the overgrown factory warehouse.

Tears filled my eyes immediately, but before I could speak, I was shoved inside another building—this one small and square like an efficiency apartment—stumbling back, then falling to the floor. Pain radiated up my wrists and I hissed, scooting until my shoulders hit a wall.

Only then did the man formerly known as Chop, the Red Dragon, lose his hateful glare and say, "You're safe now, Emily. I won't let anyone hurt you."

CHAPTER TWENTY-FIVE

Archer

A cold rag was on my head when I finally came to. This time when I saw her, I knew I wasn't hallucinating.

"So glad you're awake. You gave me quite the scare."

I squeezed my eyes shut and pushed myself up in the bed, but chains rattled my legs, sadly keeping me trapped.

"You… a ghost?" I croaked out, wincing at the burn in my throat, the throb in my head most of all.

Ma snickered under her breath and shook her head. The sound was so damn familiar I felt my throat close off from the memories this time, the emotions that never stopped coming when I thought about her.

"Ain't no such things as ghosts," she told me, wiping blood off my hands and arms that looked like it'd been there for days. Her movements were rough; I supposed it had been a while since she'd been a mother. But she was real, and here, and I couldn't stop staring at her, even though I only had one good eye to look with right now.

"H-How…" I managed, then looked around, needing a drink for my throat. When I spotted one, I tried to nod my chin toward it, but my shoulders were too weak to hold my head up.

Thankfully, she picked up on it, putting the straw to my lips. I drank greedily, knowing if I kept at it, I'd likely puke again. But the water was cold and I couldn't speak without it. I also couldn't get out of here until I got my shit together—drinking was just one step toward that goal.

Ma put the cup back down and I looked around, trying to get the layout of the room. I didn't recognize shit, other than it looked like I was in some sort of office with a hospital bed. The light was a tiny desk lamp that sat in the corner of the room. There was nothing else, which meant this couldn't be a permanent locale for Pops and his little rogues. They were on the move again. Question was, were they running south or coming for us?

I curled my lip at the thought, only for the water still in my mouth to drip over my bottom lip and slide down my neck.

My heart raced at the thought of Emily being here somewhere. I needed to find her, hold her in my arms. I needed her to know that what had happened between us wasn't something I'd expected, but if I got out of here alive, then I'd accept it, open my fucking arms for as long as she'd let me have her.

"Em…" was all I could get out.

Ma frowned at me. "What are you trying to say?"

"Em…"

Her face softened. She nodded. Which could only mean one thing. She knew who I was talking about. She'd seen her or met her and that meant she was here, maybe close by. I tried to sit up again, a little faster this time, but dizziness hit me full force and all the water I'd managed to get down me was threatening to come up.

"Rest." Ma touched my shoulder. "She's safe right now. Angel's keeping his eye on her."

Who the hell was Angel?

Ma smiled at me, and it hurt to look at because I'd gone without seeing it since I was twelve years old. She'd died. Dad and I had buried her.

"You love her, don't ya?" Ma asked, pulling me out of my head.

I frowned.

"Emily," she clarified, then brought the water back to my lips. Even still dizzy, I drank that shit down.

"She's a pretty one. But she's spoken for, I'm afraid."

My eyes narrowed.

Every ache and burn and throb was nothing in comparison to thinking about Emily being with someone else.

"Sorry. But Chop's claimed her—"

"No," I hissed and shook my head. Emily was mine, not fucking *Chop's*. That traitorous bastard. I'd kill him first. Bare hands, gun to his head, it didn't matter.

"You need to rest." Ma sighed. "I know you have questions for me. And I'll try to answer as much as I'm allowed. But if you wanna make it out of here alive, boy, then you're gonna have to play like you've switched sides, you hear me?"

I gave my head a fast jerk, instantly regretting it. The pain shot down my back and arm, my ribs too.

"It's got to happen, Nicholas." Nicholas. She was the last person to ever call me by my real name, other than Dad. That's not who I was anymore though. "This isn't your world here. This is Pops's—"

"No." Never fucking ever would Pops be a part of my world.

"So stubborn, just like that Da of yours." She ruffled the top of my hair, which was about as affectionate as she'd ever been, then set both hands on her lap when she'd finished. "He should've let me go. Coming to the States was the worst thing he could've done for you."

"You... should've... lived."

She winced. "Yeah. I know it's gotta be a surprise for you. And I'll explain in time, like I said, but I am pleading with you, Nicholas. Do not try and be a hero. You're too weak right now."

"Let me... call..."

"Absolutely not. Nobody here has phones except for the big boys."

"Get... one." I needed to call my brothers.

When they arrived, this place would burn to the ground, and if she wasn't careful, Ma might go along with it. I wasn't sure whose side she was on, whether Pops and her were together. I wasn't sure if I could trust her or love her or what. But I didn't have time to think about that right now. Not when I knew Emily was close by.

The door opened then, and in walked a kid. I frowned at him. He couldn't have been much older than fifteen or sixteen. All lanky legs and arms, skinny frame, green eyes.

I stiffened, taking him in through narrowed eyes, watching his movements, the way he stood at my ma's side, hovering protectively.

"Who the fuck… are you?" I managed.

He glared at me, arms folded. The kid was pale, like he never saw the sun. Loaded with freckles too. Red hair, a little curly at the ends.

But his eyes… Good Christ, I knew those eyes. It was like I was looking in a mirror. My chest burned with every throbbing beat. And when I looked to Ma, seeing her head down, tears on her face, I knew right the fuck away what was going on.

This was her son.

This kid was my blood.

The first thing I could see in my mind was my old man. He looked like hell, just as I remembered him, but he was smiling in my memories. We were back home in Ireland. He and Ma were on the back of his bike, telling me they'd be out late. They looked so damn happy as they drove away that afternoon, Ma's braid blowing behind her. And because I liked being home alone so I could look at my old man's titty mags, I was damn excited that they'd gone off together.

But then everything had changed.

My world.

My dad.

"Archer?" Ma whispered, jerking a thumb back toward the kid. "This is Angel. He's…"

I looked at her again, away from the blood, eyes narrowing, lips pursed…

Spit it out. Spit it the fuck out.

But she didn't. Instead, she stood, wiped her hands down the front of her dress, and said, "I can't do this right now. I'm so sorry."

Then she left me and my new little sibling alone there together to bond.

Just what I needed right now.

As if being trapped in this damn bed and reunited with my ma who I thought was dead wasn't bad enough. Now I had to do it with blood I didn't know I had? A long-lost sibling? Fuck that.

Still, once Ma left the room, I couldn't help but be curious about the kid. Most of all, I wanted to know if he'd seen Emily.

"C'mere." I motioned him over with a finger. At least I think I did. I was just thankful I could feel the damn things now.

The kid didn't come over though. Instead, he stood against the wall, arms folded, staring at me.

"Get… over here… damn it." The words were coming easier now, but that didn't mean shit. I may have been a little more alert, but that didn't mean I was ready for a full-on conversation.

He lifted an eyebrow at me in challenge. And that's when I saw it. His smart-ass smirk. *My* trademark smirk. Not his.

Or should I say our *dad's* smirk.

I sucked in a sharp breath, stomach twisting as I counted the years back in my head.

Holy shit. This wasn't just Ma's kid but my old man's too.

I shut my eyes, lowered my head back against the bed. How? How the *fuck* was this possible? I needed answers. I needed real answers. But first, I needed to break out of this shithole and find Emily. And I hoped to whatever entity was out there that this kid, my blood, would become my key.

CHAPTER TWENTY-SIX

Emily

"Just listen to me, would you?" Chop covered his face, shook his head too. "I'm sorry I hurt you. I really am. But Pops threatened my family. My mom and little sister. He threatened my ex too."

I lowered my head back against a wall, not willing to look at him while he told me the truth. About how he'd got involved with the club in the first place. How he'd spied on and betrayed his friends to make it happen.

"When?" I asked.

"Right after I joined up. I got… I got this email…" He ran his fingers through his hair. "I didn't think much of it at first, thought it was a prank put on by one of the brothers. But…"

"But what?"

"Remember that night we first met in the bar last year? Before I started following Summer?"

I nodded, remembering alright. Not because of the memory of meeting him, but because of the encounter I'd had with Archer that night. I'd gone to the club on one of the rare occasions where I'd left my tiny house in search of something to make me stop thinking about Sam. He'd called that afternoon, begging me for another chance, and my heart ached because I'd had to tell him no again. Keeping him away from me and all of my baggage was the most important thing I'd ever done for our relationship, despite the fact that I missed him fiercely. The guilt had nearly killed me, to the point where all I'd wanted was to get drunk, something I didn't do very well.

Archer had found me at the bar drinking before Chop was around. He'd sat beside me, wordless, our thighs grazing like he couldn't have cared less who I was, or about the lack of space between our bodies. I remembered feeling a spark then. A tiny, electric jolt that I'd played off as annoyance. But it hadn't bothered me like I thought it would. Out of all the men at the club, he was the one who bothered me the most. I thought it was because he was the most controlling, but it seemed it was because he was the only one who let *me* lose control.

My entire body had heated up. I thought something was wrong with me for feeling such opposing emotions. For a second, I'd felt something. And I'd wanted the distraction too. But then another woman had sat down beside him and blatantly grabbed his erection through his pants while his hand was still on *my* thigh and his lips were still against *my* ear.

I was so mortified and angry with him *and* myself that I'd pushed him off his stool and left. Embarrassed tears had slid down my face, disorienting me to the point where I'd gone down the hall toward the dorms, only to wind up finding a crying Chop on the floor outside his room, face in his hands.

"What happened that day?" I asked Chop, sitting up against the side of the shed he'd taken me to.

"I got a call from the hospital that morning. My dad was hit by a fucking car. Almost died. I knew then that the messages were serious."

I winced, turning to him. "That was Pops's doing? Why didn't you say anything to Flick or Slade or my brother? Archer even?"

He laughed. "I was barely patched in." He shrugged. "I didn't have a pot to piss in, let alone clout to get them to believe me."

"You had the emails though." I frowned. "And your dad was in the hospital."

"Nobody cared, I'm telling you." He growled then pushed to his feet, pacing in front of me. "I was their IT guy. The guy they counted on to get them details about stats and shit like that. A smart kid but a low man on the totem pole."

"That's not true." I shook my head and stood. "The Red Dragon brothers care—"

"The fuck they did. Not that it would've mattered." He laughed, but nothing about it was funny. "Pops said he'd kill my family if I didn't help him. That's why I did it." He stopped in front of the door, choking on his words. "You were the only real thing I had, Emily. And… and you left. I could've helped you. A hell of a lot more than Archer."

"How did you know that I was going to leave?"

"Who the hell do you think's been delivering all those letters to your school, huh?" He shook his head at me as if I was stupid.

"But Angel—"

"He only came that night because I had to be there for Flick's return." He grunted. "I'm the one who let him through the gates." He ran a hand through his hair. "It's not like *I* could give it to you. Not without blowing my cover."

But he could have, was the thing. Even if all he'd done was leave the letter, like all of the others.

I looked down at my hands, too confused and tired to question this anymore.

Chop said he could have helped me, yeah, but if he was so adamant about not angering Pops and keeping his family safe, then there was no way he would've risked his family's safety just for me.

"I'm sorry," I told him, feeling bad in a minuscule way. Not because I liked him or even wanted to help him, but because I knew what it was like to have to choose between two things you loved. "I wish things were different."

"Whatever. Nothing you can do to help me."

I blinked, watching him move to the door. So many things were left unanswered, and I did not want to be stuck in another closed-off room, waiting for rescue.

"Let me come too. I know they're keeping Archer somewhere inside that building, and I want to—"

"Archer's as good as dead."

I stiffened. All the blood drained from my face, and I was suddenly so cold. "No. That's not true. I just saw him."

Turning back to me with blank, empty eyes, Chop smirked. "Yeah. He is. You can trust me on that."

Chop closed the door and I decided there was no way I'd stay in his place like some damsel. I needed to find Archer. Get him out of here. The both of us. I just didn't have a clue where to start looking.

I found an unlocked and un-boarded window in the bathroom and slipped outside. Thankfully it was only one floor so the drop was more of a step. There were no armed bikers in the surrounding wooded area. No cars or anything like that. It was really weird to think this entire place was right there in the open, easy to find, no protection.

It was dark out now, close to midnight. My feet were light as I stepped toward the main building, but the ground was littered with sticks, and no matter how many times I tried to avoid them, the crunches were inevitable.

I went from dark window to dark window, trying to find an open one, almost giving up until I saw it. A propped-open door, no light from beneath it. It was a risk I was willing to take at this moment. I needed to get to Archer, find him, explain that the rest of his brothers would be here either tonight or tomorrow—at least I *hoped* they would.

Slowly, I slid in through the door, the hinges creaking so much I had to freeze just to make sure nobody had heard me. Voices sounded from somewhere, fading to the point where it was almost too silent to be real. There were no rogue Red Dragons sitting around standing guard, not that I was hoping otherwise.

Against a wall, I scooted down a hall, peering into rooms, holding my breath whenever the floor would squeak beneath my feet. Left and right I looked, only a few hall lights flickering above, each one making clicking or buzzing sounds.

A soft murmur just up to my left stopped me short. It sounded like a woman, whispering. Hope had my stomach circling and dropping at the same time. Was it my mom? That woman I'd seen earlier? I sped up my pace, pausing just outside the door. I put my ear to the wood and held my breath once more, waiting and praying the halls stayed empty.

That's when I heard the accent. Irish. It *was* the woman from earlier. Angel's mom? Hope had me twisting the knob, but before I could get it open, a figure popped up to my left.

I jumped back at the sight of Angel, a hand to my chest.

His hands balled into fists and he moved in closer, distrust in his gaze.

I held my palms out. "Please don't hurt me. I just… I need to find my friend."

He stopped in place, cocked his head to one side too. With an unnerving intensity, he studied me, reaching up then touching the end of my bangs. It was odd—not just his weird touching but the fact that he did it with just the tip of one finger.

Holding my breath, I waited for him to finish, all the while thinking the worst.

The door burst open a moment later. "Angel, have you come with…?"

The Irishwoman peered her head out fully, eyes widening at the sight of me. She looked left and right then grabbed my arm, yanking me inside then shutting the door once Angel was in the room as well.

"Are you out of your mind, child?" she asked me.

Before I could clarify that I was not, in fact, a child but a college graduate and teacher, the woman went on a quiet tirade.

"I see why he's so fond of you, but Lord in heaven, you must have a death wish to be walking around here like you are." She shook her head. "You're lucky everyone's in Church planning the run."

The run? What *run* was she referring to? As in the run to attack back at home? My hands shook at my sides at the thought of my family.

My family. Summer was my family. Niyol was my family. The Red Dragons, even though I didn't know them well? They could've been part of that family too. They'd sheltered me, protected me. They'd let me stay on their land and… God. They were everything that Archer had told me they were. I'd just been too blinded by the possibility of finding my mom to truly get it until now.

The woman took me by the arm and sat me in a chair, mumbling something under her breath I couldn't hear.

"My name is Anne," the Irishwoman reached for my hand, shook it once. All business. Hard, even. But there was still something about her that I respected already.

"I'm Emily," I managed.

"I know who you are." She nodded at me. "But what I don't understand is how did you get inside the main building? It should have been locked."

"There was a door propped open." I swallowed hard, nervous that she'd tell someone. I didn't know her well enough to trust her yet. I was just hoping she was different enough to care.

"I suppose you're looking for your ma?"

My heart jumped into my throat, anger and sadness combining inside. I hadn't seen her since this morning, but she'd also been the furthest thing from my mind. It's funny how priorities tend to change over time. I'd come here to help her escape… but she didn't want to escape. Now, I would do just about anything to get out of here myself, but with Archer, not my mom.

She'd made her choice, picking Pops over me. It hurt, yes—more than I wanted to admit right now. But I had a new goal to distract me: Get Archer out of here. Get him home. And maybe, just maybe, escape with him.

"I…" I bit my bottom lip, not sure if I could trust this woman completely. Then I looked over at Angel again, and he nodded once as if knowing what I wanted to ask. For some reason, I found myself relaxing enough to say what I needed to say. "I'm actually looking for a man who was taken in around the same time I was. His name is Archer."

Something flashed through the woman's eyes. I couldn't tell what it was, exactly, and that worried me. Maybe I'd said too much.

"You can't see him." She lifted her chin. "His room is heavily guarded and you'd be asking for trouble if you tried."

"Is he okay? He's still alive then?" I held my breath.

"Yes. The doctor was here earlier to treat him. He's going to be okay."

"So, will you tell me where he is? Please? I need to get a message to him."

"No, lovely. I'm sorry. I can't help you."

My shoulders fell and tears gathered in my eyes. I knew it was a long shot, that it would be far too easy just to walk inside and take him out of here. But the thought of never hugging him or kissing him again left me all sorts of crazy.

A hand settled on my shoulder then, and soft words of reassurance filled my ears. "Let me rephrase this for you. I can't help you. But Angel can."

I lifted my head again, hope flickering in my chest.

"Would you like to give him a message?" she asked.

"Yes, please."

She walked over to a desk and returned with a pen and a small piece of paper. "But you have to do it right now and then go back to wherever you were, do you understand me?"

I nodded, relief flooding through me. Even as my hands shook, I penned him a letter on my knee, spilling everything in me, including the tears as they fell on the ink.

I told him what I could. About Chop, and my mom's loyalty to this club most of all. Then I told him how I felt about him. And that because of that, I'd texted Niyol and told him what was happening, where we were headed. That I wanted Archer safe and they needed to be here to help make that happen. Archer would be mad at me for telling his brothers, but in the end I'd done it because I cared about him… though *cared* was a mild word compared to how I really felt about Archer Benedict.

The woman touched my arm in reassurance when I finished. She took the letter, not reading it, then folded it up and gave it to Angel. "Alright. Angel will drop this off tonight."

I nodded again. "Okay. Yes. Thank you."

She smiled but chose to stay quiet.

"What about my mom? When do you think I can see her again?" Even if I was going to leave without her, I wanted to say goodbye.

"You'll see her in two days when we leave this place. I'm guessing since you're Pops's daughter, that you three will be riding in a car together."

My stomach dipped into my toes. "Leaving?"

"Yes. We stay in places for only one or two weeks at a time."

I licked my dry lips. "Um, do you know where we're going next?"

She shook her head slowly. "That's never disclosed to the women, I'm afraid. But I've heard rumors…"

"What kind of rumors?" I stiffened.

"Pops is ready to move in on his territory in Rockford."

"Oh, God." I'd been right, which meant everyone at the Red Dragon club was in danger.

For now, there was nothing I could do about them. But maybe getting this woman and her son on my side might help.

"Can you tell me how you became a part of this place?" I winced, wondering if it had been a choice.

She hesitated, looking at Angel, then Maisy, and finally me, blowing out a long breath as she did. "We don't have much time, and I fear we're always being watched." She looked to Angel, who'd moved across the room to stand closer to the door. He crossed his arms like a warrior, and it made my heart swell.

So young, yet so brave. I could tell just by looking at him that he was one of the good guys.

"Please." I looked back to the woman, taking her hand in mine. I didn't even know her name. "You can trust me."

She patted my hand, and a small dimple formed on her right cheek when she smiled. I studied it, frowning. Archer had one there too.

"I was stolen from my husband and family in my country fifteen years ago, sold to a cartel that traded women and young girls for money and drugs and weapons."

I put a hand to my mouth.

"It's okay. I was one of the lucky ones. I managed to escape, and thank God too, because I was pregnant." Pregnant. Alone in a country she wasn't familiar with.

"Did you ever try to go home? Back to Ireland, I mean?"

She nodded. "Yes. I very much did. But I had no money, no way to contact them. Angel and I lived in homeless shelters, hiding out from my kidnappers for years."

"And you never went to the police?"

"No. I was too scared. By the time I had enough money to leave the country, I'd found out that my husband and son had left for America, and I had no idea where they were." She took a deep breath before continuing. "Every connection I had with them back home was lost. But then last year, I heard…" She paused, and tears filled her eyes. I stood, if only so I could hug her, but Angel had moved away from the door and was by her side in a blink, his arm around her shoulder.

"I'm fine." She tried to shoo him away, but he was determined not to let her go. It was there in her son's arms, though, that she was able to finish her story.

"I was working at a convenience store in Missouri about six months ago, just barely making ends meet. Then one day I looked up and there was a man standing in front of me. He told me he knew my husband and son. And he'd take me to them, but I had to do him a favor first."

"What kind of favor?"

She rubbed a shaky hand over her mouth. "Help him with his cause when it comes to the club. I serve him and the brothers, as a mother, a wife, a cleaner, a nurse, a vessel to their, um… needs. Whether sexually or any other way." She laughed bitterly. "It's sad that a group of men like this still needs a woman to help them with their daily needs."

In other words, she was a slave.

"How did Pops find you?" I asked, struggling to hold back my shudder.

She shrugged. "I'm unsure."

I listened with a lump in my throat as she continued to speak about the things she'd gone through. How Angel, who had just turned fourteen, had been forced to be a brother, to bulk up and be a man, to prospect, she'd said. If he didn't, then he'd never see his mother alive again.

As the words began to spill out about her family before, the ones she'd lost after being taken from Ireland, I realized without a shadow of a doubt who this woman and her son really were. They shared the same haunting eyes, the same light skin too… They were a family. *She* was Archer's mother. And Angel was Archer's little brother.

There was a lump in my throat when she finished, one I couldn't swallow away. I barely even knew these two people, but I'd still do whatever possible to help them get out of there.

"I'm so, so sorry." I bowed my head, setting my chin to my chest.

"Nothing about this is your fault, dear," she said as she stood from her seat and moved in front of me, setting both hands on my shoulders.

"But I brought Archer here and put him in danger. I—"

"Yes. You did. But you are also saving lives, don't you see?" she asked.

I looked up, meeting her eyes. "*How?*"

"Because, my dear, you're the key to our escape."

CHAPTER TWENTY-SEVEN

Archer

Angel was there in the room with me this morning. I still couldn't wrap my head around the fact that I had a brother. An actual *blood* brother. Of course, he wasn't alone—Chop was with him, sitting at the table, looking bored out of his damn mind as he watched on.

"Watch the blade, would ya, kid?" I hissed as the razor in Angel's hand nicked my skin. I knew he couldn't help it. He was young. Probably never shaved a day in his life. Still, one wrong move, and he'd slit my fucking throat. I wasn't too big on dying before I had a chance to kiss Emily again.

Her soft lips, meeting mine, the stuff of fantasies come true. I'd been reliving that kiss we shared every time I shut my eyes. It was the only thing that was keeping me alive right now. The only thing that encouraged me to push through and get out of here.

Of all the goddamn things they could be doing, the fact that Chop insisted on the kid shaving my hair off this morning was the most messed up part of this day. Not that it mattered. Half my skull was hairless now anyways, what with Pops and Chop both yanking it out.

The buzz echoed throughout my skull like thunder. I likely had a concussion. Probably some broken ribs too. I had no idea why they were keeping me alive at all. Did they think Flick would barter with them for me when the time came? Because he wouldn't.

I was VP, yeah. But that didn't matter if it meant Flick would be giving up the land and power he'd gained by taking over the club.

"Yeah, you're lucky I don't use the damn things to cut other shit off your body right now." Chop pulled a cigarette out of his box and tucked it between his lips.

I smirked. "If you think I'm gonna apologize for being with my woman, you're wrong."

"She's not yours." Chop stood, pushing his chair over and crouching down in front of me. The Angel kid stopped with the clippers, moving away just in time for Chop to grab me by the chin and get in my face. "Not after what I did to her last night."

"You shut your damn mouth, motherfucker," I growled so loud my throat burned. The harder I tugged on the cuffs around my arm, the more my already blistered skin burned too. The pain meant nothing to me at this point. Not when all I could think about was taking the razor in my kid brother's hand and shoving it down Chop's filthy throat.

"How's it feel?" He lowered his mouth to my ear. "Knowing her pussy's all mine?" His loud laugh echoed throughout the room, like he'd just won some kind of game.

When I got out of here, I would kill both him *and* Pops, then tell her I was ready to become a reformed man once and for all, if she'd have me.

"Not so pretty anymore." He took a towel and slapped at my shaved head.

The stinging pain he'd caused was nothing in comparison to the rage boiling in my veins. Hot liquid, poisoning my already darkened soul. Even though I wanted to tell him what he could really do with his towel—hang himself would be nice—I felt my head falling forward again, as if I had another stream of drugs running through me that I didn't know about. Two days of sitting upright, sleeping upright, cuffed to this wall… I wasn't anywhere near where I needed to be in order to fight back and get out of here.

Chop finally left the room, leaving me alone with the kid—the kid who hadn't moved since Chop had shoved him out of the way. I frowned, wishing I could look him in the eye and tell him there was a better way to live out there than this. But I couldn't lift my head. Instead, I kept my eyes to the ground, watching it blur in and out of focus.

"You good, kid?" I managed.

He didn't answer. Or move.

"I know you're there," I told him, lip curling as I looked to the wall. "Kinda hard to talk though when you're behind me, don't you think?"

I could hear him shuffling, moving closer. Somehow, I managed to glance over my shoulder at him, wincing at what I saw. His hands were at his sides, elbows locked, eyes down. He looked just like my old man. But the terrified version.

Casper. That's what I'd rename him. A ghost.

"You're the spitting image of him, you know," I said, already out of breath. "He'd probably call you ugly like he did me." I chuckled at my own joke.

His answer was to look at me again. Then blink.

What would it take to crack the kid? I bet Emily would know.

"You don't talk a lot," I continued, clearing my throat. My eyes were blurring around the edges, proof that I'd be passing out again soon.

His lips moved, opened, then shut. Then he looked to the ground and shook his head. Bet he'd been taught to shut up like that. Bet Pops had fucked him up real good to make it happen too. The thought pissed me off. Made me mad at my ma too. How could she let this happen?

"How long have you and Ma been with Pops?" I questioned, needing answers. As many as I could get. We didn't have much time.

He hesitated, looking at the door, which was closed still, then back at me before he finally said, "S-six months."

"Huh." I nodded. "Wanna tell me how you all got together?" What I really needed to know was where the fuck my ma had been all this time. Most importantly, why she hadn't tried to find me and my old man.

"Pops."

"He found you?"

The kid nodded, fidgeting a little more.

"Sit." I pointed to the chair across from me. "I'm not gonna ask you for help here. I just want some answers." I cleared my throat once more, my mouth drying up, my tongue getting thicker. "Me and the old man thought Ma was dead. Thought someone killed her."

His green eyes went wide; I could see that clearly. "You… know Dad?"

"Yeah." A knot built in my throat at the thought of the old man. "*Knew* Dad."

The drunk protector. The guy who'd nearly given everything up after he thought his wife was gone for good. Then one day when I was fourteen, he'd remarried after knowing my stepmom for two weeks. It was his way of trying to help me, no doubt in my mind, but my old man never loved that women. His heart lost the ability to love the second they found Ma's body. Or what was *supposed* to be her body.

Then one day, six months after he'd married again, he ended that shitshow, packed up our shit, and said to me, *We're moving to America.* I'd tried to ask why, didn't like the idea of leaving my friends and school, but he'd told me I'd make new friends where we were going. The best kind too.

Never did finish school, only got to the middle of tenth grade actually. But I did find the best damn friends a guy could have, and a family I thought I'd never know, in the RDs.

Later I found out from Flick the reason why he came to the US in the first place. Apparently, he'd thought there was a lead here when it came to Ma's killer, which never made sense to me because she'd been shot back home in Ireland. But a month into this supposed lead, Dad found himself down a dead-end road and called it quits after nearly getting shot up himself.

Then his spiral into the bottle happened, and his heart was too broken to heal this time. When he died, I didn't shed a tear. Because that man wasn't my dad. That man was a ghost.

Fitting, as his unknown *new* son acted like one.

"Where… is he?" Angel's voice cracked. I almost asked what was wrong with him, but didn't wanna be a dick.

I shrugged and looked at the floor. "He's dead, kid."

Angel's shoulders grew stiff, and both of his eyes narrowed. Already I could tell he was Ma's fierce protector, even if it was obvious Pops could squeeze his little neck with one hand and end him in a heartbeat. Still, I admired his fight.

His face relaxed after a while but he didn't look away. Brave little shit he was. He'd make a good RD—the right kind of RD. I bet he and Mute would get along real well.

I watched then as he stood and pulled something from his pocket. A piece of paper. He opened it slowly, glancing quickly over his shoulder toward the door before giving it to me. I could see the ink there. Curly words in black. Feminine. I blinked at it then looked at him again; everything was too unfocused. I wasn't sure how the fuck I was gonna read it.

"What's that?" I nodded at it with my chin.

He turned it around, letting me see, only to whisper back the most important word in my life: "Emily."

CHAPTER TWENTY-EIGHT

Emily

I'd been locked up for two days since that night I'd met Archer's mom. She'd told me to go back, that she had a plan, and I'd been waiting here trying to believe her.

Chop had been checking on me—he'd told me that I wasn't allowed to leave without him. That it wasn't safe. So, he hated me but still chose to protect me for some reason. I half wondered if he felt bad about what he was doing or if, all along, he was still working under Flick.

Today was the day we were supposed to be leaving. And another day where the Red Dragons hadn't shown to rescue Archer. I didn't want to lose hope… but it was fading with every breath I took. If Anne didn't have a plan to leave after all, then I'd be doing this all on my own.

I was tired of being a prisoner.

It was time to get out of here. Jumping up off the floor and onto my feet, I straightened the front of my shirt out and lifted my chin. Sacrificing myself for the sake of Archer's release would be the easy part. Getting Archer to agree with it would not. Even still, I'd do what was necessary. I'd give up my life just so he could continue living his.

If Pops was that generous, of course.

Before I could make the move to leave, the front door opened and slammed against the wall with a loud bang. I jumped, covering my ears as Angel appeared in the door frame like, well, an Angel.

"What are you doing?"

He scowled at me and shook his head as he said, "No… time."

A second later, he moved in closer and grabbed my arm, pulling me behind him out the front door.

"Angel, what's going…?"

Then everything happened so quickly that I barely registered any of it.

A huge explosion sounded, and within moments of the noise, the front of the building across from Chop's place was in flames.

"Oh, God," I murmured, pushing around Angel.

Pops was at the building's entrance, holding Anne by her hair. He shoved her to the ground with an audible grunt, causing her to cry out.

"N-no," Angel growled.

Pops dug his foot into the back of Anne's skull, forcing her forehead to dig into the cement. I covered my mouth with both hands, fighting the urge to scream. Another explosion sounded in the distance, and smoke billowed up into the sky toward the back of the building. I looked around, frantic, thinking I'd see my mom or Archer, but neither of them were there.

Angel's body shook behind me. He wanted to go to his mother, protect her, but for some reason he was staying by me. I wouldn't let that happen. I wouldn't let his mom die for me.

"Go, Angel. Go."

He hesitated, eying me.

"Please. Don't let him hurt her."

Nodding once, he took off down the road toward the building, yanking a gun from his belt along the way. As if he knew Angel was coming, Pops left Anne alone and raced to the other side of the building, opposite where I stood. It took him only seconds to get lost in the smoke and scrambling bikers, which only sent my heart racing faster. What if he was going for Archer? Or even my mom? I had to get to them first.

Shouts were barely heard over the roaring of the fire, which now took hold of the skies with its black smoke. Chaos ensued, in the form of bodies being dragged from the building. With every lifeless form that wasn't Archer, my heart thumped more wildly in my chest. Where were they?

"Emily!" A voice called my name from behind a large truck that sat off to the side of the building. Chop ran toward me, his arms waving frantically. "We need to go. Now."

I blinked, looking into Chop's eyes the closer he got to me.

"Now!" he shouted. "Come to me."

Slowly, I shook my head, refusing to move. Not when the fire was growing thicker, blocking the doors, the windows, overtaking every inch of the building. Archer was inside there somewhere. My mom, possibly, too.

"Come on. Now." He yanked at my arm and dragged me toward the gravel road to the left.

"No. I'm not going with you." I tugged my arm out of his hold and took off toward the building. If I had to run into the fire to find the people I loved, so be it. I'd die for them both.

"The hell you're not." He grabbed me by the waist from behind and yanked me against his chest.

"Don't touch me."

"I will touch you because you're mine now," he growled low into my ear.

"I'm *nobody's*." I shrugged out of his arms, launching my foot back. I knew I'd hit him where it counted the second he started to groan.

Frantic, I ran forward, not caring about death or destruction, fire or whatever stood in my way. I had to help.

"Emily!"

I froze before the door when I realized who that voice belonged to. My mom.

Seconds before I could go to her, a blast of fiery heat shot out from the building, forcing me to step back. I coughed, holding my arm up and over my face. Smoke was filling my lungs already and my eyes burned like someone had poured acid in them.

I bent over at the waist and gagged, wishing I could puke up smoke.

"Emily, honey!" I lifted my head in time to see her there before me, her frantic eyes searching my face. "We need to get you back. The building is going to explode."

"What… happened?" I coughed.

She shook her head. "I did it for you. For all of us. So we could be together. Not the club, or the brothers, or anyone else. Just us. We can go get Niyol. Charles will tell him he's sorry. We can work this out as a family. I know we can." Tears fell down her face, dirt and sweat mixing in with them.

"*You* did this?" My eyes widened and my chest grew hot and tight.

Before she could answer, another rumble sounded as the front of the building began to crumble. Siding melted onto the ground and fell to our feet, all while the building's frame seemed to bend in half.

Mom stumbled back, grabbed my hand, bringing me with her.

"Please. We need to go, now. We have to go find your father. He'll take care of you. Of me. I promise, sweetie. We—"

"No!" I screamed, shoving her off of me. "I need to find Archer. He's somewhere in there and—"

Mom gasped, her eyes widening at the same time, body stiffening, then falling, falling, falling…

"M-mom?"

She fell to her knees, lips parted, looking up at me. Horror filled her face, and when I looked above her, I saw why. Pops was there, a knife covered in her blood in one hand, a gun in the other.

"That's what happens when you stab someone in the back." He wiped the knife along the front of his shirt. "You'd be good to remember that, daughter."

I blinked. Then I screamed.

The gun in his hand was raised. Soon after, he was in my face, forcing me to my knees. "You're a lying bitch. You don't deserve nothing."

My throat closed off, blocking even my sobs. I shook my head, hands held up. "No, please."

His upper lip curled, the beard on his face stringy and soaking with his sweat and soot. Before I could beg for mercy again, he took the gun and smacked me along the cheek with it.

"Charles, no, please," Mom murmured from the ground when I landed next to her.

Face numb, I reached over and touched her hand, squeezing. Blood dripped from her lips and her bottom one trembled.

"It's okay." I shut my eyes, dizzy. "It's okay."

"He lied to me. He s-said he wanted… family…"

"Mom, don't talk," I whispered, heart in my throat, tears burning. All she'd wanted was a family. A sick delusion with a man who had been filling her head with lies from the moment he'd met her. Mom was going to die because she believed in the one person she shouldn't have believed in. Shouts sounded around us, fighting, another shot went off… and a body fell beside me, eyes wide open, blood on his head.

Chop.

He was dead.

And I felt… nothing.

Mom's cry of pain pulled me back to her. I turned too fast, dizzy, but still managing to sit up. With shaking hands, I reached over to try and stop the blood from coming out of her chest, but it wasn't working. She was losing too much.

"Can't… feel…" Mom managed before the blood dripped out from between her lips… before she paled. Before she went silent.

"N-no, Mom, no, please." I shook my head, reaching for her again, only for Pops to grab the back of my hair and slam me onto the ground beside her.

"You're both crazy bitches. I know you did this, Emily. You're the reason those fuckers attacked first. You ruined my plans, damn it. You always did." Even through the pain, I ignored the hovering man and scooted closer to my mom, touching her face, her parted lips… But I knew I was too late. She was gone.

He'd killed her. My *father* had *killed* my mother.

I saw hell then. The fire and the devil, waiting with greedy, open arms. I looked up, not thinking much past his eternal damnation as he stood over us still, hands at his side… smiling.

"Should've done that a long time ago." He reached down and grabbed my arm. I let him pull me to my feet, completely numb.

I'd just lost my mother.

The only thing I wanted was revenge.

Was this what it felt like to the RDs? Was that why they never let anything go? Did the promise of vengeance motivate them to go through hell?

"Let's move."

"No. I'm not going with you!" I screamed, fighting back, shaking him off, failing but never letting it deter me.

Pops laughed bitterly, moving closer. Hot, stale breath washed over my face as he spoke. "They've *ruined* my club, those men." He grabbed me by the neck, squeezing.

I gagged, scraping at his wrists.

"It was my life, not theirs." He shook my body, somehow lifting me up onto my toes. "I control things, not my *son*. Not that bastard Flick. None of them. And I will make my point known by ending you now."

"S-screw… you," I hissed, eyes bulging.

That's when the bullets came. The gunfire from the woods surrounding the building. I should have been scared. Should have been afraid of getting shot. But right then, with Pops's hands around my neck, squeezing, the strangest sense of peace washed over me.

Find Archer, I begged inside. *Please don't let him die.*

Pops dropped his head back and laughed, letting go of my throat. I fell to my knees and put both hands to my neck, struggling for air.

"You know how I can tell that bitch mom of yours cheated on me?"

I coughed as an answer. If Mom cheated on him, then good for her.

Pops crouched down in front of me, elbows on his knees, teeth yellow and gnashing like a wild animal, untamed. Around him, nobody gathered; nobody even seemed to care he was there. This supposed *leader* could've been dying and I was fairly certain no one here would have batted an eye. All these months and everyone was so terrified of him, yet he seemed to have nobody but himself.

"Because any kid of mine would know what was good for 'em. You don't." Then he slapped me.

I fell back, trying to rub the sting away, only for him to grab me around my waist and scoop me up and over his shoulders. He took off toward the woods, racing to a path. His breath was shallow, yet fast; the thud of his feet against the ground vibrated in my stomach as he ran with me.

I let it all go then: my screams, my anger, my fear. Using my balled-up fists, I punched him in the back. I kicked his chest with my feet too.

But it was no good.

CHAPTER TWENTY-NINE

Archer

I moaned, wiggling my fingers and toes, lifting my head to see nothing but blackness surrounding me. This wasn't a dream but a nightmare, a fiery hellstorm of smoke and death. The hall was on fire. The room filled with smoke. I was still a prisoner in this abandoned building in Kentucky, but there was one positive thing: I wasn't cuffed to the wall anymore. Don't know how it happened, who did it for me either, but I wasn't about to look a damn gift horse in the mouth.

I managed to get to my knees, but the sudden sharp pain in my gut, likely from my ribs, was so lightning fast that I hissed like a damn snake. It was as though my insides were seconds from falling through my skin right there on this dusty-ass floor.

Voices roared in the hall, loud and echoing... until they weren't. Until the only thing I could hear was the loud roar of the fire. Emily's face flashed through my mind then. Fear for her, wherever she was, was forcing me to do something. *Anything.*

Using the wall as support, I pushed myself up and got to my feet, hissing through the pain again. I may have been okay with dying, but I sure as hell wouldn't let her go down too. Ahead of me, smoke filled the hall. I was alone. Everyone was gone.

I grabbed the table I'd been staring at for the last few days then took a few steps, somehow managing to stay upright even though it felt like my ribs were gonna slice through my gut at any time.

"Motherfucker," I growled, limping toward the hall despite the orange flames I could see spiraling up the opposite wall.

Slowly, I made it out of the room, taking my time because that was the only option my body let me have.

The drugs were out of my system, it seemed, which also meant I'd be passing out from pain sooner or later. Still, I had to get to Emily, find her before it was too late. Before Pops or Chop took her away from here… or worse.

I gritted my teeth at the thought, more terrified than I'd ever been in my life.

In the hall, everything was pitch-black from the smoke. I turned my head into my elbow and coughed, wincing through the pain it caused my ribs. Something thick started dripping from my mouth then, tasting suspiciously like blood. That probably wasn't good. Still, I needed to get to a window or door and I refused to let the possibility of a little internal bleeding keep me from doing it.

I'm coming for you, Em. I swear I am.

If I crawled through the smoke, I'd be dead weight, the pain too much for my ribs to take. So the best option I had was to find an exit, upright, possibly a window.

Grabbing an old T-shirt I found on the floor, I stuffed it over my nose and mouth then took off down the hall, eyes burning every time I looked into a room. To the right, most of the offices had windows that were boarded up. *Not good.* To the left, though, was nothing but blank walls and supply closets.

Just when my head started spinning so bad I thought I'd pass out, I made it to the last door on my right. My knees throbbed when I kicked at the wood, my stomach lurched, and I puked up blood. *Fuck.* That really wasn't good.

It was black as sin in there, even more than the hallway. Still, when I finished getting most of my guts up, I managed to lift my head in time to see what I'd been searching for. A window.

Orange flames from the hall gathered closer to the door, catching my eye. I cursed, needing to move. Now.

I looked around, and grabbed the curtains, yanking one off the long, metal rod that hung above the window. I tied it to the other curtain and let it dangle out the frame like a white flag in the hope that someone would see it. The window itself was wide enough that I could get through it fine. But the fall down, in my state? It'd be impossible.

"I'm so screwed." I scrubbed both hands over my face, falling to the floor on my ass this time. Leaning back against the wall, I couldn't stop from wincing when my stomach began to throb and burn against my shirt. Instead of checking out my injuries and seeing if there was something—anything—I could do for myself, I counted down the seconds in my head until this entire place collapsed, all while wondering if Emily had gotten out of here before it had gone up.

"God, let her be okay," I said out loud.

I couldn't stand it if she didn't get out, that's all I knew. Especially knowing I was the reason she was here at all. If I hadn't taken that side road to get away from that fucking black car, then we wouldn't have gotten stuck in the flood. Either way I looked at it, everything that had happened since I'd cuffed her was on me.

It felt like hours, but was probably more like minutes, before the fire started lighting up the walls and door like I figured it would. My eyes were shutting, and my lungs burned nearly as bad as my skin and gut; my breaths grew less frequent as I struggled to get air from the open window. When I couldn't take it in much more, I decided now would be a good time to shut my eyes and pray to a Big Guy I didn't even believe in for this one final miracle…

Save Emily. Save her, please.

Something slammed against the window frame then. When I opened my eyes and turned to look, I noticed, first, a ladder… a ladder with a dude on it who had bright-red hair. Then I saw his freckles as he peered inside and I knew right away I'd been given a second chance. Angel was there.

He spotted me first, his face staying stoic with that look I'd come to know over the last few days as his don't-give-a-shit look. Kid wore it better than Slade, even.

I nodded then coughed again, throat too tight and covered with smoke that I couldn't say jack. He finished his climb inside, one long leg after another, like some sort of gymnast, or maybe a badass ninja warrior. Reaching down, he took my hand, got me to my feet, and urged me toward the window. The fire was in the room now, filling with smoke, flickering flames licking the walls.

I winced, speaking through the pain as we moved. "A damn hero is what you are. Like brother like brother."

His response was a nod—always with the damn nodding.

I don't remember the walk to the window, but I could feel the air on my face, his nails in my skin too, pulling me along behind him. He urged me to go first. I wanted to argue, but the look in his eyes wasn't one I'd mess with. So, I lifted my leg and started my climb down… only to feel the rush of gravity as I missed the last four steps.

Slow-motion style, I fell backward.

Not even ten seconds later, Angel rushed to my side, eyes panicked as he stared down at me.

"I'm fine, don't worry about me."

Standing above me like that, he looked like fucking Banshee, a former X-Men—an Irishman too. My little badass bro. I think I loved the kid already.

Pushing myself to my feet once more, I held a hand against the aluminum siding and said through a dirty cough, "We gotta—"

Then I heard a scream, and my good eye went wide. "That's Emily."

Angel nodded, yet-fucking-again with the nods. I wasn't sure why this time, until I saw him reaching into his pocket and pull something out. My eyes narrowed when I caught sight of the black barrel.

"You even old enough to handle that thing?" I asked.

For the first time since meeting him, he rolled his eyes.

"You little shit." I laughed, but it was more like a hacking cough. Then I took the gun he held out to me, my vision blurring double when I got it in my palm. If I had to shoot this thing, I was pretty sure I'd miss my target.

"Thanks for this, kid."

He gave me another nod, motioned his head back, took a step that way too.

"You got a plan, don't you."

He nodded again.

"Then get to it."

Our eyes held a second longer, an unspoken question there in his eyes that said, *You got this?*

"Go." I nodded him on with my chin and only then did he turn and run, the opposite way from the fray.

Fear for Emily was the only reason I could put one foot in front of the other and make to the front. And when I got to the corner, I pulled in a breath, coughed again, then peeked around the building's edge, freezing when I saw the shit show going down in the front yard.

"Holy shit." It was like a damn war zone, only nobody was actually fighting.

Bodies lay burned on the ground in front of the building. Half were dead, some were nearly there. The rogues who were left stood fifty or so feet back from the building, hands in their hair, cowering, or crouched down and crying. I took them all in, counting the live ones and the dead. The bodies were... endless.

The ones still up? Not so much. Twelve. I counted twelve fucking dudes still breathing, yet I couldn't see Emily anywhere.

I heard another scream, this one less familiar. Thoughts of Emily had me hauling ass again, as best as my ass could haul, giving the building a wide enough berth that if it started falling, I wouldn't get caught beneath it.

Next to a small garage, I found the source of the scream. It was my ma on her knees, hovering over another woman. I blinked a couple of times, watching her shake the body, sobbing.

Another step closer and I froze, right away taking in the dark hair. The short legs…

"No, no, no." My heart leaped into my throat, my eyes burning. I tripped but didn't fall, ignoring the eyes of the rogue wannabe soldiers, and focused only on the unmoving woman.

Emily.

Fuuuuuck. It couldn't be her, damn it. It just fucking couldn't be.

"Move!" I yelled at my ma, who was hovering over her body, and I fell down beside her… then froze when I realized it wasn't Emily lying on the ground.

It was Lisa.

My heart stopped. I looked to my ma, breathless when I realized Lisa was dead.

The only thing I felt in my chest right then was pain for Emily; she may not be dead but the pain of losing her ma might just kill her.

"Where is Emily?"

Ma shook her head, tears falling down her cheeks when our eyes met. The woman never cried. In all the years I'd known her and loved her, I'd never seen her shed a tear.

For some reason, the sight of it pissed me off.

"Stop crying and tell me where the fuck Emily—"

Gunfire popped in the air again, and I fell on my stomach, bringing my ma down on top of Lisa's lifeless body. *Son of a bitch!*

Ma was shaking, speaking in Gaelic, and if I'd stayed up on my studies, stayed in Ireland even, then I might've known what she was saying. At the same time, it didn't take a genius to know she was praying, the words running on repeat, over and over… When the fuck did my badass-biker ma become so religious?

I turned my head away, trying to see through the trees—Emily, Pops… anyone. But instead, I saw more bodies. A shit ton of them. One more familiar than the others.

Chop. Dead, just ten feet away. *Holy shit.*

I blinked, no time for questions, only to notice more bodies… these ones alive. Tall, black jeans, cuts with red dragons… Thirty or forty of them rushing through the trees like warriors, guns drawn.

I smiled. Despite the body beneath me, the destruction surrounding me, and not knowing where Emily was, I fucking smiled.

The cavalry was here. The RDs… minus the Texas crew. Flick hadn't let them come after all.

CHAPTER THIRTY

Emily

It happened so fast that I didn't see it coming. First I was on Pops's shoulder, being rushed through the woods surrounding the building, and then I was falling, landing with a thud that stole the breath from my lungs. Flick stood over me, a hand on his gun, while Niyol held Pops against a tree, forearm to his neck, a gun to his temple.

"You're a pussy," Pops growled. "Ain't got the guts to end my life."

"The hell I don't." Niyol shoved the gun to Pops's temple even harder, hissing. For the first time in my life, I feared my brother. Not in the sense that he would ever hurt me, more in the sense that he had murder in his eyes—even if his intended victim deserved to die a horrible, vicious death.

This was the Red Dragon life I didn't ever want to be part of.

But there I was, at the center of it all. Only Archer wasn't with me.

Archer, who might still be inside that building.

I choked on a sob, eyes squeezing shut. I pulled my knees to my chest and didn't get up off the ground as I stared at the smoke rising in the distance. Even as the gunfire slowed, then stopped, a sense of desperation hit me in the stomach as if I was bound for death, though I had no real wounds.

If Archer didn't make it, how could I? I'd pushed him away. I hadn't wanted any part of him or his club. But now I'd do anything to have him in my life, in any way he'd let me.

A gun went off then. I jumped, turning to see Flick standing over Pops's body as it fell to the ground. Flick mumbled words I couldn't understand, and I could have sworn I heard him laugh. It wasn't time for laughter now, didn't he understand? Didn't he know that Archer probably hadn't made it?

I cried out at the thought, sitting up, determined to go back and see for sure.

"Hey, hey," Niyol said, crouching beside me, his dark brows pulled together as he searched my face. "You alright? Don't move, you're bleeding."

"I... I..."

"Shh, it's okay. You're good." Niyol pulled me against his chest, hugging me to him. I didn't understand. I didn't get it. He should hate me. Everyone should. I should be the one dead, not Archer. Dizziness washed over me before I could say so, and the next thing I knew, I was passing out in my brother's arms.

CHAPTER THIRTY-ONE

Archer

I crawled forward, passing my ma, and Lisa's dead body, and grabbed a fallen gun, just as more shots were fired from my left. One by one, bodies began falling, and I knew then that my brothers had zero mercy for the army Pops had created. Anyone affiliated with that man was dead. It didn't matter if they were young or old, pawns or not. They'd teamed up with the wrong man and messed with the wrong MC.

The first person I recognized was Crazy, who jumped in front of me with wide arms and wild eyes. "Ho-lee-shit," he said with a long whistle, taking me in, then my ma, then finally, Lisa's dead body.

"Don't just stand there, you fucker," I hissed, wrapping an arm around my waist. "Make yourself useful." Somehow, I got to my knees again, then my feet, the gun in my hand shaking right along with my fingers.

Slade was there next, sweat dripping down his temples, his dark eyes even wilder than Crazy's. At the sight of me, his face paled. "How are you not dead?" Then he pointed to the ground with his gun. "Sit down before I make you."

"Nuh uh. Emily's—"

Another shot was fired, this one from somewhere ahead in the woods. I looked up, eyes narrowing as if I could see where it was coming from, knowing deep down that wherever it was, Emily might be there too.

The thought had me panicking, shoving both Slade and Crazy aside as I raced up the hill to the edge of the woods, over branches, mud, past a tree, then another… until I spotted her, unmoving, with her head on Hawk's lap.

My stomach twisted at the view. I took off even faster, stumbling some more. And then I was there, falling to my knees at Emily's side, swearing I'd never get up again if she didn't get up too. Is that what love does to a person? Make them feel fucking helpless and lost at the thought of ever being without their partner? I couldn't lose her. I knew right then and there that if I did, it would end me.

"Move." I shoved Hawk away, pulling Emily's limp body against my chest. "Baby, please. Wake up. Please. JP, Emily, Em, come on. Open those eyes." I searched her face, her body, lifting her shirt, only for Flick to slap my hand away.

"Get your kicks somewhere other than her." He curled his upper lip.

Ignoring him, I kissed her head, her nose, each of her eyes. *Come on, Sleeping Beauty. Don't you fucking leave me now.*

And just like that, Emily began to stir in my arms.

"A-Archer?" she whispered, lips pulling to one side as she studied my face. Reaching up, she touched my wrist, weak fingers struggling to hang on to me.

"Christ, Em. You scared the shit outta me." I touched my forehead to hers and took my first real breath in days.

She was okay. She was alive. She was also the only thing I could see and breathe and smell and… love.

Goddamn, I think I loved this woman.

No. I *did* love her. Fuck being cursed. I was one lucky son of a bitch, that's what I was.

I hiked her up higher onto my lap, needing her as close to me as I could get her. She must've felt the same because she straddled my lap, arms around my waist like she'd never let me go. The feeling was mutual. She buried her face into my neck and I knew, right then, that this was where I was always meant to be.

Death and destruction sat ahead. No doubt a crew would be by soon to help clean up the scene, but I wasn't ready to go back to the carnage. Not when I had everything I'd ever need again right there on my lap.

As if she knew what I was thinking, Emily leaned back just enough to look at my face. As much as I wanted to forget everything, I needed this moment to talk, see what she'd been through most of all, only so I could figure out how to fix it for her. For us.

"What happened? Tell me." I cupped her face and ran both thumbs over the bruises on her cheek, the one next to her eye, too.

"Nothing I couldn't handle." She reached down between us to take my hand in hers. It was likely a natural movement for two people, a couple even. But for me? Holding Em's hand felt like kissing. Real and about as intimate as I'd ever been with another person before. Hell, sex had never made me feel the way holding Emily's hand in mine did. The same went for her hugs.

"My mom…" she whispered a minute later, her eyes watering, her breath a shudder.

I squeezed her fingers as tight as I could, letting her know I was there. That she could talk all she wanted, and I'd do my best to listen. Letting her know, too, that if she just wanted to cry and forget it all, I'd be the best damn hugger she'd ever have again.

"She didn't make it, Archer. I-I couldn't save her."

"I know." I brushed my nose against hers, felt her pain so fucking deep in my chest I could've called it my own. I'd lost my ma once. Knew what that felt like, even though she'd come back from the dead. The ache Emily was feeling? It'd never go away.

Emily sniffed, stroking the back of my hand with her free one. "Your mom though…"

I cleared my throat. "Yeah."

"Did you know?"

"No." I winced as pain shot through my ribs.

Her fingers moved from the back of my hand to stroke my newly buzzed hair.

"Who did this by the way?"

"Angel," I said. "But Chop made him. Guess he… didn't like my pretty…" I coughed, wincing again, "golden locks."

Instead of laughing, she frowned, shaking her head at me.

She started stroking my head again, finishing with, "If the guy wasn't already dead, I'd kill him for this alone."

I hummed and shut my eyes, taking a quick breath.

"Hey, don't you close your eyes," she said, rubbing at my cheek. "A little help up here!" she hollered through the trees, then looked at me again. "You're really hurt, aren't you?"

"Nah. Just banged up is all."

She frowned, obviously not believing me.

"I'm sorry." I winced.

"For what?"

"Not being there for you like I should've been. For what happened with the flood and my bike and—"

"Don't." She lowered her forehead to mine.

"Don't what?"

"Talk like you're getting ready to say goodbye to me, Archer. It's my fault you're hurt, so if anyone should apologize, it should be me."

I wanted to argue with her, tell her that she hadn't forced me to go anywhere and that I'd made every decision up until now on my own. That other than the pain, her getting hurt, the flood, and all the bad shit that had happened, I wouldn't trade a second of my time with her. But the words were stuck and the pain inside of me got to be too much to take.

Emily hollered for someone again, even louder this time. "We're gonna get you to a hospital and heal you right up, because I'm not losing you, do you understand me?"

I winced, her voice blurring in and out of my ears. That wasn't good.

"Kiss me." I did manage that one. If I was gonna go, then I wanted to feel her lips. To take them to the grave with me.

"Always," she whispered, lowering her soft, tear-soaked mouth to mine.

CHAPTER THIRTY-TWO

Emily

Archer was in the hospital. I was admitted for a night too, suffering from severe dehydration. There was no denying I felt like crap, but I didn't have time to be sick or to think about myself. Not when I had Archer to worry about.

There hadn't been much of an opportunity for me to think about my mom. I knew her death would hit once I left this town and went back to Rockford—if I was even welcomed back at all. Niyol seemed fine with me returning, but I still got the cold shoulder from everyone else. I wondered if they blamed me for Archer's injuries, for everything that had happened. I know I would if I were them.

He'd gone through two surgeries in twenty-four hours. One for a broken collarbone and another for the internal bleeding in his stomach. They'd sealed up the leaking vessels with a heat probe, and when Archer had woken from that one, he'd joked for an hour about probing *me* again. How the guy could be so dirty after suffering through so much, and feeling so much pain too, was beyond me. Regardless, the fact that he'd wanted me there with him, holding his hand when he puked ten minutes later from the medicine, did more for my soul than any declarations between us ever would.

Now, a day later, he was back in the operating room for his eye. It'd been shattered, and they weren't completely sure if his vision would ever be fully restored. Out of everything, *that* was the surgery I'd cried about… I wasn't sure why. It could've been my lack of sleep. Or it could've been the fact that seeing Archer in pain was undoing me.

Anne had told me I needed a break. To go out and be with the brothers in the waiting room for a while. Despite the fact that I wanted to be there when Archer came back, I knew she was right. I was hungry and thirsty, and I needed to call Summer.

"Hey," I said, leaning back in the hospital waiting-room chair. Summer had answered my FaceTime call within seconds. I was using Flick's phone; he'd unsurprisingly been the one and only guy from the club to offer it up when I'd asked to borrow one.

"Don't you *ever* do that again, you hear me? You leave, I go with you. End of story." Summer wiped her wet face, her angry words biting.

I reached out to touch the screen, tracing Summer's long, blonde hair. Her eyes were brighter than I remembered them being before I left. But that also could've been her tears.

"I'm sorry. You know I had to."

She sighed, reaching out to touch the screen too. "I know. But it was so stupid, Emily."

I swallowed hard. "Yeah. And look what good it did me too."

My throat burned as memories of Mom's eyes, full of fear, peered up at me. She hadn't died heroically. She hadn't even died for a cause. She'd died for a man who'd never been in love with her.

"Honey, I'm so, so sorry," Summer whispered. I was glad she didn't ask if I was okay, because I wouldn't have been able to stop an inevitable breakdown. There'd be time for that later. For now, I needed to be strong for Archer.

"Thanks." I wiped my face with a nearby tissue, catching sight of Flick, who sat across from me. He'd been giving me creepy looks since we'd gotten to the hospital, and I wasn't sure if he was plotting my demise or what.

"How is Archer? Is he out of surgery yet?"

I blinked and looked at the phone again. "No. They said this one might be the hardest out of all the surgeries because they did so much damage."

"Damn it. I hate this. So much."

"Me too." I frowned. "But we've got to believe things are going to get better, right?"

"Yeah. Especially since my baby needs godparents," she told me. "So don't you *ever* leave me again, deal?"

I wanted to promise her that I would always be there, but facts were facts. The RDs would never forgive me for what I'd done, even though I loved a man who was at the heart of their club.

Summer blew out a slow breath, changing the subject. "Bad news on the work front by the way."

"Oh, God, what now?"

"Rumor has it, cuts are going to be made. All non-tenured teachers are pretty much screwed as far as jobs go next year."

I shrugged, not really surprised. "It's fine. I'll just look for something else. Maybe take some online classes, get my masters. Or take time off to deal with…" I was going to say Mom's wedding-planning business, the one she'd left behind when she'd left with Pops. But that was too raw of a subject to think about right now, or ever, really.

"Hey." Summer tapped the screen, drawing me back in. "Come four and a half months from now, I'm gonna be hiring a nanny."

I wrinkled my nose. "I love you. And I'll love my future niece or nephew to bits, but I'll pass."

The doctor pushed through the doors a second later. The serious look on his dark face had me shivering, standing, and saying goodbye to my best friend without even looking at the screen.

Slowly, I made my way over to Flick, Anne, and Angel, who were listening intently to everything the doctor said.

"… stable condition and should be waking up soon."

My entire body seemed to sag at that news. I covered my mouth to hide my incoming sob of relief. Anne looked at me with hope-filled eyes, giving me even more confidence that he'd get through this. We all would, actually. I didn't even know this woman. But I felt like I did.

"Can we… go back…?" Angel tried to speak then bowed his head, shaking it.

Flick stiffened, and when I looked his way, I saw the confusion on his face. Likely, he was trying to figure out what was wrong with Archer's brother's voice.

"As long as you're family," the doctor said, giving him a firm nod.

Once he was gone, we decided that I would go back to see Archer with Angel. Until Flick changed the plans.

"Need to talk to you first, girl," he told me, pulling me out of the group.

Angel moved closer to me, protectiveness in his gaze that I didn't deserve. I touched his wrist and smiled, knowing this was it. My fate was sealed. Flick was going to give me my one-way ticket out of here, no matter what was going on with Archer.

I just wished I had more time.

"It's okay," I told Angel. "You and your mom go back first."

He didn't nod. Just stared at me, then Flick, something like fear paired with anger encased in his eyes.

"Don't get your panties in a bunch, kid," Flick told him, moving to wrap his arm around my shoulder. I stiffened. "I just need to talk to the girl, is all."

Once they were gone, it was only Flick and me. The rest of the bikers got up to leave, none of them sparing us a glance as they did.

"Sit, girl." Flick pointed to the chair I'd been sitting in earlier.

I handed him back his phone and did as he asked. If I wanted to go back to Rockford with Archer, then I needed Flick's forgiveness for what I had done. Not only for running off, but for talking to my mom without telling anyone.

"Listen," I said as we sat down, one chair between us. "I don't expect your forgiveness, but I need you to know how sorry I am about the letters—"

"Don't give two shits about some letters. I knew where Pops was all along."

My eyes widened. "You *what*?"

"You gonna rat me out to my boys?" He arched an eyebrow, looking like it didn't matter what my answer was. "You're not exactly their favorite person right now."

"I… I don't…" *He knew?* All this time?

He leaned forward onto his knees and grunted. "Looks like we've got ourselves a quandary, huh?"

If I wasn't so angry, I'd have laughed at that big word coming out of his dirty, filthy, bearded mouth. "So, what, are you, like, blackmailing me?"

He shrugged. "Maybe."

"Why tell me at all, then?"

Slowly, he pulled something out from the inside of his cut. An envelope the size of the ones my mom had been sending. I recognized the handwriting instantly.

"Damn conscience, that's why."

I blinked, mouth opening, then shutting, then opening once more as I asked, "Is that…?"

"Yeah." He chuckled a little, but his face didn't display the humor. "Started getting them in Texas. Thought it was a fluke. Had some guys check it out."

"And…?"

"Not a fluke, girl. Your mom was writing to me too."

My eyes burned with tears. All this time, I'd held onto the secret, fearing what would happen if someone from the Red Dragons found out I was in contact with my mom, yet the president of that very same motorcycle club had been getting letters too.

"What did she say to you?"

He handed over the letter then ran a hand down his long beard. Flick looked the epitome of casual and calm, though a tiny shake seemed to take over his left hand as he rubbed it up and down his jeans.

"Read it. Find out for yourself." He stood then, not looking back as he hollered at me, "See ya in Rockford… daughter."

My jaw dropped.

And then he left.

Without hesitating, I opened the letter, spreading it out onto my lap as if it was made of silk. It was crinkled at the corners, and there were tiny holes in the middle, as if he'd stubbed a cigarette out on it a time or two. The ink was smudged in many places as well, as though he had run his fingers over certain words. I could bet he'd balled this up, thrown it away, only to reopen it more than once. I'd done that with the first letter I'd gotten.

The tears came the second I started to read, and by the time I reached the second line, my bottom lip was all out shaking. Covering my mouth with a hand, I read the words, sometimes twice, only for them to make less and less sense. Soon, I wasn't just crying. I was sobbing, the letter like a dagger in my back, my chest, my lungs too. I couldn't breathe. I couldn't think. And I also didn't understand.

This letter.

This truth.

Pops wasn't my father.

Flick was.

CHAPTER THIRTY-THREE

Archer

"Turn the damn lights off, would ya?" My head hurt like it did that time I drank a fifth of my favorite whiskey, all in one afternoon. Only this time when I swallowed, it tasted like chemicals instead.

A soft sigh sounded from my right as the lights flickered off. Then I felt her hands on one of mine a second later when she sat back down beside me.

"Are you always this crabby when you wake up?"

I smirked, then winced from the pain of doing so. "Don't make me laugh." I breathed through my nose, and it felt like a thousand needles were prickling the inside. "Shit hurts."

Lips pressed against the back of my arm, my hand, whispered words softly against my skin as she spoke. "I'm sorry this happened to you."

"Me too." I cleared my throat. "You good?"

"Now that you're awake and out of surgery I am."

I smiled. That didn't hurt at least.

"I've been sitting here for an hour trying to figure some stuff out though." She moved onto the bed beside me, laying her head on my chest. She was so little I barely felt the pressure of her against me.

I wrapped my arm around her waist and kissed her temple, more than thankful to have her here, safe in my arms. "Your brain hurting again?"

"I wish it was. Then maybe I'd stop thinking so much."

I didn't wanna say it out loud. Fresh wounds like that were shit to bring up. But maybe she was waiting for me to ask. "You thinking about your mom?"

She nodded. "Among other things."

"What other things?" I shut my eyes, worried she was second-guessing us… me as a whole. We hadn't been able to figure out what this thing was between us. No time, no real knowledge either.

"What other things am I thinking about?" she asked.

"Yeah. Tell me."

At first, she was quiet, and I thought maybe she'd changed her mind about talking at all. But then she asked me something so easily remedied, I knew she'd be saving the tough shit for the end.

"What does JP stand for?"

I grinned, but it hurt and I could only do it halfway. "You really wanna know?"

Her warm breath grazed my neck as she put her chin on my chest. "Yes. It's been driving me nuts."

I sighed. So much for never telling her. "It stands for 'junk puncher'."

I waited for her to yell at me. Call me a pig, or tell me I was an ass. Lo and behold, she did none of those things and started laughing instead.

"You think that's funny?" Hearing her laugh like that was something I didn't think I'd ever hear again. So even though my gut hurt, I couldn't help but laugh with her. The pain was well worth the pleasure.

"I mean, it's original." She snorted. Actually fucking snorted.

"And you're damn good at it, too."

Tears dripped from her eyes from laughing, and I couldn't stop from reaching up and wiping them away. Thankfully my pain meds were awesome because I couldn't feel nothing in my broken collarbone.

"From the moment I met you, Archer Benedict—"

"Pulling out the full name now, are ya?" I poked her in the ribs and she jerked, her thigh falling over mine.

"Let me finish." She rolled her eyes.

"Go for it. Nobody's stopping you."

She groaned and set her forehead on the center of my chest. "*As I was saying*," she drew the word out. "From the moment I met you, you've done nothing but fluster me or anger me, or make me feel… alive. Even all those years back when I came to the club with my mom, I used to watch you. And I hated the fact that out of all the men there, you were the one that intrigued me the most. I'd been taught never to want the bad things in life, you know."

"I should probably be offended, huh?"

"Nah. It's a good thing." She shrugged. "Besides, I see the real you now, Archer."

"And what's the *real me* like, huh?"

She laid her ear back against my chest, but not before I noticed the smirk. "Strong-willed. Still too cocky. But you're brave, and caring, and you sacrifice yourself for the people you love. You're nothing like I once thought you were."

"Hmm." I grinned a little, desperate to stroke the back of her long hair.

"The point I'm trying to make is, I think that there was a reason I was drawn to you, even though I never actually liked you back then. Like, maybe all those years ago, I knew that somehow our lives were… you know."

She rubbed a slow circle over my sternum. That soft movement alone had my cock jumping under my hospital gown, and damn if I wasn't happy that he was still alive and ready. Because as far as I was concerned, he and the space between Emily's legs had only just gotten acquainted.

"Spit it out. Everything in that mouth of yours. I wanna hear it, JP."

"Fine. The truth is, I'm in love with you. And before you start telling me that you don't do love, that it's a curse, let me just point something out first."

My heart jumped into my throat as I stared down at her red cheeks, those brown eyes so sincere and honest that I wanted to fucking live in them.

"I'm listening," I whispered, running my fingers over her cheek, her eyes, her nose, her lips, all while she told me her truth.

"Statistics show that people who go through trauma together, and fall in love while they're at it, don't always last. But sometimes they do, and I'm banking on that with you, because as much as I once thought running away was the answer, I know the truth now. Even if my mom had made it…" She paused. I saw the tears there and lifted a thumb to the corner of her eye to catch them when they fell. "Even if she had," she continued, "I would have come back."

"For Summer, right? And Hawk and the baby?"

"No, Archer. Because being away from you? It would've killed me." Emily lowered her forehead to mine, breathing me in like I did her. "I want *you*, Archer. I want you for as long as you'll let me have you."

Despite the fact that I was all messed up from the meds, my cock reacted to those words like she'd just put her lips around it. I couldn't help it. I was wired one way, so being trained to be the man Em deserved was gonna take some time.

"Got a hypothetical question for you first." I ran my hand down her cheek, tucking some hair behind her ear. "Say you get an inkling to leave the club again—would you? Because I'm all in with this thing, but if you leave me, I need time to prep."

She shook her head, tears falling from her eyes. "You'd leave your club? For me?"

"I would." In a heartbeat. I loved my brothers. But I loved her more.

"I wouldn't ask you to do that. Not ever. They're your family and… I want them to be my family now too."

I blew out a low breath, chuckling a little with relief. Leaving the RDs would hurt, yeah, but losing Em would hurt more.

"I get it now."

She frowned. "What do you get?"

"The reason you ran was the same reason I ran with you."

She blinked then laid her head back on my chest again. "We protect who we love, right?"

"Always, Em. Always." And though her ma hadn't made it, I was determined to help her find a new family in the one she left back in Rockford. With me and Hawk and all the brothers. She belonged there. With me.

I lowered my hand to her hip then slid it up to her waist. She arched her hips over me, a tiny gasp leaving her mouth as I squeezed. Pushing her forehead up with mine this time, I looked her in the eyes and said, "You gonna kiss me again, or what?"

Her grin grew impossibly wide as she raised her lips and hovered over my mouth. "Soon." She winked. "We got lots of time for lip kisses. But I'm thinking right now, I want to kiss you somewhere else first."

"No shit?" I smirked.

She nodded, slowly lowering her body over mine, kissing my neck, the middle of my throat, tugging my hospital gown up just enough to get lips on my stomach. I flinched, but not from pain; her hot breath over my skin was full-on pleasure.

And then she gave me that curse-sealing kiss—the best kind a man could ever ask for—in the form of her perfect lips wrapped tightly around my cock.

When she was done, and I was panting and pulling her hair and dying from how good her mouth felt on me, I finally yanked her right back up my body and sealed the deal between us with her mouth connected to mine.

EPILOGUE

Emily

One year later

"Oh, good Christ, babe. Feels so damn…" His words turned into a low moan as I rubbed and pushed my thumbs deeper into his skin.

"You like that?" I settled my mouth to his ear, grinning as I kissed the lobe. His hair had grown out, not long but enough to where I could run my hands through it and it tickle my palm when I did.

"Fuck yeah. Don't stop. God, don't ever—"

"The hell's going on in here?" Flick yanked open my car door, his eyes latching onto me… straddling Archer's lap.

"Fuck you, cock-blocker," Archer moaned, laying his head back against the seat. His eyes were so narrowed I thought for sure he'd give himself another headache.

We were completely dressed.

There was no sex happening either.

Just me, being a good little girlfriend, giving my boyfriend a massage outside the club, in a *very* compromising position. Archer, though, must've thought this was about to be something entirely different.

"Hawk's running all over trying to find your ass. The guys are getting ready to leave, for fuck's sake."

Leaning back against the steering wheel, I stared at my, um, *father*, wondering if I'd ever get used to the fact that a man who I barely knew was suddenly trying to be a man he should've been years ago.

My mom's letter had shaken me to the core.

Flick was my father.

Flick also hadn't *known* that he was my father.

Mom, feeling guilty during her months of chasing Pops across the country, must've grown a small conscience over time which had then inspired her to admit the truth.

Flick wasn't an ideal dad in the least. And I wasn't sure if I'd ever call him the d-word. But over the last year, we'd talked a little. Spent some time together too, where he'd told me about him and my mom, their relationship, and how he'd wanted to protect her. He'd been willing, at one point, to go against his president to make it happen, he'd said. But my mom had been too scared, dumb, and clueless about loyalty and what mattered and didn't. In turn, she'd nearly ruined everything in my life because of it. But you know what they say about things happening for a reason.

Still, Flick did what he could, even trying to help me revamp my mom's wedding-planning business, only for me to decide after one wedding that I absolutely *hated* that job.

"He'll be there in a second." I smiled down at Archer, tracing the small scar by his left eye.

He narrowed his eyes up at me, squeezing my hips just beneath my crinkly dress. "Yeah, sure we will."

"Do not make me fucking remind you, asshole, that this is my *daughter* you're with now." Flick slammed the door shut at that, leaving us alone, only for the two of us to burst out laughing with our heads pressed together when he was gone.

A few seconds later, when I was sure my mascara wasn't dripping down my cheeks from cry-laughing so hard, Archer buried his nose against my hair.

"Yeah, and I'm gonna make his daughter scream real good when I get her under me tonight."

My giggles turned into moans and I shut my eyes at the feel of his teeth nipping my neck. "That a promise?"

"Fuck yeah it is." He bucked his hips up, the hard erection beneath the zipper of his dark jeans rubbing at my wet center. My panties were soaked from massaging his shoulders alone, so much so I feared a person might see it.

Regardless, I'd *really* missed this between us.

"You're home, then?" I gasped. "For good now, right?"

He nodded, lifting his hands out from under my dress and grazing both thumbs against the bottom of my breasts. "You miss me, JP?"

"Terribly." I pulled back, cupping his cheeks in my hands. Then I did what we'd gotten amazing at, kissing him so softly, so lightly, that my head began to spin.

For the past month, he'd been in Ireland with his mom and Angel. They'd planned the trip after Anne had found out her aunt was still alive. More than anything, she'd wanted Archer and Angel to meet the woman, and Archer, who'd developed quite an attachment to his little brother, had eagerly gone along in hopes of getting to know the quiet, protective boy who'd saved us both. At seventeen, Angel, who Archer had affectionately nicknamed Casper, had truly come into his own. He'd begun prospecting under the Red Dragons three months ago, and would soon be a full-fledged brother of the club. I was protective of the boy myself, mostly because he was still so quiet, but I also knew he was in good hands when it came to his brother, and the rest of the men here.

Who would have thought that a lifestyle I had once hated would become a lifestyle I now reveled in?

Archer's tongue slid expertly between my lips, soft and smooth, if not a little overeager. Fingers skimmed higher up my thigh, toying with my panties, and I sighed, completely content with it all. Yes, I would've loved it if he'd slipped a finger beneath the elastic, but after nearly losing him and after what we'd gone through? I'd learned to appreciate the little things in life, like a make-out session in my car, ten minutes before our best friends were set to get married.

The mint of his breath rushed through me and I shivered when he dragged his dull nails down to my knees. I smiled, loving the taste of him, feeling so much like a teenage girl it wasn't even funny.

"Love you." He breathed the words like he always did, leaning back to look up at me. Sometimes I wondered if he even knew he was saying it at all, but I felt it. So much so. Always. Archer loved like he'd never done it at all: expressive and tender, rough and real. I was determined to make him my forever.

"I love you too." I kissed his nose, grinning, feeling my nerves kick up when it hit me all at once—that feeling, that question…

"What's wrong?" he asked, concern pulling his deep-green eyes together.

I blinked, smiling wider, the words sliding up before I could even think about their consequences. "Marry me."

He stiffened, then he blinked. Yet his words stayed locked inside.

Crap, what have I done?

"I'm not saying now, or within the next year. I'm not saying it's a deal-breaker if you don't want that. I just—"

He yanked me close again, his mouth to mine, his fingers in my hair, his body shaking…

Crap. Was he telling me no, doing it the only way he could, by distracting me?

Seconds later, there was another tap on the window. This one tinier. I jumped, sweat dripping down my temples and tears in my eyes. Archer stared up at me like he wasn't sure what to say, and I gave him the out we both needed, opening the door.

"Finally," Niyol growled, looking handsome as ever with his dark hair, his dark vest, a white button-up dress shirt beneath, and his signature black jeans and boots.

"Sorry." I cleared my throat and smiled at the little thing in his arms.

"Yeah," he barked, handing me his daughter as I got out of the car. "You'll be sorry when Summer's beating my ass down the aisle with a ruler."

Archer jumped out of the car then. His distance from me couldn't be more obvious. His voice was smooth though, casual. The act he was so good at putting on for everyone but me.

"Sorry. JP owed me." He wrapped a hand around my waist, fingers squeezing at my hip. He dropped a small kiss to my niece's head, then winked at my brother. "You know how it is, right?"

"It's my fucking wedding day, asswipe." Niyol, always the gentlemen, smacked Archer alongside his head.

Right away, the tiny blonde laid her head on my shoulder and yawned, calming me like a drug. I hiked her further up into my arms, thankful for the millionth time that I had this little thing in my life. Despite my previous disinterest when it came to being a nanny for this kid, I'd realized just eight weeks after she was born, when Summer had been struggling to find a caregiver for her, that I, indeed, was the best person for the job. Someday I planned on working again, preferably as a science teacher. But for now, this job was perfect for me.

Eleanor "Ellie" Lattimore, named after her grandma—Summer's mother. If it weren't for her, I'm not sure how I would've gotten through my mom's death without losing my mind.

Once Niyol took off, running through the gravel of the compound and heading toward the tiny field which they'd turned into a place to have the ceremony, I let go of my breath, praying that the tension I was feeling would keep away and not ruin this day.

"You ready?" Archer cleared his throat, sticking his hands into his pockets.

I nodded, stroking my hand down the back of Ellie's sleeping head. Her body had grown limp in my arms, proof that she'd likely sleep through the entire ceremony.

I didn't look at Archer when I nodded, but my chest ached from the thunder of my heart. He cleared his throat, keeping a good foot between us as we walked. Damn it, I hated this. So much. I knew what his stance was when it came to marriage and families, but it had hit so hard, so fast, that I hadn't been thinking with my head, but my heart.

Just outside the gates of the compound, when tears started stinging my eyes, he touched my arm, pulling me to a stop.

"Were you messing with me in the car? Or are you being real?"

I blinked, and tears slipped out. The guitar player Summer had hired to play their music had already started.

"Let's talk about this later, okay?"

"No." He shook his head despite the fact that I could now see Summer and her dad coming out of the clubhouse.

How she'd gotten the man to agree to have this entire wedding at the compound was beyond me, but that was beside the point.

"Emily." Archer lowered his voice, moving closer, his hand to my face, drawing it up. "Tell me you weren't fucking with me."

I bit my lip, knowing eyes were on us now. Summer and Niyol didn't have attendants, but they'd wanted me and Archer to come in last with Ellie.

"I'm not doing this right now."

"Tell me, damn it," he growled.

"No, I wasn't fucking with you, alright?" I hissed, louder than I intended, but damn it all to hell, this was not the time or the place to discuss this.

His eyes widened in amazement, but he wasn't smiling. Oh, God. Archer didn't want marriage. What was I thinking?

Summer's and her dad's footsteps could be heard to my right, crunching against the gravel. Ellie stirred in my arms right then, lifting her head just in time to see her mom. She let out a huge wail, reaching for her, and I hustled toward the crowd of onlookers, thankful for the temporary distraction from my obvious mistake.

I was pretty sure I'd never learn.

Ellie cried louder as I struggled to get us to our seats up front. I smothered my face into her soft curls and whispered calming words into her ear. Realizing that it was me holding onto her, she finally settled, her entire body shaking from the tears. This was a frigging nightmare.

The wedding march began, and I stood, turning to watch my best friend walk down the aisle, all while ignoring the glares of the bikers who stood surrounding me. Obviously, they didn't know what the hell was going—

"The answer's yes."

Arms wrapped around my waist, pulling me and Ellie back against Archer's firm chest.

Shutting my eyes, and missing the moment when Summer approached Niyol for the first time, I whispered the only word I could, tears falling fast down my cheeks. "Yes?"

"No, Em, not yes. I mean hell yes."

He nuzzled my hair, pulling my face toward his by the chin. We looked at one another, smiling with our eyes as much as we were with our mouths. And then slowly, painstakingly so, his lips descended to mine for a kiss. The kind of kiss that sent sparks into my toes and said, *I absolutely just got engaged to a biker.*

A LETTER FROM HEATHER

I want to say a huge thank you for choosing to read *Her Hot Ride*. If you did enjoy it, and want to keep up to date with all my latest releases, just sign up at the following link. Your email address will never be shared and you can unsubscribe at any time.

www.bookouture.com/heather-van-fleet

I hope you loved *Her Hot Ride*, and if you did, I would be very grateful if you could write a review. I'd love to hear what you think, and it makes such a difference helping new readers to discover one of my books for the first time.

I love hearing from my readers—you can get in touch on my Facebook page, through Twitter, Goodreads or my website.

Thanks,
Heather

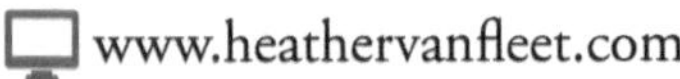

ACKNOWLEDGEMENTS

It takes a village to create a book, like it does to raise a child, and I'm so thankful I have a full life with wonderfully supportive people to make that happen for me.

Chris. My husband. My best friend. Some days I can't seem to thank you enough for everything you do for me and our family. The extra hours you put in at work, the scrapyard trips, the side work… You make it possible for me to stay home and write, and though you don't always understand the turmoil of authoring, you're always the first person there to hug me through my tears and serve me up fruity adult beverages when the going gets tough. I love you like nothing else in this world.

Kelsey, Emma, Bella. You ladies are my queens, and *my God* am I lucky to be your mom. Love you three to the moon and back. Oh. And thanks for always understanding if Mom needs a few moments to rage-cry it out in the shower. You know what I mean. 😊

Jess, J, Jessica. My sister. My best friend. I'm pretty sure I'd lose my mind without you. We're in this together until the end, and no matter what happens in life, our connection and our friendship is only going to grow stronger with time, no doubt in my mind. Thank you for being you. #NMFTG

Lana! You're amazing and so freaking supportive. I'm blessed to have you in my life. May we strive together to write the dirtiest, raunchiest sexy times ever. #TeamAwesome2.0forever

Jen! My badass CP and amazing friend. Archer found his ending (finally) and would never exist without your eyes. I'm so thankful to be able to call you a friend. And the day we meet? It's going to be hug-crushingly epic.

And finally, to the entire team at Bookouture. Thank you for giving my series a home, for giving my steamy romance a shot, most of all. Jennifer, especially… There is not a single soul out there in this business who has believed in me like you have. I'm blessed to call you my editor and my friend. Thank you, from the bottom of my heart, for everything you've done.